Hope In Cripple Creek

CRIPPLE CREEK SERIES, BOOK 1

SARA R. TURNQUIST

MOUNTAIN
SUMMIT PRESS

If you would like to stay up-to-date on this and all other series from Sara:

https://saraturnquist.com/list

For my Lord who keeps me going.
And to my friend and mentor, Hannah,
who keeps me honest.

CHAPTER 1

Home

The stagecoach moved along, bumping and rocking as it went. Trees and other green scenery whisked by the window. Views of mountains and open plains were visible from the seat of the coach, vistas familiar to its occupant. Katherine Matthews was coming home. She returned to Cripple Creek, no longer the scared, unsure teenager who had left to further her education so many years ago with hopes and dreams of a new life in a new place. No, she had matured into a confident young woman who had grown in stature and in beauty. Her hair was no longer the mousy color she always hated, for it had deepened into the same beautiful chestnut brown she had always admired in her mother's appearance. She'd grown out of her awkward teenage features, and was now well regarded among her peers as a rather handsome woman.

Returning to Cripple Creek brought many rather-mixed emotions to the surface. Imagine, one of her first postings would be at the same schoolhouse where she received her educational start. When her mother wrote to her of the interim need, she was glad to help out. What an odd coincidence that the letter would find her, too, in transition. Would this turn into a permanent placement? Did she want it to?

The mountain scenery became more recognizable, and she thought back on her childhood. There were so many happy times here. Unbidden, her mind wandered to the day of the great tragedy that had marred her spirit—the day Ellie Mae died.

Even all these years later, she carried the scar in her heart. The events of that day had left her broken. Why must thoughts of Ellie Mae plague her so? And all the more as her return became imminent? She shivered as the images from her nightmares the previous evening flitted across her mind. They would not stop. These same visions visited her in sleep night after night. All the more frequently these last weeks.

Closing her eyes, the hazy images took form and became memory. It was as if no time had passed. She and Ellie, walking through the school-yard just as they did every other day . . .

Hooking arms with Ellie Mae, Katherine stepped out of the schoolhouse and into the yard. A rather large group of students gathered off to the right near the old tree. It didn't bother Katherine. She turned her attention toward the path that would lead home.

"What do you think they're up to?" Ellie Mae whispered.

Katherine glanced in that direction and noticed Betsy Callaway at the center, flapping her jaws. Why would anyone listen to anything she said? But they did. The class at large seemed to adore Betsy. It didn't make sense. Clenching her teeth, Katherine grabbed for Ellie Mae's hand. "Whatever it is, we don't want to be involved." She pulled Ellie Mae along as she walked on, trying to pass the gathering.

"I know Miss Matthews couldn't do it," Betsy said loudly.

Katherine froze in her tracks. What had she just said?

The crowd of students parted and glared at Katherine and Ellie Mae.

"Let's keep going," Ellie Mae pleaded, tugging on Katherine's hand.

She should listen to Ellie Mae and not become a part of whatever game Betsy played. But she could not let Betsy get the best of her. What would everyone think of her?

So, she turned to face her accuser. There stood Betsy with Wyatt Sullivan, the most popular boy in school, right beside her. Betsy's blonde pigtails, tied back with perfect pink ribbons, shone in the sun. Her dress was no less perfect, pink with just the right amount of lace and even a slight puff to the sleeves.

"Do what, pray tell?" Katherine shot back. Her heart beat furiously in her chest.

"Go down through the mine shaft." Betsy folded her arms in front of her chest and raised an eyebrow.

Katherine's heart skipped a beat then, but she tried not to show her fear.

Ellie Mae's grip tightened on her hand.

"I assure you, Miss Callaway, it's not that I can't do it. It's simply that I have better things to do than to be traipsing about a mine shaft." She turned to leave and hoped that would be enough to silence Betsy.

"Prove it." Betsy's voice rang out after her.

Katherine's eyes slid closed. Was there any way around this? "I have nothing to prove to you," she called back over her shoulder.

"Fraidycat!" Betsy laughed.

The other students joined in.

Katherine's face burned. A fire had been lit within her. She was not afraid of anything! Releasing Ellie Mae's hand, she then whirled around. "I am not afraid!"

"There's only one way we'll believe that." Betsy's hands moved from her chest to her hips.

There was no way this would be a one-way challenge. "Are you going?" Katherine poked her chin out, putting her own hands on her hips, attempting to puff up her chest as much as she could.

"Of course," Betsy said, though her voice caught.

"Then, let's go." Katherine grabbed after Ellie Mae's hand and headed out in the direction of the old mine shaft. She hoped Ellie Mae didn't feel how her palms had started to sweat. Perspiration covered her whole body. How was she to keep up this façade?

The group of students followed, a din of voices behind. As they neared the cavernous opening, they became quiet as they halted several feet short of the forbidden place.

Wyatt pushed through the crowd once they had stopped. "Now, girls, this is foolishness. Talking about it is one thing, but you're not actually going down there, are you?"

Katherine glanced at the mine opening. It looked dark and ominous. Not what she wanted to see. Then she eyed Betsy. She had everything—the popularity, the most handsome boy in school ... But she would not have Katherine's pride, too. "I am."

"Then I am, too." Betsy stared at Katherine, matching her glare through slitted eyes.

"Kath-rine," Ellie whispered, tugging on her hand.

Katherine looked over at her friend. Ellie's eyes begged her not to go. Katherine wondered again at the danger. Her friend had every right to be concerned, she supposed. But it would not last. Betsy would go but a few steps in and give up. Katherine was sure of it. So, she would not be dissuaded.

Wyatt's eyes moved from one girl to the other. A couple of years older than the girls at their thirteen years, he stood a good head taller than Katherine. At last, he threw his hands up in the air. "Then I'm going too."

"And so am I," came Ellie Mae's quiet response.

Katherine leaned toward her friend. "Ellie, you don't have to go." Her eyes held Ellie's. What was she going to do? She couldn't take Ellie into that place. But something had eased in her when Ellie Mae volunteered to go. Was it selfish of her to want her friend to accompany her?

"Yes, I do." Her voice was firm, though her chin quivered. "I'm sticking with you."

A bump in the trail jolted Katherine from her reverie. The scenery outside became blurred. Or was it her? Touching her face, she felt moisture. She wiped at the tears. This would not do! Whatever happened when she returned, Katherine was determined she would face it with as much bravery as she could muster.

Not for the first time, she wondered what had become of Wyatt Sullivan and Betsy Calloway. She had avoided this subject in her correspondence with her parents over the last few years. Knowing Wyatt, he had gone on to bigger and better things and gotten himself out of Cripple Creek. And Betsy had probably caught the first stagecoach that took her wherever Wyatt went. So that was that.

The coach slowed and the town she knew so well appeared in the distance. In a matter of moments, she would be home. What a state this trip had left her in! With gloved hands, she smoothed over her dress and straightened her jacket. Her fingers worked to once again secure the pins that held her hat in place as the coach turned. Then they trotted down the main stretch into town.

Some of the changes her parents had written her about became visible. Cripple Creek had become a mining town. When Ol' Bob Womack filed his claim, which he'd named the El Paso Lode, he'd started another gold rush, this one in Cripple Creek. She remembered the old man. Everyone thought he was crazy and at first no one paid attention to Ol' Bob until a mining man formed the Cripple Creek Mining District, bringing in thousands of miners and prospectors within weeks. And then a stranger to their town, a Mr. Winfield Stratton, struck gold as well. Not just a little bit of gold, but such a lode that he became the first millionaire to grace this part of Colorado. That did nothing to deter interest. Some of these things were part of her memories, some her parents had told her through letters, but the events blurred between the two.

The stagecoach came to a slow stop, and the door opened. Katherine coughed at the burst of dust that flew into the coach. Once that settled, she was thankful for the fresh air. She gathered her things and stepped out of the coach.

Taking in the sights around her, she was struck at the amount of activity that filled the main thoroughfare. The main street appeared quite different with tents, makeshift cabins, and lean-tos set up all along the way. At the same time, it amazed her how little Cripple Creek had changed. As she gazed down the street, she spotted the bank, the church, the General Store... Katherine could almost see Ellie Mae standing there at the corner of the street, waiting for her so that they could walk the rest of the way to school. Blinking back tears, she fidgeted with the hem of her jacket.

"Ma'am?" a man's voice interrupted her thoughts as fingers touched her arm.

Turning her head in the direction of the sound, she found a well-dressed man looking at her. He seemed to be expecting an answer. Had he asked her a question?

"I'm sorry, sir. My mind was elsewhere." She fought the urge to touch her face and wipe away any incriminating tears.

"That's quite all right. I'm John Jacobs, the town mayor. Katherine Matthews, I presume?" He stuck his hand out to shake hers.

She slid hers forward, forcing a smile she didn't truly feel. "Yes, nice to meet you."

"And you as well. Welcome to Cripple Creek. Rather, I suppose I should say 'welcome back.'"

Katherine nodded, her eyes drifting past Mayor Jacobs to the town once more. The voices from the past called to her. But she drew her attention to the present and to Mayor Jacobs. "Yes, it's good to be home. Although it has changed."

"That's what I understand. The population of this town has grown in the time I've been here. I can't imagine how much it's changed for you."

She nodded again. How much indeed. *The streets are full, Ellie Mae isn't here, and I'm doing business with the Mayor.* A loud clap on the wooden boards of the sidewalk startled Katherine. Turning, she placed a hand on her chest. Only her trunk and bags being unloaded from the coach.

Mayor Jacobs gestured toward the stack. "Shall I have these things taken to the boarding house? That is still your plan, I take it?"

"Yes, I thank you." She released her grip over her heart and let out a deep breath in hopes it would slow its beating.

He nodded and then continued with some hesitation, "I hate to impose, Miss Matthews, but I hoped you would be agreeable to meeting with the town council. They are eager to speak with you."

The trip had tired her. She had traveled for many days, and the emotions of being back in Cripple Creek had begun to overwhelm her. What she truly wanted was a couple hours of rest before her parents came to collect her for dinner. This delay would affect her plans. However, this was her job, and she didn't want to disappoint the town council. After all, they hadn't had the opportunity to interview her properly before offering her the position. So she tipped her head in agreement.

He smiled. "Good. They'll be at the schoolhouse within the hour. Do you need some refreshment after your trip? The boarding house has a nice café."

Maybe this would help her relax before the meeting. "Perhaps a glass of water or lemonade. I am parched."

"Of course you are." The mayor ushered her toward the lower level of the two-story building. "We have time for a bite to eat as well."

Eat? She was far too anxious to put anything in her stomach. "No, but thank you. I'd rather get a look at the state of the schoolhouse and I don't want to keep the council waiting."

"All right."

Mayor Jacobs opened the door, and Katherine stepped off the wood planked porch and into the cooler rooms within. The space was open and smelled of coffee and pot roast. Katherine's mouth began to water at the enticing aroma, but she reminded herself she did not wish to chance a meal. Simple oak tables covered with white linens were scattered about, and burgundy curtains lifted in the breeze that flowed through the space from the open windows. Altogether, a pleasant sort of place. Nothing quite so quaint existed in San Francisco where she'd gone to receive her higher education. But it fit Cripple Creek.

Once inside the small café, they were acknowledged and seated quickly. The mayor ordered two lemonades. As they sipped on their cool beverages, the mayor made small talk about the town, the townsfolk in general, and the mining operations. He inquired after her family, and they concluded their visit with some chitchat about her father's ranching business.

By the time Katherine finished her lemonade, the mayor had long since drained his glass. She blotted her mouth with her napkin and stood. Mayor Jacobs left enough money on the table to cover the bill and escorted her out of the café and back into the hot sun.

Now on the main stretch, he held his arm up in the direction of the schoolhouse. "This way, ma'am, as I'm sure you remember."

Katherine moved through the town, taking the same steps she had so many times before. Her view of the road changed and before her eyes she saw the ghosts of her past. As if the townsfolk she had known were before her, and her childhood classmates moved through the streets to get to the schoolhouse on time.

As they neared the old tree in the schoolyard, Katherine took a moment to touch the sturdy trunk. How many times had her younger hands touched this very spot? How many games had she played around its frame? A fine bench had been put in underneath its branches. She sat on it and ran her hand over the smooth wood. It was unimaginable the hours two friends could pass here, telling stories and sharing secrets.

The new playground lay nearby, but as she gazed at it, it was not face-less children she imagined there; it was her classmates. And Ellie Mae . . .

Ellie Mae had been Katherine's best friend for as long as she could remember. They had grown up together. Her friend's raven-colored hair and blue eyes made her one of the more intriguing-looking girls in class. She also had Katherine's pale complexion. However, Katherine thought it much more becoming on Ellie Mae.

"Hey," Ellie Mae said, waving, having spotted her friend.

Katherine rushed over to her. Pleased, as always, that her friend waited to walk the rest of the way to school with her. "Hey, Ellie."

They linked arms and turned toward the schoolhouse.

"Did you see Betsy this morning?" Ellie lowered her voice as if she shared a great secret.

"No." Katherine rolled her eyes. What was Betsy up to now? Always something with her.

"She is wearing quite the dress today. And mooning over Wyatt."

"I'll bet." Betsy was always throwing herself at Wyatt. Even more so now with the fall dance coming up. That girl would do anything to get him to ask her to the dance. Katherine was curious why he hadn't. Why did he continue to make everyone suffer Betsy's through antics?

Not that it truly bothered her. He wasn't her beau. And she didn't have a crush on him. Heavens no!

"She is so obvious. I wish he would just ask her already." Ellie Mae's eyebrows furrowed.

"I think he likes the attention." Katherine scowled. Wyatt was just plain vain.

"Shhh!" Ellie Mae elbowed her as she stifled a giggle.

Katherine looked around. Why had Ellie Mae cut her off?

Now in the schoolyard, they had just passed Betsy, Wyatt, and their classmates gathered by the old tree. But as Katherine glanced in their direction, Wyatt stared at her. Their eyes met. Katherine turned away. Why would he be looking at her? Did he hear what she had said? Did he know she was talking about him?

Katherine, her face warming, ducked her head and quickened her pace to get inside the schoolhouse.

Ellie Mae wasn't able to keep up. As they reached their seats inside, she caught her breath at last.

"What was that all about?" Ellie Mae's eyes sought Katherine's after they did a sweep of the area. "Why did Wyatt look at you like that?"

"I don't know. Do you think he heard us?" Katherine's heart raced, and her body coursed with energy as if she could run away. And that's just what she wanted to do — run a million miles away!

Ellie Mae shook her head. "Surely not."

Katherine looked in the direction of the door. "I hope not." But the warmth continued to creep further into her face. She was hopeless!

The school bell rang and a flood of students came through the doors. Katherine's eyes remained fixed on the open doorway until Wyatt appeared. When she spotted his tall, slender frame, she spun around and dropped into her seat with a thump, dropping her head into her hands.

As the rest of the students took their seats, Miss Johnson, the schoolteacher, moved through the room toward the front of the class.

Katherine pulled her head up, but couldn't focus. Had Wyatt heard her comment? Did he know it was about him? Wyatt was by far the most handsome boy in the whole schoolhouse. His sandy blond hair and blue eyes weren't all that remarkable, but the strength of his features won him acclaim among the females.

To Katherine, he was her greatest rival. She might not be much to look at, but she knew she was smart. Well, so was Wyatt. For every high mark she made, he made one point above or below her. They always challenged each other for the top score. How unfair that he could have both the smarts and the looks! But that was life.

Everything became quiet around her.

Ellie Mae poked her.

"Wha—?" she startled in response. One look at Miss Johnson silenced her.

Miss Johnson stared at her.

And so did everyone else.

Had the teacher just called her name?

"Um . . . present," she said, rubbing her offended arm. She shot Ellie Mae a mean look.

"Are you sure?" Miss Johnson raised an eyebrow.

The class laughed.

Though she did not think it possible, Katherine's cheeks heated several more degrees. "Yes."

Miss Johnson moved on with the roll.

Mayor Jacobs coughed, drawing her attention back to the present.

"I'm so sorry, Mayor. I seem to have lost my sense of time again." Katherine stood and strode over to the schoolhouse stairs. She ducked her head as she passed him, almost as embarrassed by this lapse as she had been that day so long ago.

The town had kept the building up quite well. It appeared to have recently received a new coat of paint. Taking the few stairs, she stepped inside the one-room structure and pushed a fresh flood of memories to the side to focus on what lay in front of her. The student benches and desks all seemed to be in good repair, and the leg of the teacher's desk, which Miss Johnson had propped up with books, had been fixed.

Forgetting the mayor was with her, she moved among the desks, letting her hand graze the tops, hearing Miss Johnson calling roll. Walking toward the front of the classroom, she let her hands run over the edge of the teacher's desk and chair. Now at the chalkboard, she shifted to take in the whole room. Her eyes drifted across the room, seeing her classmates as Miss Johnson would have seen them. And the desk she shared with Ellie Mae.

"Well, what do you think?" the mayor's voice interrupted her reverie.

She must get control of herself. Katherine shook her head and cleared her throat. "Quite nice. Rather well kept."

"Thank you." His voice was soft.

Did he know she was struggling to stay in the present?

"We do what we can. Our children and their education are important to the people of this town."

"That's good to hear." She swallowed hard, attempting to quell the myriad of emotions welling up within her. This always had been a good town. Full of heart.

The stairs creaked outside. Katherine's eyes darted toward the door and she guessed they were about to be joined by the first of the town council.

A tall man dressed in black entered the room. His pastoral collar caught her eye. But as she looked at his face, she knew this preacher was familiar to her. He had grown into a man and a beard hid some of his features, but she would know the eyes of her first schoolyard beau anywhere.

"Timothy," she said as he closed the door behind himself.

He grinned. "Katherine."

They moved toward each other, meeting in the middle of the classroom, embracing as old friends.

"It is so good to see you." Katherine found herself leaning into his strong frame. It did feel good to be received so well. Not all of her classmates would have done the same.

"You too, Katie," he said as he pulled back. "My goodness, look at you."

Katherine's face warmed. "And you, the town preacher." She straightened the lapels of his jacket. Why had she done that? There was time and distance between them, but he still smiled at her. And so the edges of her mouth formed a wider smile as they continued to gaze at one another.

While they had kept up correspondence when she left for school, over time, her letters became few and far between. And then she stopped writing altogether. Katherine just couldn't make herself stay so connected to home. The last she knew, he had gone off to seminary and hoped to return as Cripple Creek's preacher. She had suspected her chances of coming across Timothy were good and she prayed for understanding. And now here he was, welcoming her back with open arms.

"Does it suit me?" The pride in his eyes could not be mistaken.

She nodded. "It does." There was much of the boy she knew in the man before her. Yet he had grown up. What had changed? What was the same?

"I guess no introduction is necessary here," the mayor interjected, stepping in from somewhere.

Katherine had forgotten anyone else was present. "No." She took a step back. "The Reverend and I are old friends." Referring to Timothy as 'Reverend' seemed odd. When she said that word, the face that flashed through her mind was that of old Reverend Jones. May he rest in peace.

The door opened again and two men Katherine did not recognize joined them. They were introduced as Michael Hammond, the town's banker, and Phillip Yerby, who ran the General Store. Once Mr. Yerby was made known, Katherine could see in the older man's face the features of the man she had known as a girl. The years had been hard on him.

"We're just waiting on Doc, as usual," Mr. Yerby said. "And who knows when he'll be free?"

Was the doctor not to be inconvenienced for council meetings? Or was it that he felt his work was more important than meeting the new teacher?

"Our town doctor is the fifth member of the council," the mayor explained. "He'll be here as soon as he can. What with emergencies and whatnot. That being said, we might not see him at all."

Emergencies? Were there that many emergencies in little Cripple Creek?

"Why don't we start without him?" Timothy offered.

The men let out a chorus of agreement. Mayor Jacobs pulled the teacher's chair around to the front of the desk, indicating for Katherine to sit, and the councilmen took seats at the students' desks.

Katherine took the offered seat and turned her thoughts to the men in front of her, attempting to give the man who was not present the benefit of the doubt.

"First, we want to thank you for coming to fill our interim position. We are so pleased to have a qualified teacher with our children during this time of transition," the mayor said as they all got settled.

"I'm glad to be here." Katherine smiled. It was true after all, right? She didn't know anymore.

"The Reverend tells us you are from Cripple Creek." Mr. Hammond gave her a curious look.

"Yes, sir. You might know my parents, Tom and Lauren Matthews." She had this. Her parents were good people, strong people in the community. They were certainly well regarded.

Murmurs of acknowledgement rumbled among the group.

Mr. Hammond's features relaxed, but his questions continued. "And you went away to further your education?"

"Yes, to San Francisco." They didn't need to know that it wasn't the only reason she'd gone away.

"And how long have you been a teacher?" Mr. Yerby piped up.

"Since I graduated, three years ago."

While she spoke, the door opened to admit the final member of the town council. The long awaited doctor had finally arrived. The man nodded in her direction as he entered, his features masked as his head was tilted forward. But as he came closer, she began to make out nuances of his face.

A chill ran down her spine and she froze.

It was none other than Wyatt Sullivan.

"Miss Matthews?" Mayor Jacobs's chair squeaked as he leaned forward.

"Yes?" She caught herself. Had he been speaking to her?

"I said, 'I believe you may already know our doctor as well.'"

She nodded, unable to speak. Yes, she knew him. Better than she wanted to. So much so that she would do anything to erase the memory of everything surrounding him.

"I hope you don't mind, Wyatt. We got started without you." Timothy waved to a nearby student desk. "But jump in whenever you'd like."

How could Timothy just speak to him so amicably? Had he forgotten?

Wyatt nodded, sliding into the chair that was much too small for his tall frame. "Certainly." He turned toward Katherine. "Good to see you again."

Katherine nodded at him but still couldn't find her voice. She looked at his shirt, his hair, everywhere but his eyes.

"Did you spend those three years teaching at the same institution?" Mr. Yerby pulled out his handkerchief and wiped at his brow.

So the room was warm, it wasn't just her. She longed to fan herself or loosen her collar. Anything to relieve some of this heat inside her. A moment lapsed before Katherine remembered she still sat in a session with the town council. "Yes," she said, closing her eyes to focus her thoughts. "The Billingham Boarding School for Girls."

"Katherine," Wyatt leaned forward on his elbows. "If I walked into your classroom on a typical afternoon, what would I see?"

Meeting his eyes at last, she blinked a few times before finding an answer. "You would find students learning." She bit her lip. It was not her intention to be snarky. "But I don't think that's what you mean." Taking a deep breath, she continued, "You would find the students and I engaged in a discussion about a book or a topic in science. Perhaps we would be doing math on our tablets, but I prefer most of our learning to be done through discussion." There, that was done. His question had been answered. Her eyes moved toward the other men, but Wyatt spoke up with another question.

"Why did you want to become a teacher?"

Pause. Breathe. She met his gaze. "Because I love learning and I want to share that with the next generation."

Wyatt's next inquiry came within a breath of her answer. "Tell us about your discipline philosophy."

She stared at him. This seemed more like an interview and less like a 'get to know you' session thanks to Wyatt's questions. Still, she responded, shoulders back, chest tight. "I think it's important to reduce behavior problems by offering students a stimulating environment." This time, she continued to stare at him, daring him to continue questioning her.

He rose to the challenge. "But how do you handle discipline issues?"

Her heart started to pound. She became rather uncomfortable under his scrutiny. The others eyed her, and she decided it best to do what she could to remain calm. "I prefer to remove privileges and have the students do write offs."

"What are your classroom rules?" Mr. Hammond interrupted the back and forth.

Somewhat relieved for the respite from Wyatt's steel blue eyes, Katherine shifted her attention over to the banker. "My rules revolve around the students respecting myself, other students, and the school-house. That involves things like no talking when someone else is talking, raising hands to be recognized to talk, no behaviors that would be destructive to the schoolhouse or the desks . . ."

"What about students who are not performing as they should?" Wyatt interjected.

"It depends on whether it is a discipline issue or a capability issue." Katherine raised an eyebrow at him. Would his questions never end?

He leaned back, folding his arms across his chest as if he had not considered that fine point.

Not wanting to give him any opportunity to gain on her, she continued, "If the student is willing, I can give him or her extra attention and time in order to support them."

Wyatt opened his mouth, but the mayor cut him off.

"Miss Matthews, thank you for answering our questions. Do you have any questions for us?"

"Whom do I take any of my concerns to?" She had been dreading the answer to that question since Wyatt had walked into the schoolhouse. Holding her breath, she waited for the mayor to confirm or alleviate her fears.

"You will work most closely with the Reverend," the mayor said, tipping his head toward Timothy. "Most issues and concerns will be addressed by him."

Timothy offered her a winning smile.

A deep sigh of relief escaped her. Was it audible?

"Serious issues that, for whatever reason, need to go beyond the Reverend will be handled by myself." Mayor Jacobs placed a hand on his chest. "But we only want to support you."

She nodded. Nothing would faze her as long as she didn't have to answer to Wyatt. "I understand."

"Anything else?"

Katherine shook her head. She hadn't expected to end this session with such an elated feeling in her heart. "Unless something has changed from our most recent correspondence as far as salary and start date?"

The mayor shook his head. "Everything is the same."

"Then I have all the information I need." Still aware of Wyatt's gaze on her, she fidgeted with her hands in her lap.

"Well, gentlemen," Mayor Jacobs said as he looked at the other men.

"I think we need to let Miss Matthews rest after her trip." He turned back toward her. "Thank you for meeting with us."

And the men rose, each nodding in her direction in turn before shuffling toward the door, making small talk with each other.

Katherine stood as well, only to realize how weak her knees were. But she maintained her posture as the men clustered near the back of the room, still chatting.

Timothy alone stepped toward her. "Might I walk you back to your parent's house?"

Was he being forward? Did she want him to be? "I'm actually staying at the boarding house in town."

"Oh." He looked toward the floor.

Did he think her refusal was a rejection? She had not intended that. "But I would welcome your company back into town, if it's no trouble."

The other men had already started moving in the direction of the doorway. Was it her imagination, or did Wyatt linger? Was he eavesdropping? It wasn't long though before even he had vacated the schoolhouse, leaving her and Timothy alone.

"No, no trouble at all." The corners of his mouth twitched and turned upward.

A warmth spread through Katherine. Yes, she still rather enjoyed the way Timothy's smile made her feel.

Katherine took one last long look around the room where she'd be spending most of her time in the days to come. She allowed herself a few more moments to lose herself in her memories. Perhaps she should rearrange the schoolroom to prevent these flashbacks.

Turning back to Timothy, she offered him her best smile. Maybe he would come to like her smile too. "Ready when you are."

With that, they made their way toward town.

"So," she couldn't help but say, grinning. "Find any good lizards lately?"

When they were but schoolkids, Timothy had been well known for his obsession with all things creepy crawly. He tried to share this love with her, but her obsession had been books. Hopeless even then.

He shook his head, stifling a laugh. "I haven't been on a good reptile hunt in quite a while."

"That's a shame. I think you must take my students on one of your famous reptile hunts!" Had she just said that? Was she flirting with Timothy? Would that be all right?

"Truly?" One of his eyebrows shot up.

"If only you would." She tugged playfully at his arm.

"I think I would like that."

"It's settled then." She once again surprised herself and slid a hand into the crook of his arm. It was her turn to be forward.

He seemed surprised by her familiarity, but soon fell into step with her, bending his arm to create a better space for her handhold. A silence fell between them for a few moments. The time and distance hung in that space. She needed to speak about it. If it remained unsaid, it would only create a greater gap.

"I'm sorry I stopped writing." Her voice became quiet.

"I understand why you did," he said, his voice soft. With his free hand, he reached across to lay it on hers.

She nodded, biting at her lip to contain her emotions. "Thank you . . . for understanding."

"I'm glad you're back in town." His voice seemed deeper somehow when it was so quiet.

Katherine kept her gaze on the ground for a few seconds before looking over at him. How much should she trust him? He was the closest thing she had to a friend here. Ever since . . . "I have mixed feelings about it."

She didn't have to say anything further. Timothy would understand.

That same silence fell on them again, only this time it was thick with memories.

He slowed their steps, breaking the spell. "I wanted to say, don't let Wyatt's questioning bother you. He's just that way about things. It's nothing to do with you."

Surely Timothy meant to reassure her. That could not be so. "I wish I could believe that," she confided.

Timothy pressed her hand, but said nothing.

Katherine drew her attention from Timothy to her surroundings. Long had they left the grassy surroundings of the schoolhouse and entered the dusty streets of town as they approached the boarding house.

"Here we are," Timothy said, turning to face her, but not releasing her hand.

"Yes, we are." She glanced down at her captive hand. Why did he hold her hand so? Was it possible he maintained his interest in her?

"What would you say to dinner tomorrow night?" His breath quickened and his voice shook, almost imperceptibly. As if he were that same young kid asking her to the fall dance so many years ago.

Her stomach flipped. "I think that would be nice, Timothy." Smiling up at him, she gave his arm a little squeeze.

"Good." He beamed. "If you need anything before then, don't hesitate to stop by."

"Thanks." She thrilled at the thought of spending more time with Timothy. He would also be an invaluable ally with Wyatt in town and on the council. Not to mention how relieved she was that their friendship was still intact despite her actions.

With that, he released her hand and moved in the direction of the church.

She watched him go, thankful again for her old friend's presence and help during this transition. And perhaps the hope of something more.

Katherine's father would be by to collect her for dinner soon, so she'd best get out of her travel clothes and into something more comfortable. What a day it had been! The memories, the interrogation, the promise of an evening out. She stepped into the boarding house and moved toward the stairs at the back of the café.

As Katherine passed the small mass of tables, she paused. Was that . . . ? She turned her head to get a better view of the café. It was – Wyatt and a blonde woman. But why should it stop her in her tracks? Why should Wyatt's dining habits concern her? Still, she couldn't help but chance another glance in his direction, letting her eyes drift over to his dinner companion. Her breath caught. His dining partner was none other than Betsy Calloway.

Betsy hung on Wyatt's every word, eyes glued to his face. But Katherine watched Betsy's face, every bit as beautiful as Katherine remembered, a clear step above her peers. It irked Katherine, and she chided herself for feeling that way. She was no longer the preteen girl who felt lost among her peers. As a grown woman, Katherine had become well regarded and respected by those who knew her. Why should it matter to her what Betsy looked like? But Betsy's presence here with Wyatt did strike Katherine.

So, after all this time, she had finally gotten her man. Good for her.

Katherine turned her attention to the stairs and made her way toward her room, trying, for the millionth time, to put Wyatt Sullivan out of her mind.

CHAPTER 2

Changes

Lauren Matthews sang as she worked in the kitchen, preparing her daughter's favorite meal for her first night home. It was, after all, a momentous occasion. When Katherine moved away after finishing school, she had tried to understand. But that didn't keep her from plotting how she might get her daughter to return home. She never dreamed such an opportunity would surface or that Katherine would be so easily convinced. Perhaps deep down, Katherine wanted to come back.

Either way, Lauren would make everything of this opportunity to persuade Katherine this was where she belonged. It would take little effort for the town council to see that it would only be to their benefit to make Katherine's placement at the schoolhouse permanent. She could see it all falling into place. What mother wouldn't want her children close to home?

Step one would be to make her homecoming as welcoming as possible. Her expert hands worked the oven, checking the pot roast to ensure the meat and vegetables were coming along. They were perfect. She closed the oven and wiped her hands on her apron. Nothing to do but wait for her husband to arrive with Katherine in tow.

They would have their whole family gathered at the table once more this evening. David and his family would be joining them once he got off work. Now that was another issue altogether. While he had married a local girl and stayed close to home, he had also decided not to follow in his father's footsteps as a rancher. Why he had chosen a different path as a miner was beyond her. The life of a rancher wasn't easy, but it wasn't all that bad either. But, oh, how she hated him working in those awful mines. Still, he earned a fair living and supported his family.

Mining had taken this little town by storm. Since Ol' Bob Womack discovered his lode of gold and it set off a gold rush, things had never been the same. Within the next year, Mr. Stratton made one of the largest strikes in history. In the midst of all of this, their little town had a population boom of prospectors, gamblers, and fortune seekers, all looking to make their own million-dollar claim. No, this wasn't the same town Katherine left. Many, many things had changed.

Cart wheels driving across the rock and dirt path outside drew Lauren from her thoughts. She set her kitchen towel down and rushed over to the window, watching as Tom helped his daughter out of the wagon before he moved toward the barn to put the horse away.

Smoothing shaky hands over her dress, Lauren turned toward the door. How long had it been since she had seen her daughter? Too long.

When the door opened, Lauren stood beaming, with bated breath and open arms.

"Katie!" Lauren took those last two steps onto the porch, closing the gap between them.

"Ma!" Katherine walked into her mother's arms. She needed her embrace. It must have been Christmas since she had last seen her family. As she enjoyed being caught firmly in her mother's arms, Ma rubbed her back the way only she did.

Katherine's eyes watered. Why had she not made more of an effort to come home and visit? Why had she let her fears of Cripple Creek and the ghosts here keep her from her own mother's embrace? Those thoughts dissipated as soon as they came; she was home now and all was well. Pulling back, Katherine saw that her mother's eyes were glazed with the same tears she fought.

"Come in, come in." Ma pulled her into the house and closed the door. "How was your trip?"

"It was fine. Long." Katherine did not want to revisit her travels. First the train, then the stagecoach. She was certain her backside would be bruised tomorrow.

"And how do you find Cripple Creek?" Ma indicated Katherine should sit at the table. She then moved toward the kitchen.

"Quite different. But, still the same somehow." Her mind wandered to the Cripple Creek of years past, but she forced herself to stay present.

Ma nodded as she checked the meat.

Katherine took a moment to close her eyes and drink in the smell of her mother's pot roast as the aroma escaped the open oven door. But then, Ma had just asked her something. What was it? Oh, yes, Cripple Creek.

"You wrote about this mining craze, but I hadn't expected to see so many people camping on the main street." It had disturbed Katherine, the number of miners fairly littering the main stretch. How was anyone to move about?

Ma began cutting the bread on the counter. "I hope I don't have to tell you it's best to not find yourself walking alone at night out there anymore."

Katherine nodded, waving off her mother's concern. But that's the way mothers are. Always looking out for their little chicks, no matter how old. "Yes, mother."

Pa walked into the house just then, taking off his hat and hanging it by the door. "I heard another buggy coming. I think David will be by soon."

"Wait until you see how Jessie has grown." Ma clapped her hands. "And Peter has started walking."

Katherine smiled, trying to ignore the heaviness of regret in her heart. She had missed so much of her family's lives these last few years. Her parents visited her in San Francisco a few times, but she had only returned to Cripple Creek to see David and his family for a couple of holidays during her schooling and not at all since she completed her studies. Her mother's comment lifted her spirits and touched her heart. Ma was such a proud grandma.

"Katie, would you mind setting the table? The good plates." Ma glanced in the direction of the dish cabinet as she busied herself with the final stages of the meal.

"Sure, Ma," she said, standing.

Katherine walked over to the same cabinet that had stood in the kitchen for as long as she could remember. She ran a hand along the front, enjoying the feel of the solid wood. Its surface smoothed even more so by additional years of wear. Once she opened the door, she pulled down enough of her mother's good plates for each individual. These were the plates Ma reserved for special occasions. Her heart warmed that she, too, was special.

No sooner had she carried the dishes over to the table then she heard a commotion outside, a sure sign her brother and his family had arrived. She hurried along with the silverware so her hands were free to get her hugs once the door was opened. Her hands were shaking and fumbling as she did so. Was she truly this excited to see her brother? Just as she finished placing the last piece of dinnerware down, the door was flung open. A brown-haired six-year-old girl bounded into the house.

"Aunt Katherine! Aunt Katherine!" the wiry bundle screamed as she ran straight for Katherine.

"Jessie!" Katherine squatted and caught the child in a fierce embrace. Her eyes closed. She wanted to etch this moment into her memory. Soon enough, the clomp of boots alerted her to the presence of her big brother. Opening her eyes, she watched over the small girl's shoulder as David and his lovely wife, Mary, walked in.

Mary held a squirming ball of limbs, Peter. But as soon as the door was closed, Mary turned him loose. He wasn't free for long before Pa swooped him up for a quick hug.

Jessie pulled back from Katherine's embrace only to start chattering on about anything and everything. Her words spilled out so fast, Katherine wasn't able to catch many of them.

"Whoa," Mary admonished. "Slow down. Let Aunt Katherine say 'hello' to everyone first."

Katherine nodded her thanks. Her mind whirled enough as it was without attempting to interpret child speak. "How are you, Mary?" She stood and gave her sister-in-law a warm hug.

"Never better," she said, beaming. "Glad you're here for a while. And hoping we can convince you to stay forever."

Forever? She had only just arrived here. Katherine wasn't sure if she wanted to stay . . .

David stepped forward and embraced his younger sister. "I'll second that."

Katherine smiled at her brother. He seemed tired. Not just from lack of sleep, but from continuous overworking. Was he taking on too much? She would need to remember to talk with him about that later.

"Here's someone else who needs a Katherine hug." Pa came up behind her, still carrying Peter.

"And I'm so happy to oblige." Katherine beamed, taking her still squirming nephew from her father and hugging him to herself.

His little arms pushed against her in protest. But Katherine knew better than to take it personally.

The little man had some fight in him! For one so small, he was strong. "I know, I know, you want to get down. But you have to give me a hug first." Once she had adequately tortured him with a hug, she set him on the floor and he was off.

"Dinner's ready," Ma called from the kitchen. "Let's all get in our seats." She carried the pot roast over to the table.

"Ma, you've outdone yourself," Katherine said as she looked over the main course, her stomach grumbling. "And I'm glad you did." She loved that her mother had made her favorite meal. Not at all surprised, but grateful all the same.

Ma winked at her. "Now, sit down so we can say grace and get started."

Katherine took her seat and let her gaze wander around the table at her sweet family, all getting seated and ready to eat. This is what it meant to be home. And it was good.

A bright morning touched the town streets of Cripple Creek, a typical late summer day in which the sun beat down on anyone who dared venture out and about. But workmen, farmers, ranchers, and even doctors had to brave the blazing sun for the sake of their livelihood.

On this day, Wyatt Sullivan found himself out in the heat working on his homestead. He'd recently acquired the property and had grand visions of what it could be. So, he spent every spare afternoon and Saturday here, working with his hands to reform the already sizable home into something he could be proud of.

This property bore little resemblance to the one room cabin he grew up in. Wyatt couldn't help the memories trickling into his consciousness as he nailed away at the doorframe. His childhood home had been small, claustrophobic. All the more so with his father's frequent outbursts. He hammered into the boards with all his strength as an image of his father's face filled his mind, making him bend the nail he worked on.

He was tempted to throw the tool but restrained himself. Only then did he realize he was heaving. Sweat trickled down his face and back, soaking his shirt. But he had not been over-exerting himself. Could it be the memories?

Closing his eyes, he leaned against the interior wall, out of the sun, and took a few deep breaths. He did his best to focus on his plans for the new homestead rather than his childhood home or his father. After some moments, his heartbeat slowed and his body calmed.

With fresh determination, he moved back toward the doorframe and pulled out the bent nail, now useless. He reached for the box of nails only to discover it was empty. Sighing, he hunched his shoulders. No more work could be done until he made a much-needed trip to the General Store.

Bending forward, he let the air rush out of him and drew in a deep, refreshing breath. Only then did he gather his hat and move to saddle his horse, Rusty. As much as he loathed pausing in his work, if he wanted to get anything else done today, he'd need to make the trip as quickly as possible. And so, he pulled himself up into the saddle and urged the horse onward toward town.

He didn't often venture out to the main streets of the small town on the weekends. As long as there were no emergencies. That was his time. And he wasn't much of a social creature.

Pulling Rusty up to the General Store, he slid off the saddle and tethered the reins to the post there. Nodding politely, he tipped his hat to a few passersby before heading into the store.

Phillip Yerby stood behind the counter checking his ledger when Wyatt walked in. Looking up from his work, he waved at his most recent customer. "Good day to ya', Doc."

"Hello, Phillip. How's the store?"

Wyatt liked Phillip Yerby. He was a pleasant sort of fellow. Kind, genial, only enough in your business to be neighborly.

"Good, good. Can't remember the last time I saw you in town on a Saturday though. Maybe when Mrs. Parsons had her baby."

Wyatt nodded. Now that had been a long day. "Doctoring sure keeps one busy."

"I imagine so." He turned his attention back to his ledger. "I've heard talk you're working out at Ol' Bob Womack's homestead."

"That I am." Wyatt moved among the shelves, gathering the few supplies he needed. On second thought, maybe the man did listen to too much gossip. Although Wyatt's purchase of the Womack homestead was hardly a secret.

"I'd heard Ol' Bob ended up moving to Colorado Springs and opening a boarding house. I guess after his father passed, they just didn't want to try to keep up the ranch." Yerby moved from behind the counter and appeared to be counting sacks.

Wyatt decided he was checking his inventory. "Is that so?" Wyatt could not be less interested in what happened to Bob Womack. What had happened to the man was a shame, but his decisions were not Wyatt's concern.

"He sure did put this town on the map." Yerby folded his papers and set his hands on the counter, giving up on his tallying and turning his full attention to Wyatt.

"I'll say he did." Though Wyatt wasn't sure it was a good thing the man had struck gold in the first place, bringing in the lot of fortune seekers and, eventually, the gold miners.

"Wish I'd believed him, to tell you the truth." Yerby gazed out the front window of the store.

Wyatt grunted and moved toward the counter with his items in hand. He had only been a child when Ol' Bob ranted and raved like a lunatic to anyone who would listen, proclaiming there was gold in the valley. No one believed him. Then, against all odds, he had done it. Had found gold. But then he lost it all. It was a sad tale.

"Will that be all for ya'?" Yerby reached over and grabbed the few things Wyatt set in front of him.

Wyatt nodded. He was all too ready to have this trip into town over with before someone decided they needed doctoring. The homestead called.

Yerby started calculating Wyatt's total, but stopped after the second item, looking up at him. "It just occurred to me that you and the reverend must have been schoolmates with the new interim teacher."

Wyatt's face flushed at the mention of Katherine. "That's right."

"Well, I don't know what the rest of the town council is thinking, but I was right impressed with her." Yerby went back to his tallying.

Wyatt nodded. "I'm sure she'll do right by this town." He wished they weren't talking about this. When her name came up as a prospect for the interim position, Wyatt had done everything he could to search out a better choice. But, as it turned out, she had been the only qualified teacher willing to take an interim position. That had perturbed him—to know he would have to face her again, fearing nothing had changed since the last time he saw her. Was she still angry with him? Was she still as feisty as ever? Would that still be every bit as enticing to him as it had been when they were young?

"As far as I'm concerned, I don't see any reason why the position couldn't be permanent."

Katherine here, permanently? How would that work out? Wyatt wasn't sure. "I guess we'll just have to see how this interim period goes."

Yerby finished with the items and met Wyatt's gaze. "You want this on your account?"

"Yes, sir." Wyatt reached over the counter to gather his wares.

"Take care of yourself now, Doc."

As Wyatt left the store, Yerby picked up his ledger book again and went back to his inventory. But Wyatt's mood was far more sour than it had been when he arrived.

The Sunday service drew to a close and Timothy dismissed the congregation. Katherine stood and did her best to smile as the people around her turned to shake her hand, but her heart was heavy. Today. It had to be today. She had already put it off for too long.

As the small crowd moved toward the back of the church, she followed. But her eyes were downcast, her thoughts filled with the task that lay ahead of her. If only her legs didn't feel like lead as she pushed them onward. How impossible her errand seemed. She wished she could ask someone to go with her, perhaps Timothy or Ma. But she knew this was something she needed to do . . . alone.

Sooner than she would have liked, she stepped out into the sunlight. A hand reached for hers. Timothy. Her face shifted so she met his gaze.

"I hope you enjoyed the sermon today." He smiled, but as he watched her features, his smile fell.

She forced the corners of her mouth to turn upward. No reason to bring his mood down. "Yes, I enjoyed it quite well."

One of his eyebrows raised in an unspoken question.

"I, um . . ." She wanted to avoid the issue, but saw no reason to lie to him. "I have to visit her, Timothy. I've waited long enough."

His features softened, and he nodded slowly, his eyes kind and concerned. "I won't be much longer here. If you would like, I can . . . "

How she wanted to take him up on his offer! But she could not. She put a hand on his arm. "No, I thank you, but I think it's something I need to do by myself."

He pressed his lips together in a straight line, but she saw in his eyes that he understood. "I'll say a prayer for you."

She dipped her head. "Thank you." And then she removed her hand from his arm, stepped away, and moved down the stairs, allowing the next person to speak with their reverend.

Once at the bottom of the stairs, she closed her eyes and took in a deep breath. She could do this. When she opened her eyes, she couldn't help but spot Wyatt across the churchyard. He spoke with Betsy about something rather intently. How dare they. How dare they enjoy this fine day as if nothing was wrong when her world was crumbling! A thick, hard substance filled her chest. And it settled there, heavy. As much as she wanted to continue to watch them and nurse her anger, Katherine tore her gaze away and moved toward the meadow adjacent to the small church.

Among the tall grasses there, Katherine began to pluck flowers. In a short time, she gathered a fair-sized bouquet of wild daisies, buttercups, and violets. They were lovely. Violets had always been her favorites. She stuck her nose into the petals of the delicate blooms and breathed in their fragrance. It calmed her. A gentle breeze drifted by and she imagined it carried all of her sadness, grief, and despair away. But she knew it was just wishful thinking. The heaviness in her chest remained. And the burden of the task ahead dragged on her consciousness.

Katherine glanced behind the church. There it was—the town cemetery. Surrounded by a short fence and shaded by a large weeping willow, it was everything a final resting place should be. But Ellie Mae had been too young. Far too young.

Tightness clamped around Katherine's chest and her feet turned to solid rock. How was she going to do this? She had faithfully visited her best friend's grave when she lived here. But that had been years ago, so many years ago. And now, it seemed impossible.

Somehow she made her legs move forward and carry her toward the rows of gray grave markers. Almost as if some invisible force drew her toward the lone stone that stood off to the north side of the tree. It seemed almost pitiful, off by itself. Ellie Mae's name was faded from the years of weather, but Katherine was still able to make it out on the smooth rock's surface.

"I'm sorry, Ellie," she whispered. "It should have been me."

Now standing over her friend's grave, she could not stop the tears that came. Why did Ellie Mae have to insist on coming with her into the mine? Why? She had been such a loyal friend. And that day was no different. The soft petals of the bouquet fell from her fingertips.

Katherine raised her hands in hope of stemming the tide threatening to overtake her. Her knees wobbled and became weak. She sank to the ground, the cool earth underneath her, the dirt between her fingers. She smelled it in the cloud of dust drifting upward, disturbed by her movements.

The air smelled stale. They continued on their journey that seemed to last forever. In the darkness, with only the small torch Wyatt had lit as their guide, it was difficult to discern any progress. Still, they made their way through the cavern, inching along as the tunnel became darker and darker.

Wyatt insisted they let him lead. The girls didn't argue. The mine was dark, cold, and damp.

Katherine felt enclosed, as if encased in a tomb. Every step of the way she regretted letting Betsy goad her into this. But with each step, she became more certain they neared a point when Betsy would admit defeat and they could turn around.

And then the tunnel split.

"What now?" Wyatt turned to Betsy.

"I think we should go this way," Betsy pointed down the shaft to the right, her eyes meeting Katherine's, gleaming in the light of the flame.

"You can't be serious . . ." Wyatt started.

We should turn around. But Betsy wasn't backing down. What will the others say if I do? "Suits me." Katherine met her gaze, unwavering. "Shall we?"

Betsy's face dropped for a moment before she regained her composure. "All right," She spoke with confidence, but her voice faltered.

Wyatt rolled his eyes, and Ellie Mae gripped Katherine's hand even tighter as they moved off in that direction.

They traveled for several feet with the thickness of the utter dark attempting to swallow them whole. That's when they hit a wall. At some point, the cavern must have become unstable and collapsed here, creating a wall of stones.

Katherine's insides did a flip-flop. Everyone had heard the stories of trapped miners. An unstable cavern was dangerous. They had to get out of there and quickly.

Looking over at Ellie Mae to see if her friend shared her anxiety over the state of this mining shaft, Katherine saw that Ellie Mae was shaking. Whether at the seriousness of their predicament or the prospect of retracing their steps, Katherine was not sure. But they had no choice; they must make their way back out. Without discussion, they followed Wyatt back down the corridor.

They had only moved a few feet when the rumbling began. The sensations of the earth quaking about them were by far the most sickening thing Katherine had ever experienced. Everything around them shook. Their small group hurried their steps, but it was no use. Between the unsteadiness of the ground and the scurrying of their bodies, Katherine lost her hold on Ellie Mae.

The cavern gave way and fell down on them all. One minute it was thunderous, the next minute, there was silence.

Katherine lay still. Was she dead? Moving her limbs, she felt life return to her. When she took a deep breath, her lungs filled with dust. This started a coughing fit. The more she coughed the more dust she inhaled. It took some time before she was able to breathe again.

As she was able to take stock of herself, she found she had a layer of dirt and small pebbles covering her, but was otherwise okay. Slowly getting to her feet, she tried to find the others in the group. There was movement nearby.

"Ellie?" she called out, her voice still hoarse and weak from coughing.

"No, it's Betsy."

She found herself thankful that Betsy was alive. "Betsy, are you okay?"

Betsy sniffed. "Yeah, but my arm hurts real bad."

Katherine maneuvered around the space. Her eyes were adjusting to the dark still. Now that the torch was out, she saw pinpricks of light coming through the rocks in places. She came across another body. It was Wyatt. He didn't respond to her. Was he alive? Dropping to her knees, she then shook him. After some prompting, he started to move.

"My leg," he groaned.

Katherine had a difficult time seeing what had injured him. One of his legs had gotten caught under a huge rock. "Betsy!"

"What?"

Where had she gone? "Betsy, I need your help."

She moaned, but Katherine heard her moving as she stumbled toward her.

"We need to push this rock off of Wyatt's leg." Katherine kneeled by Wyatt's legs, prepared to work on the rock.

"But my arm," Betsy whined.

Katherine had no time for Betsy's childishness. "Use your other arm."

Wyatt managed to sit up and position his hands on the rock as well. They all worked together to push the rock off his leg. He let out a loud cry as the rock moved, but that, too, was silenced as quickly as it started.

"Are you all right?" Katherine leaned closer to him than she realized in the dimness.

"Yes, I'll be fine." His warm breath grazed her cheek.

Katherine moved back a few inches, almost losing her balance. "Now we have to find Ellie." Katherine scanned the area and saw no sign of movement or another body. Where was Ellie?

Betsy helped Wyatt to his feet while Katherine moved around the cavern.

"Ellie!" Why hadn't they heard from her by now?

Wyatt felt along the wall created by the rubble. Was he searching for any weakness in the structure near the top? Hoping they could pull stones away and crawl out?

Katherine didn't care about any of that. She had to find Ellie Mae.

"Ellie!" she called and walked further away from Wyatt.

"Betsy, help her find Ellie Mae," she heard Wyatt instruct Betsy. Scrapes and gravel shifting sounded as if he dragged his wounded leg behind him as he continued to seek out an exit.

Moving her hands and eyes along the cavern walls, she searched for her friend. Seconds ticked by into minutes, though it felt like hours as they searched.

Katherine became frantic by that time. "Ellie, Ellie!"

Wyatt came back over to where he had parted ways with Katherine and Betsy.

Shaking, Betsy moved toward Wyatt. "We've searched the cavern and can't find her. Do you think she's under the pile of rocks?" Betsy's voice betrayed her fear at the prospect of Ellie Mae's death.

Katherine closed her eyes against that possibility. It just couldn't be. Ellie was here. Alive. She had to be. A sick feeling settled into her stomach.

Wyatt responded after some moments. "Betsy, go to the other side of the wall and wait for us there. I made a small opening for us to get through.”

“No, you come with me.” She pulled at his arm.

“I need to help Katherine.”

Katherine, only half listening to their exchange, continued to search. She maneuvered into a corner of the cavern they had passed before and spotted something pale poking out of the fallen rocks. Kneeling down, she felt the object. A hand! Working quickly, she brushed the dirt and rubble off of her friend's face and hair.

“Ellie! Betsy, Wyatt! I found Ellie!” Tears of hope filled her eyes. They had found Ellie!

“Wait here,” Wyatt told Betsy.

The sound of his leg being dragged across the dirt-covered ground allowed Katherine to track his movements. He came to where Katherine crouched now trying to rouse Ellie Mae.

Something wasn't right. She was cold. Only her face and arm protruded from the rocks, the rest of her had been buried under the fallen rocks.

Wyatt knelt down beside her and felt Ellie Mae's wrist and neck.

“Betsy, come help us move these rocks off of her,” Katherine called. Her own voice betrayed that she was crying. But she didn't care. They had to help Ellie Mae.

“Betsy, stay where you are,” Wyatt called.

Katherine moved to work on another rock that trapped Ellie Mae's body and Wyatt grabbed her hands.

“No, Katherine! You'll cause this whole wall of rocks to come tumbling down on top of us!”

What was he saying? They had to. This was Ellie Mae. “We have to get her out.”

“Katherine, she's gone.”

“No,” Katherine insisted. That couldn't be. They had found her. Her face and hand were here. “We just need to get her out. She'll be fine.”

Wyatt stood and pulled Katherine to her feet, but she fought to free herself of his arms.

“We have to get out of here.” He tugged at her arm, making some progress toward their escape route.

Betsy didn't need Wyatt to ask her to join him, she was a step ahead.

Katherine shook him off again. Hot tears stung her eyes. What was he doing? "You can't leave her. Ellie!"

Wyatt grabbed Katherine around the waist and pulled her toward the small opening he had created. He set her down just short of the opening as Betsy made her way through. Maneuvering his face so he was nearly nose-to-nose with Katherine, he spoke. "Listen to me. This cavern is unstable. If I could go back for her, I would. But I can't. We need to get out of here, Katie."

The rumbling started again around them, and she felt the instability of the cavern in the vibrations under her feet.

"No," she choked out. How could he ask her to leave Ellie Mae? How could she do such a thing?

Wyatt turned her and hoisted her up, pushing her through. She didn't want to leave her friend behind, no matter what, but Wyatt was behind her. So, she grasped for a handhold and pulled herself through. The cavern continued its grumbling protest.

As she popped out on the other side of the wall, she fell to the ground, sobbing. What had she done? She had left her best friend in there. To die.

There wasn't much time to mourn as Wyatt came through the opening not long after and urged her onward. She wanted to fight him, but it was no use.

He pulled her the rest of the way through the cavern until they were in the sunlight. As soon as he released her arm, she sat on the grass and wept. She wasn't sure how much time passed before she sensed someone kneeling beside her. Looking up, she saw Timothy. He pulled her into his embrace, and she continued crying on his shoulder.

"It's Ellie," she mumbled through her tears, "He wouldn't help me save Ellie. I'll . . . never . . . forgive . . . him."

Katherine found herself in the present, hunched in front of the tombstone, sobbing just as she had so many years before. She slammed her fist into the earth and was rewarded with a stinging sensation in her hand. Why had God let Ellie die instead of her? Why couldn't Wyatt have helped her save her best friend? Her heart ached with the heaviness of these unanswered questions.

She didn't know how long she remained there, caught up in her grief. But dusk had fallen before she found her way out of her memories. By then she was seated with her legs folded in front of her, tears pouring out until there were no more. And she became aware of a presence. Someone watching her.

Turning, she spotted a figure dressed all in black at the edge of the cemetery. Timothy? She let out a broken sigh. Katherine didn't want him to see her like this, her tear-streaked, dirt-marred face. Yet, here he was. And, from the gentle sounds of the crunching grass, she guessed he moved toward her.

He came to a halt just short of where she sat. But he did not speak for several long moments. She didn't mind. The silence was more comfortable for her.

"Are you all right, Katie?" Came his soft question at long last.

She nodded, still resisting the urge to look up at him.

He eased himself down to sit next to her. And they sat in that comfortable silence again for some moments more.

"It wasn't your fault."

She sniffled. He didn't know what he was talking about.

"It was an accident. Tragic. But an accident all the same."

Rubbing a hand across her face, she became more determined not to start crying again. Timothy didn't know the whole story. How could he? He only knew what he'd been told.

"Katie," Timothy said after some time as he leaned toward her.

She shifted to look at him. His eyes were kind, sincere. Glossy as if fighting back their own tears.

"Let me walk you home." He put forth a tentative hand, reaching for hers.

Sliding her hand into his, she allowed herself to take comfort in the strength of his warm hand closing around hers.

Then he rose to his feet and tugged at her hand, encouraging her to stand as well.

With some reluctance, she lifted her other hand to him and let him lift her to her feet. Once standing, she became all too aware of how she must look. She turned her head.

"I must be a sight," she said, her face warming.

"You are." Timothy rubbed his thumb against the back of her hand. "A lovely sight."

Her eyes met his, certain to find anything but the intensity she saw there. The warmth of his gaze held hers comfortably.

His face broke in a smile. And, turning sideways, he offered his elbow to her. "Shall we?"

Nodding, she took his arm and allowed him to lead her back toward the boarding house. And, as much as she felt spent, she also knew comfort.

Dr. Wyatt Sullivan made his way to the church. The time for another monthly town council meeting had come. As he did so often on his walks through the town, he considered the small city under his care. Buildings lined the quaint city street, which stretched out, cutting through a section of wilderness. This town had been his home. And these people had been his friends, his neighbors, his family. Now they were also his patients. While the responsibility of that was a heavy burden, he tried to bear it well.

Moving beyond the main street, he came closer to the church building. Happily situated near enough to the town to be under its protection and jurisdiction, yet several feet away from the hubbub of activity, the church stood in quiet assent to the passage of time. It was one building that had not changed much these many years. Like the schoolhouse, the townsfolk had kept up the appearance of the building, but it had neither been rebuilt nor expanded in the booming years Cripple Creek had seen.

Wyatt thought about all the changes he had seen in Cripple Creek. Even this past month had brought plenty of change to the town. It seemed every week there were more fortune seekers flocking to the town in hopes of striking it rich.

Here, in its happy situation, the things of the church felt . . . separate somehow from the mayhem of all the goings on in the town. Nothing, it seemed, could force the church forward. Must they always lag behind the times? Any new discovery in science was usually deemed "witch-craft" or "heresy." But Wyatt could not help himself. He was intrigued.

At last, Wyatt reached the church. Taking a deep breath, he opened the door and entered. Piano music greeted him. He allowed the simple melody to wash over him but found the tune indistinguishable to his ears. The reverend, the only other occupant of the church, sat at the instrument, his hands moving expertly across the ivory keys. All too soon, the music came to a halt. Wyatt's eyes met Timothy's. So, the reverend had noticed the intrusion. It must have distracted him from his playing.

"Wyatt," Timothy said in greeting, turning his body sideways on the piano bench. "I didn't hear you come in."

"Timothy," Wyatt tipped his hat. "That's all right. I was enjoying the mini-concert." It didn't matter that the rest of the council, or the town for that matter, referred to Wyatt as "Doc" and to Timothy as "Reverend." They referred to each other by name. While they were not friends as schoolboys, they had come to hold a mutual respect for each other.

Timothy smiled at the compliment. He waved Wyatt into the space. "I've got the table set up." Timothy stood, straightening his jacket as he moved toward the raised platform.

The council preferred to meet at a table so everyone could see each other during discussions. It also afforded them a surface on which to place any documents or take notes if they had need. Timothy was faithful about clearing a space on the pulpit for the table and setting up chairs so everything was ready for the council members.

Wyatt nodded and took his seat. Might as well enjoy the silence. It wouldn't be long before the crowd showed up.

Just then, the door swung open and Phillip Yerby walked in.

"Phillip," he called to the man. "How's business?"

"Same as ever," Yerby said, heading straight for a chair as usual. The man's girth and age demanded he sit often. As Yerby settled into his seat, Wyatt heard the man's breath heaving from the walk to the church.

A few of the townsfolk began trickling in. Timothy stepped down from the dais to greet them. That was Timothy. Ever the cheerful outgoing one. Wyatt did not have that gift.

Soon thereafter, Mayor Jacobs joined them.

Their group was nearly complete. Seated, they awaited the last member's appearance. Jacobs and Yerby exchanged talk of the recent heat as Jacobs took out his pocket watch. He would hold out a few more minutes for the banker. It wasn't quite time for the meeting to start yet and more townsfolk were filling the pews.

Wyatt drummed his fingers on the table's surface. These minutes ticking down to the start of the meetings always made him anxious. His eyes watched the door, waiting for the moment Mr. Hammond would come and they could get started.

Betsy entered and flashed him a grin before taking a seat on the front-most pew. He managed to smile back. She always seemed to show up wherever he was. Rather supportive of the town that way, she was. Or of him. Either way, she was a good friend.

It wasn't long before Mr. Hammond entered and joined them on the raised platform. He muttered his apologies before taking his seat.

Wyatt cared not for his reason; he simply wanted to get this over with. His eyes scanned the small space for Timothy and caught him near the back of the room. He was speaking with Katherine Matthews. It did not escape Wyatt's notice that Timothy stood rather close to Katherine. Closer than he needed to.

Why should that bother him? Because it was improper for the town's reverend to behave so? Yes, that must be it. Only, it wasn't. He had every right to court a single woman of his choosing. Warmth began to creep up Wyatt's neck.

At that moment, Timothy turned from Katherine and moved toward the empty seat on the dais.

Wyatt continued to track Katherine as she took a seat by her mother near the middle aisle. He didn't realize he still stared at her until her eyes met his. Then he turned his attention to other men at the table.

Mayor Jacobs stood and opened his mouth to bring the room to order and called for the meeting to commence. Timothy read the minutes from the last meeting. They were accepted and the way was cleared for new business.

"There is one matter I think we need to settle first and foremost," Jacobs spoke up, his voice more timid than Wyatt would have expected.

This was his town. He was charged with presiding over it. Where was his confidence?

"I know we have discussed this before, but I think we can no longer deny this town needs more deputies. Our population continues to grow, the saloons are full to bursting, and our town streets are rowdy at night and no longer safe for the common folk to walk."

A chorus of voices sounded from the congregation. But such a din of voices were they, that nothing could be discerned.

Wyatt wanted to reserve his opinion until he'd heard everyone out. But he couldn't help his reaction. More deputies would mean more taxes. While, yes, it sounded nice, that was not something he wanted to put on the townsfolk.

"I agree," Mr. Yerby said, eyebrows furrowing. "Things get awful shady when the sun goes down."

"And it will only get worse with the influx of silver miners," Jacobs reasoned.

"Silver miners?" Wyatt's eyes lit up. "I'm afraid I don't understand. Has someone found silver in our valley?"

"No," Jacobs said, his voice slow.

Sounds of stifled laughter came from the people.

Wyatt chose to ignore it and focus on the problem. His fellow council members spoke as if this was something he should know. Had something significant happened? How was he not in the know?

Jacobs tried to prompt his memory. "Because the whole silver market went bust? All the silver miners out of work? Looking for work in gold mines?"

Wyatt shook his head, mouth quirked. This was news. He had not heard anything about the silver miners.

"Goodness, man," Mr. Hammond said, appearing equally as shocked as Jacobs that Wyatt didn't know what was going on. "Where have you been? Under a rock?"

More sounds from the congregation. Wyatt tapped his finger on the tabletop. His eyes cut over to Katherine. He was somewhat relieved to see she appeared every bit as confused as he felt.

"Are you not aware of the Sherman Silver Purchase Act?" Jacobs offered.

It sounded vaguely familiar. But not enough that Wyatt could rely on his memory for anything. So, he shook his head again.

"Do you ever read the paper?" Mr. Hammond asked, exasperation evident in his voice as he waved his hands in the air.

Jacobs put a hand on Mr. Hammond's arm. "The long and short of it is that a lot of silver was being mined, and people wanted to be able to bring in silver to the bank and exchange it for silver dollars the way you exchange an ounce of gold for a minted ounce. The Sherman Silver Purchase Act was a compromise. It increased the amount of silver the federal government would buy. So, when a silver miner brings his silver to the government, he gets a silver note. Only, this silver note can be exchanged for a silver dollar or for gold.

"What do you think people wanted? Gold. This drained the federal government's reserves of gold. So now, the government is in desperate need to replenish those reserves. The price of silver went down, the silver market went bust, and every business that touched the silver market went bust. So now all those silver miners are out looking for work. Where do you think they're going to go? The gold mines."

Now it made sense. "So we'll have an influx of miners," Wyatt said.

"Yep. And I think we're crazy if we don't prepare for it." Jacobs' gaze shifted to the other members of the council.

"Not only will the increased population be a problem, but those extra miners will stir up trouble at the mines for sure. No one likes their job being threatened," Mr. Yerby said, his breathing getting more rapid.

"So it sounds as if we're all in favor," Mr. Hammond's booming voice interjected.

Timothy remained quiet. He struggled. The council had this debate before, privately and here in these council meetings. He wasn't as ready to realize that Cripple Creek had become the bigger town it was. In his mind, it was still the small town where he had been a boy.

"Reverend? Are you in?" Jacobs set his eyes on Timothy.

"How many deputies are we talking about?" Timothy was ever the practical one.

"Good question." Jacobs turned to the others. "Sheriff has two right now. What say we extend his force to include five?"

Wyatt considered the stakes. They made a valid point about the incoming miners. He didn't want their streets to be unsafe. Extending the force seemed the right thing to do.

Wyatt, Hammond, and Yerby nodded. Then all eyes settled on Timothy. He remained pensive. After some moments, he made a slight nod and everyone in the room let out a collective breath. No one enjoyed outvoting other members of the council. Seemed too much like forcing someone's hand. It was much better when they came to a consensus.

And so they were on to the next matter of business.

"See that frog?" Timothy pointed to a brownish-green and white frog in the distance.

Katherine squinted to get a better view of the amphibian in question. The small creature sat on a rock apparently sunning itself, ignorant of its audience.

"That is a wood frog," Timothy said with admiration in his voice. He couldn't hide it; there was still a great love for all manner of creatures in him.

Class had only been in session for one week and already Katherine had taken the class on their first field trip. To say the students and Katherine were still learning each other would be an understatement. They had tested her boundaries. But that was to be expected. This outing had proven to be a good break from the classroom for all of them.

They had been out on their reptile hunt for an hour, and Timothy had already unearthed several types of lizards, a couple of snakes, and a few salamanders. As quiet as they tried to be, the students still were not the stealthiest. So Timothy had to catch most of the animals and then bring them over to show the children. Once an animal was in his clutches, he was better able to talk about its unique features. Katherine had no doubt they were all learning a lot.

Timothy and Katherine had decided to take the students into the woods behind the schoolhouse. And they had traveled quite a ways back, perhaps a couple of miles. In his enthusiasm, Timothy continued to take them deeper and deeper. Katherine, on the other hand, watched the sky with growing concern. There weren't storm clouds to observe, but something just didn't seem right to her. Was it the way the wind blew?

"See how it has what looks like a mask on its face and an almost white stripe along the middle of its back? Those are its most distinctive characteristics." Timothy's smooth baritone drew her attention back toward the focus of everyone's attention.

The students hung on Timothy's every word. Today they had come to discover there was much more to their preacher than they had ever thought. He earned great admiration among her pupils. Even now, they all crowded around him, trying to catch a glimpse of the frog he pointed out.

"I think," Katherine spoke up, unable to keep silent about her concerns any longer. "That it's time we take all our newfound knowledge and head back to the schoolhouse."

A disgruntled chorus of "aws" from the students followed. Katherine hated to disappoint them, but it was best they start the trip back sooner rather than later. Could she find a brighter side of the situation for them to look to?

"We don't want to miss the dismissal bell, do we?"

They all shook their heads begrudgingly. It wasn't quite the "brighter side" Katherine had hoped it would be.

"Miss Matthews is right," Timothy interjected. "I'm glad you have enjoyed our reptile hunt. Perhaps we can do it again another day."

All eyes turned on Katherine, begging her to agree to such a prospect.

She was pinned, but she smiled in spite of it. Another reptile hunt would suit her just fine. "I guess that's that, then," Katherine agreed. "We must do this again."

Another chorus sounded from the children. Cheers and "yays" this time. The students weren't so forlorn then as they turned back in the direction of the schoolhouse and began the long walk back.

Katherine shared a smile with Timothy, grateful for his offer. How did he always know just what to say?

They resumed their traveling order, but in reverse. Katherine led and Timothy took up the rear to ensure there were no stragglers.

She continued to worry about the possibility of the weather turning, with no real evidence that it would, other than the chill of the wind. So she hurried the students along as quickly as they could go. Her niece, Jessie, was the youngest at six and her little legs rushed to keep up.

Only a few minutes had passed when the sky opened up and unleashed a torrent of blinding rain upon them. Katherine met Timothy's eyes over the heads of her students. They needed to find shelter, but they were in the midst of an open field. Where would they find such a place that would hold them all? She scanned the area for some abandoned structure or at least enough tree limbs to make a lean-to.

Small hands were upon her skirt. Lowering her head, she looked into the wide-eyed face of Jessie. Of course she would be nervous. Katherine lifted her easily into her arms.

"Over here," Timothy called out, waving in the direction of a nearby hillside. "There's a little cave over here."

Katherine glanced in the direction he indicated but couldn't make anything out. All she saw were bushes. But as she peered more closely, she could just make out an opening beyond the branches of the shrubs.

Timothy did not wait any longer for Katherine. He turned the group, leading the children to the safety of the small cavern. Holding up a hand to pause the students, he stepped in first. They didn't want to disturb a dangerous animal that might be living in their newfound refuge. Seconds later, he appeared again, waving them into the small space.

Katherine, with Jessie clinging to her, began herding the children into the cave, but stopped short when it was her turn to step inside. She froze to the spot.

All of a sudden, Timothy appeared, holding out a hand for her. "Katherine, come on," he shouted to her.

She shook her head, her mind just as frozen as her body. Why couldn't she just step inside? What held her back? Jessie squirmed in her arms.

Timothy stepped out to her in the pouring rain, taking her hand.

"Katherine, you're upsetting Jessie. You must come inside. You're getting drenched!"

She then allowed him to take Jessie from her and lead her into the small cavern. With him holding her hand, she could go wherever he led her. He sat her down near the opening and turned to see that the other children were okay.

The cavern was small. Had it been an animal's shelter? Carved out by God's hand or humans'? She swallowed, but it seemed to catch in her throat. Her breath caught and she began to feel a bit dizzy. But in the midst of her swirling came a moment of clarity—the reason this was so difficult. A cavern so many years ago . . .

Closing her eyes, she tried not to think about the tunnel they had walked into on that fateful trip. Or how it started like this, an opening in the ground that became darker and more enclosed . . . and then there was no way out. Her eyes flung open and she gasped for air.

She couldn't breathe!

Clawing at the top of her dress to loosen it, Katherine became frantic. Her hands were shaking and she couldn't control her movements.

Then hands were on hers—Timothy's. He placed his body between her and the children, doing his best to block their view of her.

"Katie, what is the matter?" he whispered, his gentle voice now harsh.

"I can't . . . " She felt faint, she had to get air. "I can't breathe."

"Yes, you can. Look at me," he said, his voice firm.

She stared straight ahead. The walls of the cavern closed in on her.

"Look at me," he commanded her.

She turned her head toward him. His eyes on her were deep. And kind. They were an anchor.

"Now, breathe with me." He took a few exaggerated breaths.

Katherine tried to obey, tried to breathe with him. Drawing in ragged breaths. But she ended up coughing. It was no use. She couldn't control her breathing. Continuing to fight for air, she felt her breaths come faster and faster. Light-headed and faint, she seemed to float farther away from the cavern.

"Stay with me."

Her eyes locked with Timothy's once more and when he drew in a deep breath she fought to suck in air. When he exhaled, she pushed air out. He squeezed her hand and it grounded her to the moment. After some more exaggerated, deep breaths, she was able to breathe more easily with him. Then, as she continued to concentrate on her breathing, it normalized.

"Good," Timothy said, his hands now on her arms. "Keep breathing like that."

She nodded and his hand slid down to capture hers once more. He then turned toward the children to tend to their needs and fears, something she should have been doing. But it took all she had to hold it together. And she gripped Timothy's hand as if it were her only hold on reality.

CHAPTER 3

Trouble

Nearly an hour after school dismissed, Katherine sat hard at work grading papers. She smiled at the answers to this most recent assignment. Yes, she was pleased with her students and their progress. Although a few gave her pause, and a couple gave her trouble, it wasn't anything she couldn't handle. The most important thing was that they showed improvement under her tutelage. And they did.

Her stack of papers dwindled, and she curled her back in a stretch. The muscles protested but relaxed into their natural position, now soothed. Movement just beyond the walls of the schoolhouse drew her attention from the final papers. Who would be outside at this hour? One of the troublemakers up to no good? Or did one of the students return to collect something left behind? Katherine's eyes scanned the schoolroom as she stood and moved toward the window.

Sweeping the lace curtain to the side afforded Katherine a complete view of the front of the schoolhouse. As she gazed out to the yard beyond, she spotted a carriage moving closer. Who? She squinted to focus her eyes and could just make out the features of the figure—Timothy!

The rest of the papers could wait. Smiling, she grabbed for her shawl. No doubt, Timothy had something fun planned for her. Over the last several days, he had made every effort to plan special rendezvous and outings for the two of them. And so she found herself in eager anticipation of where he would pop up each day.

Stepping out onto the porch, she met Timothy as he pulled up to the door.

"Good day, Miss Matthews." He tipped his hat.

He wasn't the most handsome man she had ever met. Not that he was hard on the eyes. But he might well be the most gracious. "Good day, Reverend." She offered him her brightest smile.

"I wondered if you would be agreeable to an afternoon ride with me," he said, indicating the seat next to him.

"With you? Why of course I would." A cool autumn breeze blew across the yard, and she wrapped her shawl tighter around herself. The rustle of leaves being picked up and scattered tickled her ears as she pulled the door to the schoolhouse closed.

Timothy hopped out of the carriage and, walking around to the opposite side, offered his hand to help her up. Katherine slid her hand into his, grateful for his assistance. How good it was to be out with him again! A gentleman above all else, she felt comfortable and safe in his presence. But also cherished.

Once she was in her seat, Timothy disappeared. The carriage jerked to the side a bit as he hoisted himself up into his seat. He gripped the reins and urged the horses forward. As they got underway, a silence fell between them. But not one of those uncomfortable pauses. Katherine rather enjoyed it. With Timothy, the silence didn't seem so awkward. So she watched the familiar scenery and rested back against the gently rocking carriage seat, taking it all in—both her surroundings and his presence.

After some time, Timothy broke the stillness between them. "How are the students treating you?"

How to answer that? She didn't wish to disturb their afternoon with tales of the troublesome students. Nor did she want to seem like a braggart and harp solely on her successes. "I'd say fair to good."

"Only fair to good?"

So he wanted to hear more. Katherine sighed. "I have a couple of students who pose discipline problems, but we're working things out, finding our way to a better understanding of one another."

"That sounds promising." Timothy's voice was so confident and firm. Did he have that kind of faith in her?

Her heart warmed. But he was her overseer. Shouldn't she reassure him? "Even so, these few students don't create serious issues day to day."

"I'm glad to hear that." His voice softened. Could that comment be more about his consideration for her than for the classroom being well run? Or was she mistaken? Perhaps he did think after her ability to handle the children.

"I do think, despite our small setbacks, that the students are all learning."

Timothy nodded. "If you need help with another science lesson on reptiles, just let me know."

She smiled at that, but only briefly. The memories of their last field trip were not altogether pleasant. Unbidden, they unfolded in her mind. A small cavern, her difficult breaths, Timothy's concerned eyes . . .

"Hey," Timothy said, his voice gentle. Did he notice the change in her mood? "I didn't mean to . . . "

She drew in a ragged breath, coming back to the present. "It's all right," she lied, turning to look at him.

He took a hand off the reins for a moment to clasp her small fingers in his.

Smiling at his gesture, she squeezed his hand. He was a good friend. She hoped that wasn't all.

They continued to ride like that for a few minutes, until he needed his hand back to slow the horses. They neared the creek, one of her favorite spots. How did he know?

"Why are we stopping?"

"Because I have a surprise for you." He reached behind the seat and pulled out a basket.

"A picnic!" Katherine clapped. There were few things she enjoyed more than picnics.

He jumped out of the carriage and came around. With his hands on her waist, he helped her down. Once on the ground, they were face-to-face. The moment seemed to draw out. She held her breath. Was he going to kiss her? Would she let him?

But, true to his nature, he was a perfect gentleman. After a handful of seconds, he removed his hands and offered her his arm, lifting the picnic basket with his other hand. Taking his arm, she allowed him to lead her to a spot near the creek that offered a nice view of the mountains in the distance. One of her favorite places as a child, it stole her breath anew.

Timothy busied himself spreading out a blanket. He then brought the basket over. "I hope you don't mind," he said as they settled down onto the blanket. "But I took the liberty of asking your mother about some of your favorite dishes."

She caught herself before her mouth dropped open. Her heart did a little flip-flop. "Mind? I'm impressed. My favorite dishes. My favorite picnic spot . . ."

"Your favorite picnic spot? I brought you here because it's my favorite."

"Oh. I guess that's one more thing we have in common." She offered him another smile. Was it her imagination, or did his face color just a bit as their eyes met?

"Now I can't take credit for the food. I had some help from Mrs. Abby at the boarding house."

What did that matter? Katherine's mouth watered at the pleasant smells coming from the basket now in close proximity to her. "I can't wait."

He uncovered the basket and set out the food.

Katherine watched him, thinking of how perfect this afternoon out truly was. *I could get used to this.*

Katherine grit her teeth against the bumping of the carriage, no longer a gentle rocking. Pain tore through her at each rut they hit in the road. One glance over at Timothy's stony face told her volumes.

Reaching out a shaky hand toward his arm, she attempted to calm him. "Timothy, I'm truly all right, I . . . "

"We're almost there," he dismissed her. "You'll be fine." He said this more to himself than to her, she suspected. Did he think he was responsible for her little spill down the creek bank? If only there were something she could say.

Drawing the horses to a halt, he jumped out of the carriage and raced over to where she sat. Reaching up, he positioned his hands first one way and then another, seeming unsure how best to get her down. *This could take forever.*

Biting her cheek against the pain, she leaned toward him and all but fell into his arms. She couldn't help the yelp that escaped her lips.

The crestfallen look on Timothy's face was almost more than she could bear. She was stung anew. But not by her injuries, by her heart.

They were at the clinic door in a few of Timothy's long strides. He fiddled with the latch underneath her for a moment before the door gave way. As he stepped into the clinic, Wyatt rose from his desk.

As he laid eyes on them, Wyatt leapt into action. Moving farther into the clinic, he indicated Timothy should lay Katherine on the examination table. He did so, placing her as if she were made of the finest china.

"Tell me what happened," Wyatt barked as his hands moved over Katherine. He checked her pupils and grasped at her wrist.

This was certainly not necessary. Katherine opened her mouth to speak as she tried to wrest her hand away from Wyatt's, but Timothy spoke before she could utter a sound.

"We were walking by the creek and Katherine's foot found a hole in the ground. She slid down the bank and landed on her side." The distress in his eyes and in his voice would be evident to anyone.

Another pang. Why did he feel so responsible? It was her clumsiness that caused this.

Wyatt nodded, frowning. "What hurts?" he looked at Katherine.

She tried to sit up. There must be a way to put an end to this foolishness. "I'm fine. Timothy is just overly concerned . . . "

Wyatt pressed her back down onto the table. "That may be, but I insist you let me examine your injuries. What hurts?"

Katherine bit at her lip. She did not want Wyatt examining her. Hatred and unforgiveness filled her. It was almost a tangible thing within her as she gazed up into his steel blue eyes. No, she did not want his hands on her for any reason.

She shifted her focus toward Timothy. Would he help her? No, none would be found there. One look at his guilty face told her she wasn't getting out of here without complying. She needed to endure this for his sake.

Closing her eyes for a moment, she took a deep breath and faced Wyatt again. His eyes were hard on hers. If she could have pulled back, she would have. But she gathered her wits and met his gaze. "It's my left ankle, where I stepped in the hole, and my right side, where I landed."

Wyatt stepped to the foot of the table. As his hands moved over the already swollen area, Katherine grimaced in pain. Did he have to be so rough?

Timothy, still standing on the opposite side of the table near her head, reached for her hand. She appreciated what comfort he offered her.

Wyatt prodded the injury, maneuvering the ankle at the joint, testing the integrity of the bones. "I don't think anything is broken, just sprained," he concluded.

Katherine nodded, letting out a breath, thankful his examination was over. She didn't think she could stand much more of his inspection.

Wyatt moved back toward her head, but his eyes sought out Timothy. "I'm going to have to ask you to excuse us while I examine her ribs."

Katherine's eyes shot over to Timothy. He couldn't leave her! She would never have agreed to come if she had known there was a chance she would be alone with Wyatt for even a second. But now she felt stuck. What could she do that wouldn't upset Timothy further?

Timothy looked at her, apparently not reading the trepidation in her eyes. He nodded his assent to Wyatt. But he did take a moment to lean over Katherine, running a hand over her hair. "I'll be right outside."

She nodded, but that was of little comfort to her, as she would be left in here with Wyatt.

Timothy lifted her hand to his lips and pressed a kiss to the back of her fingers.

Katherine smiled up at him, her heart sent into rapid pacing by his caress. He laid her hand back down by her side. She could do nothing but watch him step outside the clinic doors. And then she was alone with Wyatt. Her eyes narrowed as they landed on him.

Wyatt followed Timothy and locked the door behind him, pulling the curtains closed as well. Then he turned back to Katherine.

"I need you to disrobe down to your chemise," he said, walking toward his washbasin to clean his hands.

Katherine's heart stopped. "Absolutely not."

Wyatt whirled back around, shock evident on his face. Perhaps he was not accustomed to outright refusals from his patients. "What?"

"I have no intention of disrobing for you, Wyatt Sullivan," she said as she struggled to a sitting position, leaning heavily on her left arm.

"It's Dr. Sullivan, and I need to examine you to make sure there are no internal injuries or broken ribs," he said firmly.

She glared at him. Every part of her flushed with heat. "Well then, Dr. Sullivan, I shall thank you for your services and be on my way. I'm certain everything is just fine," she returned, her tone infused with determination.

Katherine managed to sit, but if she wanted to get off the table on the side opposite where he was, she would need to lean on her right arm. When she did so, pain shot through her torso and she lost her balance and fell off the table.

Wyatt was by her side in an instant, lifting her back onto the table. He swore, cursing her stubbornness. "You're just fine, are you?" he asked, gruffly.

She bit her lip against the pain. Anger toward him still burned within her. But she became aware that a tingling sensation coursed through her as well. And it was not altogether unpleasant. It could not be a reaction to his closeness. He had no right to treat her this way! That was the truth of it.

"Here, let me help you," he said. His tone did not invite comment or argument.

His hands were on the top of her dress then. She was trapped. Her body needed treatment. So, she lay without uttering another word as her face heated. How could she meet his eyes? Turning her head the opposite direction, she shut her eyes against the reality of what was happening.

Wyatt opened her dress down just past her waist and then moved away to wash his hands again. She prayed it would be over soon. When he returned, he did not make her take the top of her dress off, rather he slid his hands under the fabric to feel along her ribs.

"I'm sorry, but this will be uncomfortable," he said more gently than she would have expected.

He was right. Pain shot through her upper body. Katherine shut her eyes, refusing to cry out in his presence.

Wyatt was a gentleman. His expert hands moved over the part of her torso that required checking, yet he did not wander into areas that need remain private. Still, it was disconcerting to have his hands on her body with naught but her thin chemise separating her flesh from the warmth of his hands. And there were sensations that arose in her unbidden. Feelings she would rather not name or give credence to.

"Nothing is broken," he said after some moments. "But you do have some bruised ribs. They'll be sore for several days, so I need to show you how to wrap them."

She nodded. All of the fight in her had dissipated, and she was prepared to focus on what needed to be done to repair her injuries and be done with this whole ordeal.

The next several minutes were spent with Wyatt showing her how to wrap her torso to support her ribs before he put a wrap on. Katherine then secured her dress before Timothy was admitted and Wyatt wrapped her ankle.

"You need to use a walking stick for a few days to take some of the stress off that ankle while it heals. And I cannot emphasize enough how important it is that you rest as much as possible so your ribs can heal." Wyatt walked over to his medicine cabinet and grabbed a glass jar of herbs, scooping some into a small container. "Take this and brew it into a tea. It's the best thing I've found for pain relief. Come back when you run out." He handed her the container.

You won't see me back here. No matter how much pain I'm in. I'd rather endure it than come to you for help again. Between the confusing emotions and the impropriety of the situation, she could not imagine it.

"Thank you, Wyatt," Timothy said, offering his hand. "I can't tell you how terrible I feel about all of this. If I hadn't suggested we walk so close to the bank . . . I feel responsible."

Then there was Timothy. Sweet Timothy. How to help him know it was not his fault?

"Yes," Wyatt said, waving him off. "Let's not have any outings for a couple of weeks at least."

No more outings? Just who did Wyatt think he was to dictate Katherine's life? But she did not speak up. She had tired of this whole ordeal and did not wish to prolong it.

Timothy nodded.

Katherine turned her attention to Timothy, reaching for his arm to help her off the table. Wyatt's hands were on her back and arm, assisting Timothy in getting her down. It made her all the more eager to get out of his clinic. Not because she despised his touch, as much as she wanted that to be the case, because it stirred something else in her.

Now that she was off the table, she leaned on Timothy with her left arm, protecting her right side. They began to make their way to the out.

Wyatt opened the door and they exited the clinic. As she stepped past Wyatt, she swore to herself this would be the last time she came to the clinic voluntarily.

Katherine glanced at the watch pinned near the collar of her dress. She shook her head. The day seemed to have passed without her noticing. More and more there wasn't the time for the things she needed to do. Nevertheless, the clock dictated it was time for math. Drills today.

Standing and straightening her skirt, Katherine cleared her throat. "Class, take out your slates and put everything else away. It's time for our multiplication exam."

Katherine stepped around her desk, leaning on the sturdy surface it provided. Several weeks had passed since her tumble down the bank. The injuries she had sustained continued to heal.

The rustle of papers and the gentle thump of books being closed told her the students obeyed. As the shuffling died down, she saw the students' desks bore nothing more than their slates and chalk. Good. They were learning to listen and follow directions. Moving toward the blackboard, she lifted the chalk, smooth and small in her hand, and began marking out the equations her students needed to answer.

As she continued to cut through the nothingness of the chalkboard, her concentration was interrupted by a knock on the door. Who would call upon the class at this hour? A concerned parent? After glancing behind herself for a moment, she turned her attention back to the board to write the final two equations. Only then did she make her way to the back of the class to answer the door, wiping her hands off on the chalkboard dustcloth as she went.

With the door in front of her, she took a breath and gathered herself to her full height in preparation to receive whoever it might be. Intrusions during the school day were quite uncommon. With a hand on the door latch, she pulled the door open to reveal the interloper. She found herself face-to-face with Timothy. Surprised and a little concerned, she fought to keep a neutral face. Why would he disturb her in the middle of the school day?

"Reverend, what brings you to the schoolhouse?" She addressed him formally, mindful of her students.

Timothy nodded toward the students who were all but staring at him from their seats before tipping his hat to Katherine. "Please pardon the interruption, Miss Matthews, but there is an urgent matter I need to speak with you about."

What could be so important that he would take her away from her students?

"Of course."

The worry etched on his face only caused her trepidation to rise.

She turned back to the class and glanced at her watch. "Becky?" she called to one of her more reliable students as she worked the pin on her broach that bore the timepiece. She moved over to where the older girl sat near the back of the room and placed the heirloom watch on the student's desk. "Would you collect the slates at 1:30?"

The red-haired girl bobbed her head in response.

Turning back toward Timothy, she motioned that they should step farther out of the schoolroom. As she closed the door behind herself,

Timothy took her arm and moved her an even greater distance from the schoolhouse. Grateful for his vigilance, she allowed him to lead her. The worried look on his face when he had spoken earlier troubled her. She did not want any of the students to overhear what he was about to say. And it seemed to be one of his concerns, too.

"Timothy, you're scaring me. What's going on?" Katherine couldn't help the shakiness in her voice. The chill of the day also pervaded her body. She had not grabbed her wrap, so she stood out in the cold of Colorado's early winter with naught but her dress to keep her warm. Moving her hands over her arms did not calm her shaking.

Eyeing her movements, Timothy's mouth opened and then closed. He then shrugged off his coat. "My apologies, Katie. I dragged you out here without your warm things."

"What about you?" Her teeth chattered a little as she spoke. Wouldn't Timothy be chilled once he gave her his coat?

But as he removed his outer covering, she saw that he still had a jacket on underneath. Not as heavy as the one he now wrapped around her, but more than she had.

"I will be fine." His hands lingered on her arms a moment longer than they needed to. But she didn't mind. He gazed into her eyes and his face inched closer to hers.

Was this the moment? Was he going to kiss her?

He stopped abruptly, pulling back and releasing his grasp on her arms. The energy between them changed as if he remembered he had come for a different reason.

"What is it?" Her voice was quiet. She tried to capture his eyes once again.

He did meet her eyes then. There was sadness there. "Katherine, they've quarantined the clinic. There's typhoid in town."

"Typhoid?" She felt the blood drain from her face. What would become of Cripple Creek? What would happen to Wyatt? She shook her head. What an odd thought to have. Besides, she didn't care what happened to Wyatt. He left Ellie behind, maybe he deserved to suffer. That thought felt bitter and odd, as if it had come from somewhere outside of herself. And she wasn't ready to accept it as hers.

Timothy's voice brought her back to the present. "Yes, typhoid. So far, there's just the one case. But, Wyatt is keeping him in the clinic and has quarantined the clinic and the man's home."

Nodding her understanding, she felt fear creep into the edges of her consciousness, threatening to close in like a vise. She had heard about typhoid outbreaks and how they had devastated towns.

"The mayor said we are to release the students and shut down the school until the typhoid is gone."

Katherine nodded again, numbed. She could only imagine her school, touched by a plague. Her students . . .

"Katherine?" Timothy's hand on her arm stirred her from her thoughts.

She brushed a tear away as it fell.

"Katie, it's going to be okay. God will take care of us and the town. We just have to trust in Him." He said all of this with a confidence she certainly didn't feel as he pulled her into his arms.

She nodded against his shoulder, wishing her faith was that firm. Closing her eyes, she prayed a simple prayer. For the town, for the school, for more faith. But it didn't change her fear. So she took what comfort she could from the strength of Timothy's embrace.

He pulled back to look at her, rubbing her arms.

"I should get back to my students," she said, reluctant to pull away from him. He had become an anchor for her. And she needed that now more than ever.

His eyes searched her face, his hands moved as if he would pull her into his chest once more, but he didn't. "Come find me after you release your students. I'll be at the church."

"Wait," she said as he turned to walk away. "What about your coat?" She began to work her arms out of the oversized sleeves.

"Bring it to me at the church." A smile pulled at the corners of his mouth. "Then you'll have to come."

Katherine nodded yet again, comforted by his warm presence but left longing as he walked away. She turned back toward the schoolhouse and sighed. This was not going to be an easy announcement.

Timothy gazed out at the congregation. His flock. What were they thinking? As a whole, they were seated and solemn. He had just delivered the final words of his thought-provoking message. Yet they remained as straight-faced as ever. The gloominess of the typhoid outbreak must weigh on their minds. Of this, he was certain. And all the more as it spread.

If only the early efforts to quarantine the clinic had been enough. They had not. The typhoid had already begun to spread and, since that time, seemed to have taken the town by storm.

It wasn't long before the patients outnumbered the beds in the clinic. This presented a problem—one the town council was well aware of, but one they tried to conceal from the townspeople. No need to create further chaos and worry. Until now.

"Before I close, I want to thank everyone for coming out today," Timothy said to the small gathering of people.

Many members of the normal congregation had fallen victim to the typhoid, and many others had quarantined themselves in their homes in an attempt to avoid the deadly disease. But these brave folks were in the house of worship this day in hopes they might beseech God to preserve them and heal their loved ones who had fallen ill.

"I know it's not easy these days," Timothy continued, "But Mayor Jacobs would like to speak now if you will afford him your attention for a few minutes."

Timothy moved to the side as the mayor stood from where he sat in his pew and stepped onto the pulpit, replacing Timothy at the small podium.

Mayor Jacobs stood for a moment in silence, perhaps gathering his thoughts, perhaps letting the people have a moment to digest this alteration in their day. When he did speak, his voice was gentle and thick with emotion. One might suspect it to be politically motivated, but Timothy knew better. The mayor cared for the people of this town.

"Good people of Cripple Creek, I know these last days have been difficult. We have seen hardship and tragedy strike at our very hearts. And we mourn together for those who have been lost. And I am greatly troubled to share a terrible problem we are faced with. We have long since run out of space in the clinic for the sick."

A collective intake of breath could be heard from among the congregation. And a few ladies pulled out their handkerchiefs. Timothy was tempted to step in and reassure them, but it was not his place to do so. Mayor Jacobs had the pulpit. He would be responsible for doing so.

"But do not fear," Jacobs was quick to add. "We have a plan in place. Even now, the schoolhouse is being converted into a makeshift hospital. This will serve as overflow from the clinic and will be quarantined as well. Dr. Sullivan will oversee the healthcare of the patients in this makeshift hospital, but we are in need of a volunteer or two who will see to the daily needs and welfare of these patients."

A flurry of whispering spread among the congregation. Who would volunteer to work with the typhoid patients? Who would risk themselves? Timothy had the same thoughts. Who indeed would take on such a daunting task?

"I'm not asking for anyone to volunteer this minute, but it is our hope that in the next day or so some kindhearted soul will step forward. I thank you for your time and I wish you and your families good health and, if any are ill, I wish them quick recovery."

The mayor stepped to the side, and Timothy resumed his place at the podium.

"Thank you, ladies and gentlemen. You are dismissed. Go with God."

Music burst from the piano as Timothy made his way down the lone aisle toward the exit. As was his custom, he positioned himself at the exit so he could speak with each person as they stepped out. After he passed to the back of the church, the members of the congregation stood and began to file out.

As Timothy touched the hands of each of his parishioners, it was as if he lived a lifetime of emotions in the span of just a few minutes. He comforted those who had lost loved ones, prayed briefly with those who had sick ones in quarantine, and shared hopes for continued health with those who had yet to be visited by the dreadful illness. It drained him, true, but it was his calling.

As the people made their way through the line, he began to think of Katherine. He had spotted her in the congregation. When would she pass through? Their last rendezvous had been weeks ago after he had alerted her about the typhoid. It had been as meaningful to him as any other, but abbreviated by the events of the day. Since then, they had been conscripted to brief encounters such as these. This plague had even seemed to steal the town's Christmas and New Year's celebrations from them. But he determined to make the most of them.

Yes, he always looked forward to seeing her smile after service. Never more so than today. And he was not disappointed. She stepped up to him in turn, her head down and her face drawn. Was something amiss? But as she drew near, she raised her face, catching his eyes and offering him a smile as she put forth her hand.

Clouded by his own emotions, he wanted to speak, yet no words came. There was only her smile and the simple contact of their hands. It refreshed him and filled him anew. Maybe, just maybe, he could manage whatever would come his way if she were by his side.

Her mouth parted and she spoke. But in the midst of his musings, he missed her words.

"I'm sorry, what?" he refocused his attention.

Then she said four words that caused his heart to sink.

"I want to volunteer."

All he could do was look at her. What was she thinking? His mind became overwhelmed with a thousand thoughts. The loudest among them were of the dangers. What would he do if something happened to her? He couldn't lose her, couldn't risk her.

When he regained his wits, he pulled her closer, glancing around to make sure no one was looking their way. "Katie, I don't think that's such a good idea," he said, his voice quiet to ensure their privacy.

"And just why not?" She didn't bother lowering her tone at all. Something akin to anger flashed across her face.

He cringed at her volume. And, though his thoughts ran a million miles a minute, and perhaps because of them, he couldn't come up with any good reasons for her to not volunteer. Except for one perhaps rather selfish reason. "Because I don't want you anywhere near this plague."

Her features softened for a moment. "I understand your concern, Timothy. But I need to do whatever I can to help these sick people."

"Your heart is in the right place . . . " Why couldn't he find any reason to dissuade her? His eyes searched hers. What he found there was determination. "Is there nothing I can say that will deter you?"

She shook her head. "My mind is made up."

Timothy could find no reason to deny her. "Let's go talk to Wyatt then."

Maybe he can talk some sense into you. It was rather doubtful Wyatt would allow Katherine to take on such a formidable task.

Grasping her hand, Timothy led Katherine away from the church and into the churchyard. There, among the people who milled about after the service chatting amongst themselves, they found Wyatt. He conversed with the mayor while Betsy Calloway looked on. Timothy brought Katherine up to the small group, interrupting their discourse.

"Wyatt, John, Betsy," Timothy nodded to each in turn.

They greeted him and Katherine, making vague comments about the sermon.

Timothy waved them off, too distracted. "Wyatt, we have our first volunteer to mind the schoolhouse and tend to the patients there."

"Who?" Wyatt's eyes widened and his brows shot up. The council had serious doubts anyone would volunteer at all, much less so quickly.

Timothy tilted his head toward Katherine.

Wyatt's features twisted.

Betsy made a noise that sounded like a snort.

Just the reactions he expected. Wyatt would not allow it. And he would be safe from having to let Katherine down himself.

"We are, of course, thankful for your willingness to help, Miss Matthews," Mayor Jacobs spoke up. "But are you quite sure you are prepared to take on the task of . . . "

"I am, sir," she interjected. Why was she so hasty? "I know this will entail a lot of unpleasantness, but I assure you, I am prepared."

"I'm not so certain she is . . . " Wyatt started, meeting Timothy's eyes.

"I am so certain," she said, her voice exuding confidence and the same determination Timothy had seen in her eyes.

Timothy prayed Wyatt wouldn't accept it.

"How could you be?" Betsy challenged. "That will be no place for a lady."

Wyatt met Katherine's eyes. They stared each other down for a few moments.

"Please," she said, her voice no longer bore the strength it had, but it was still firm. "Let me help."

Timothy continued to pray, hoping Wyatt would refuse her, that he would tell her how crazy the whole idea was.

"All right," Wyatt conceded. "We'll have a trial run."

Timothy's eyes slid closed as his heart dropped into his stomach.

CHAPTER 4

Fight

David Matthews made his way home after another grueling day in the mines. Why had he ever chosen this occupation? He wondered this many times, but he dared not say it out loud. Certainly not after he made such a big to-do about following his own path and not stepping in to take over the ranch.

The mines were not a pleasant place. They were dark, damp, and cold, and except for the sounds of the other miners, they were lonely. He spent his time doing hard labor for decent pay and the long, laborious days wore on him. To top it off, it seemed things were going to change . . . for worse.

As he approached his home, he straightened his posture and tried to push these things to the back of his mind. Nothing would be gained by weighing down his family. He would have to talk with Mary about the changes coming. But that could wait until the children were tucked in. Right now, he needed to be the best father possible for those beautiful angels.

Stepping into the simple home, he set down his few things and took off his winter hat and coat. His arms spread wide to receive the small girl's body that rushed toward him. Embracing his daughter close to himself, he gave her a quick tickle. She laughed and wiggled free from his grasp. Then he chased down his toddling son for a hug. This thrilled Peter to shrieks of joy. Holding the squirming child, David marveled anew at how full of life they were. Lives he was responsible for.

Once his kids were taken care of, he moved into the kitchen where his wife stood over the stove. Her eager eyes greeted him, and he leaned down, pressing a kiss to her lips.

"I'm glad you're home," she said, absently stirring a pot of something that smelled so good it caused his stomach to grumble.

"It's good to be home," he said, smiling, wishing he could stay in this moment, drawing strength from the comfort he found in her eyes, in just holding her.

"Now go wash up for supper. You're filthy," she teased, swatting at his black-smeared hands. "It'll be on the table any minute."

His grin widened. "As the lady wishes."

After he returned to the dining area, hands washed and face cleaned, they went through the motions of their family dinner. Then they moved on to their nighttime routines. Nightclothes, stories, and tuck-ins. All in all, it wasn't long before Jessie and Peter were in their beds and on their way to dreamland.

And so they were left in peace and quiet. David sat in his favorite chair, smoking his pipe and relaxing while listening to the sounds of Mary finishing the dishes. He closed his eyes and relished every moment of being still and warm. If only it were possible to soak it all up and take it into that dark place with him. If only. Inhaling the lingering scents from dinner, which now mingled with the smell of his pipe, he felt his soul at rest.

But he could not remain in that peaceful place. A conversation was forthcoming. How was he going to tell Mary the news?

The clanging of dishes came to a stop. Her footsteps moved about the small space as she put the last dishes away. Only then did she come to sit in the chair next to him. Without a word, she reached for her knitting and began working the yarn.

They sat in silence for a few moments. He could not make himself speak. In the end, it was Mary who broke into the stillness.

"Have you heard the latest news on the typhoid plague?" Even as she spoke, she did not look up from her work.

He shook his head and then, realizing she could not see him, cleared his throat and said, "No, I have not."

Mary had agreed to keep their children at home or at his parents' house for the duration of the plague to avoid any chance encounter with anyone infected. And though he knew she hated to miss church services, she relented for the sake of their safety.

"They turned the schoolhouse into a hospital." The clicking of her knitting needles brought a steady rhythmic sound into the silent spaces between their interchanges.

"Oh?" He closed his eyes, enjoying the remaining moments of peace before he needed to bring forth his news. Would it all be shattered then?

"And your sister volunteered to oversee the patients there."

His eyes opened, and he turned to look at Mary. She had stopped her work to watch him. Was she attempting to gauge his reaction? He was filled with concern and a bit angered.

"She's got no business being around this plague. Why, she should have packed up and moved out to Ma and Pa's house for the duration of the typhoid." He worked to contain his frustration. "But that's Katherine . . . headstrong."

"I worry about her, too," Mary agreed, turning back to her project.

He wracked his brain, but could not remember what she was making.

"But I admire her sacrifice. She is brave." That was Mary. Always looking for the better side of everyone and everything.

"Reckless is more like it." He set his pipe down with more force than he'd intended. It clanked off the end table and fell onto the floor, spilling tobacco in a small pile on the floor. A grunt escaped his lips as he reached over to pick up the pipe. "I'm sorry, Mary. I'll clean it up."

He leaned his head against the back of the chair and allowed his eyes to close again. The sound of her needles working against each other had stopped, and he felt her eyes on him.

"What's on your mind?" Her voice was soft.

"What do you mean?" He opened his eyes and looked at her.

She blinked and jerked back a little.

It had not been his intention to speak to her with such a tone.

"You've been preoccupied this evening. Anything you care to share with me?"

He leaned back in the chair once more, staring toward the fire in front of them, and took several deep breaths. It was time. "There's been an announcement at the mines."

"Oh?" Her reply was simple, yet the lilt of her voice spoke volumes. But she didn't speak further.

"They plan to increase our days to ten hours."

There. It wasn't the best news, but it wasn't as bad as it could have been. Still, it would mean he'd be getting home later. It cut into his time with the children. They would be going to bed by the time he got home. All of this he anticipated from Mary, but when she did speak, it was with a calmer voice than he would have expected.

"For how long?"

He forced himself to look at her again.

She sat motionless, poised as he had last seen her, knitting in her lap, hands folded over it. How could she be so calm?

"They didn't say." That would get a reaction out of her.

Mary let out a long breath. "That does make things more difficult. But we can manage."

Had he truly just heard what he thought he'd heard? As he watched, she took up her knitting again as if he had just told her their Sunday lunch plans had been canceled.

"Who knows," she continued. "Maybe the extra money will come in handy."

It was David's turn to let out a long sigh. "That's the thing. They're not paying us any more money. It'll still be our daily rate of three dollars."

She put down her knitting again, eyes on him. "That doesn't seem fair." Now her tone was firmer, more the reaction he had been expecting.

"I know. None of the miners are happy about it."

"Is there a plan to do something?"

"Do something? What can we do? We're at their mercy. We need these jobs. Especially now that the silver miners have come after our jobs." He hoped he could help her see the situation they were in.

"Still, there must be something you can do." Her eyes flashed.

"I wish we could." Did she think he wanted to work more hours?

"What about your union?"

"What? The Free Coinage Union? It's too small to have any real say in anything." His voice began to rise. "These mine owners wouldn't even listen if we did try to speak out. They're too powerful." He didn't have the answers for her that he should. What was he to do? This was an impossible situation. And so he turned away from her, focusing on the floor.

"I see." Mary reached across the gap between their chairs to set a hand on his, her voice soft once again. "We will find a way to manage these changes."

He nodded, not wanting to look over at her. Would he find her true emotions in her eyes if he did? Disappointment? Concern?

She squeezed his hand under hers. "I love you."

He lifted his head and met her eyes. All he found there was tenderness and support. "I love you, too."

Katherine sighed as she moved about the schoolhouse-turned-hospital. After fighting to volunteer, she poured her heart and soul into her work. She wanted to do whatever was necessary to see mothers, fathers, brothers, and sisters returned home. But she fought an unseen foe, one that had the power to steal and take at random.

As she prepared for her first patient, she went through her mental checklist for the day. There were so many needs among the people here and so many patients to care for. Truly, they needed at least one more volunteer. But no one else had stepped forward. So, it was up to Katherine to bear the workload. She had settled into a routine, which improved her time management.

Making her way from patient to patient, she checked on their progress through the night, saw to their immediate needs, and did her best to get some breakfast into them. Several had to be spoon-fed. This took up most of her day. It seemed once she finished rounding out breakfast, it would be time for lunch. *No rest for the weary.*

Refocusing her attention on her task, she moved on to the next patient.

"Good morning, Charlotte." The slender woman was older than Katherine and no doubt taller, her frame seeming to stretch across the cot. Her long blond hair splayed across the pillow, clinging to her face where she had perspired in her sleep.

"Good morning." A smile graced Charlotte's lips as she made a move to sit up.

"And how are we feeling today?" Katherine placed fresh flowers in the vase next to Charlotte's cot and assisted her in her efforts to sit more upright. Her body was weak. The same could be said for many. Still, they fought.

"As well as I can be, I suppose." Now that Charlotte was sitting, Katherine propped the pillow behind her.

Charlotte's husband had already fallen victim to the typhoid. Katherine did not know the woman at that time and could only imagine how devastating it was. She had tasted death in the loss of a close friend, but to lose your life partner . . . how does one survive that?

But Charlotte hadn't time to grieve her loss before she'd found herself a patient. And, though she hated the circumstances, Katherine found herself thankful she had come to know Charlotte. The two had developed a rather special friendship. She had become Katherine's confidant. It might not be wise. But Katherine didn't care.

"My stomach still hurts." Charlotte grimaced and laid a hand across her waist.

Katherine frowned, sorry to hear her new friend was so uncomfortable. "Dr. Sullivan will be in later to check on everyone. Is there anything I can get you until then?"

Charlotte shook her head. "Just sit with me and chat."

"For a little while." Katherine sat on the side of the cot. She reached over and grabbed a bowl from the nearby stool. "In the meantime, I've got your breakfast."

"Let me guess," Charlotte said, furrowing her brows as if she had to think intensely. "Broth?"

"How did you know?" Katherine teased, stirring the brownish-yellow liquid.

"A crazy guess." The corners of Charlotte's mouth played at a grin. "At least you could serve it with coffee."

"Sorry. Broth and water. Doctor's orders." Katherine scooped a spoonful.

"Yes, I know."

"Now, be a good girl and take your broth," Katherine admonished as she held the spoon toward Charlotte's mouth.

"As long as you tell me the latest with you and the reverend." Charlotte offered her a playful smile, weak as it was.

Katherine gave her a sideways look and a sly half-grin. "All right, but just because you asked so sweetly."

Holding the spoon out, Katherine helped Charlotte take in the broth. As she continued ladling broth for Charlotte, she told her about dinner the previous evening with Timothy. Their time together had been abbreviated once again, as she had been quite tired. Truth be told, it wasn't much of an outing, but things were as such for now, and Timothy understood. That's what was important—that he supported her work at the hospital. He was a good man.

The door creaked open. Glancing in that direction, she watched as Wyatt stepped into the schoolhouse. Drawing in a deep breath, she let her shoulders sag, relieved she was almost to her last patient's breakfast.

Wyatt scanned the small room. What was he looking for? His eyes caught hers and his search came to an end. A few long strides and he was across the room at Charlotte's bedside.

"How are you this morning, Mrs. Smith?" Wyatt appeared as put together as ever. How could he be so unfazed by this plague? How was that possible?

"About the same," Charlotte replied. "My stomach hurts."

"Where?"

She pointed to the lower portion of her abdomen off to the right side.

Katherine looked on as he leaned over Charlotte and listened with his stethoscope. After some moments, he moved expert fingers gently over the entirety of her belly. She could not help but remember those fingers moving over her own injuries. Jerking her head away, she banished those thoughts from her mind.

"Your spleen and liver are enlarged," he noted. "So we'll need to keep you from anything too active." His face broke out in a crooked smile.

Katherine resisted the urge to roll her eyes. "You should know she's been having those spells too."

"Tell me more about these spells. How bad are they?" Concern was etched in his features.

Pausing for a moment, Katherine considered her words. "She becomes confused and disoriented, doesn't seem to know what she's doing or who is around her. But nothing uncontrollable." Katherine had seen some patients with these states of delirium get quite violent.

"How often?"

"Maybe a once or twice a day." Too often.

"Let's keep an eye on it." He patted Charlotte's hand, turning his attention back to her. "Did you take all of your broth and water?"

"You say that as if Katherine lets anyone skip it." Charlotte shot Katherine a sharp look.

Wyatt's face lit up. "Good. You need plenty of fluids."

With that, Wyatt nodded at Katherine and Charlotte before moving on to the next patient.

Katherine avoided working too closely with Wyatt. Still, she had come to learn a few things about him. Like how much he cared for those under his charge, how good his bedside manner could be, and how he tried not to show his growing concern for a patient's well being. As much as she fought to hold on to her anger toward him, something akin to sympathy filled her. Was it the turn of his countenance? Or the sadness in his eyes? She did not know.

It would be better to focus on something else. Like Charlotte. Her heart twisted. Despite the ease of Wyatt's words, Katherine had seen enough of the typhoid to know Charlotte's condition needed to turn around soon.

Darkness had fallen by the time David left his house. He apologized to Mary for having to slip away instead of retiring with her. But a meeting of the Free Coinage Union had been called to discuss the new demands placed on the miners. Many were angry and ready to protest the unfair changes. Perhaps the union's reason for meeting was to ensure everyone would make a stand together. Maybe that would be all they needed.

Once David was secure in his saddle, he pushed his horse into a trot. The men agreed to meet by the creek closest to their mineshaft. David regretted venturing back out into the bitter cold of winter, but no one wanted to go into town for fear of the typhoid plague. He pushed his horse a little harder through the darkness, unsure what the night would bring. How would he even find the others? As he neared the creek, a bonfire beckoned to the coming men.

He approached the small group of miners, his cohorts and friends, then tied off his horse on a nearby tree and joined them. By the looks of it, he was one of the last men to arrive. Several of the men in the group nodded in greeting.

"We'll wait a few more minutes for any others to show up," one of the miners said. The man appeared to be older, his hair and beard well beyond graying. Was he from their mine or a representative from the Free Coinage Union? Either way, David judged this man to be the self-appointed leader of the group as he started speaking again minutes later when it became obvious the group was complete.

"Brothers, we are all here for one purpose: to receive fair treatment. And we all agree this most recent announcement by the mine owners is not, in fact, fair. For a while now, they have been assigning us to riskier work and we have been silent. But to now ask us to work longer hours without more pay is unacceptable. This must stop."

As he spoke, David understood why he was the self-appointed leader. For one thing, he was educated. Not many of the miners were. And second, he had a presence and confidence about him that demanded attention. Could the same be said of David? Not likely. He was educated, but he didn't fancy himself a leader. Just a workhand. It wasn't his place to rally a group or run a ranch. No, he belonged in the background.

"We are prepared to go to the mine owners and petition that they retract their demands or offer us more pay. What I want to know is, are we all together on this?"

"What will happen if they fire us? Are there enough silver miners to take our jobs?" One of the men from David's crew, Jonas, spoke up.

David had this thought as well. Wouldn't they just be replaced?

"They won't fire us all," the leader said. "There are miners who need jobs, but there aren't enough of them. That is a lie they have fed us to keep us in fear for our jobs."

"What if they become so angry they cut our pay further?" a voice from somewhere shouted.

"This is a negotiation. No one plans on angering anyone," the leader reasoned, holding up his hands, trying to calm the men.

"Besides," someone near David said. "They didn't seem too concerned with whether or not their decision angered us."

There were more mumbles as several of the miners agreed.

This was a bit much for David. Coming here tonight had been a stretch for him. Standing up to the mine bosses might be asking too much of him.

"Any other concerns?" The leader seemed prepared to deal with whatever question came his way. He handled himself quite well.

Despite his reservations about this union, David began to think he could trust the man, even though he didn't know his name.

"Then it's settled. We will go to the mine owners tomorrow."

There were more excited murmurs among the miners. Was it the right thing though? Then the group began to disperse.

David lingered for a few moments more, letting the fire warm him and letting what had occurred sink in. A hand came down on his shoulder. Turning, he found himself face-to-face with their leader. Now closer, he could see the man's true age. His face was weathered and worn, perhaps from the ravages of mining. Perhaps from the years.

"Do you have concerns, son?"

Should he share his trepidations? "No, sir, I'm just nervous about how it'll go. This is my livelihood, and I support a family on it."

"I understand. And we won't be foolish with the mine owners tomorrow. We'll take care of our own."

David nodded, not sure that made him feel any better. Words, after all, were just words.

"I think the best thing for you to do is to go home, kiss your wife, and get a good night's sleep."

David couldn't fault the man's advice. So, he offered the man his hand before walking back to where his horse stood. As he pulled his tired body up into the saddle, he glanced over at the few men remaining around the fire and longed for some sense of peace instead of the rock that had settled in his stomach. Only a handful remained—the one who had spoken and four others. They were already deep in conversation. Probably about tomorrow. But there was nothing more he could do, so he pushed his horse into a walk, then a trot, heading home.

Wyatt pinched the bridge of his nose. Nothing. There seemed to be nothing he could do to solve this mystery and stop the suffering he was faced with each day. The plague began to wear on him. As it prevailed, so it consumed more of his days and nights. And his emotions.

He did try to maintain some professional distance with his patients as he had been trained in school, but these were not just his patients. These were the people he grew up with. The people he looked up to and respected as he grew into the man he had become. And they were dying all around him. Would he ever get the better of it?

He pulled out his pocket watch and noted the time. Schoolhouse rounds it was. Gathering his medical bag and stethoscope, he moved toward the door. There was a slight lag to his step as he did so. And he knew he could only push himself so hard. If he wanted to maintain this pace in caring for the people of this town, he needed to guard his rest time and mind his proper nourishment. At least he had some help from Katherine. She had been a godsend.

But Katherine, too, pushed herself too hard. Not only did he find himself thankful for her help, he couldn't help but admit he rather enjoyed watching her interact with the patients. She may have missed her calling. Perhaps she should have been a nurse, she was so caring and personable with the patients. It put them at ease and that made his job much easier. They all had only the nicest things to say about her.

He had not been too sure about having a makeshift hospital being supervised by Katherine Matthews. She was smart enough. And quite good at anything she attempted. That wasn't the issue. His concern had been their ability to work together. They had never had the best rapport. But he was all too willing to admit he had been wrong. It had been a good decision. She had served this town well.

As he approached the schoolhouse, the weight of the patients' welfare fell upon him. Just beyond this door lay many who were in all stages of the illness he had yet to conquer. Many he hoped to save, but he knew there were some he could not. So he took a deep breath as he laid his hand upon the door latch and released it.

With only one foot inside, he was rushed by Katherine in a state of near panic. All around them, he heard the sounds of the patients in states of delirium.

"What is it?" His hands were on her arms. Was she hurt? What had happened? The amount of concern that filled him surprised him.

"It's Charlotte." Katherine could not contain her emotion, so it welled up in her eyes. "She's been in such a state all day, ranting and raving. I haven't been able to get anything into her!"

Wyatt brushed past Katherine and over to Charlotte's cot. Just as Katherine said, she was speaking nonsense, and as they neared her, she began flailing her arms about and kicking at them.

"My children . . . don't hurt them . . . " These were the only snippets of her mumbling Wyatt could discern. It did not look good.

"Charlotte," Katherine spoke with a gentle tone as if to reassure her. "Your children are fine. No one is trying to hurt them."

Wyatt's eyes flicked between Charlotte and Katherine. He should have discouraged Katherine's friendship. How could he not see this coming?

"No!" The woman struggled as if against some unknown assailant.

Katherine moved in closer. Perhaps to soothe her by touching her in some way.

"No, Katie, don't . . . " Wyatt started, reaching out to stop her, but he wasn't quick enough.

Katherine had stepped too close and Charlotte's arm struck out, shoving her. She fell, arms pinwheeling, smacking into the edge of an adjacent cot and landing hard on the floor.

Wyatt flew to her side and knelt beside her. "Are you all right?" Helping her sit up, his hands moved over her, checking for injuries. Nothing appeared broken.

She waved him off. "I'm fine. I think."

Confident she was indeed unharmed, Wyatt pulled her to her feet before returning to Charlotte's bedside. He made what observations he could through the woman's delirium. What he saw was not hopeful. Lowering his eyes, he took a moment to prepare himself for what he had to do. Why had he not done something sooner? It had been obvious for some time that Katherine had become too attached to this patient. And now he would have to tell her the hard truth.

Turning back to Katherine, who maintained some distance from Charlotte, he took the couple of steps to close the gap between them and lowered his voice.

"It doesn't look good. This is a critical point for her. She will either improve or . . . " He struggled to find the words. One look at Katherine's face and he wished he was one of those doctors, or maybe even a politician gifted with a golden tongue, with the ability to sugarcoat even the worst news. But he was not.

Would she break down? Perhaps begin crying? He did not do well with crying women.

Katherine's features soon became set. "Is there anything I can do?"

He let out a breath, relieved she was not going to fall apart on him. "If there is a break in the delirium, try to get some of the medicine and water into her. But that's all we can do for her now."

Katherine nodded, biting her lip and glancing over at her friend who was still in a state of complete and utter confusion. He wanted to reach out and put a hand on her shoulder, comfort her somehow, but he thought that would not be well received. She maintained her calm composure despite his distance. For that, he was thankful. Yes, she had been well suited to this task after all.

Timothy strode outside the small church and onto the steps in front of the door. He breathed in the fresh mountain air, cold as it was. The sun hung at its mid-point in the sky. Where had the day gone? His morning had been rather busy, and the hours passed seemingly without him noticing.

This day was only too much like so many of the days he had endured these last few weeks. He'd visited patients near death to counsel them and pray with them in their final hours. Never a pleasant experience. But it was part of his calling. And if he could be the bearer of some peace and comfort in their last moments on this earth, he was all too willing.

His day had also been interrupted by a number of miners seeking counsel and prayer. This was rather curious to him. He was accustomed to having someone stop by for such intervention once or twice a week, but so many in one day?

Timothy had, for some time now, thought it was time to take on another preacher in the town to help share the load. Today he felt it all the more keenly. There seemed to be no time for the things that should fill his day, this plague notwithstanding. Things such as sermon preparation, visiting the shut-ins, and walking among the townsfolk, his flock, to get a sense of how their lives were going.

And visiting Katherine.

He lingered on that thought longer than he perhaps should. Reflection on time spent with Katherine always brought a smile to his face. But instead of investing time in her, like so many days of late, he had been stuck in the church counseling or in one of the two makeshift hospitals praying over those nearing their end.

It was now well past one o'clock, and his stomach grumbled. So he went about closing up the church. But as Timothy turned to walk down the couple of stairs that would take him into the churchyard, he saw a figure walking toward him. Narrowing his eyes to focus his vision, he raised a hand to block the sun. The figure came into focus—Katherine's brother, David Matthews.

"What a pleasant surprise," Timothy called, as he continued to walk, meeting David in the churchyard. "I was just headed out for lunch. Care to join me?" Smiling, he tried to hide his surprise at seeing yet another miner away from his work.

"I can't stay long. I snuck away on my lunch break," David explained, taking his hat off, twisting it in his hands.

"Then let's head over to the café. Perhaps you can eat something while we talk," Timothy said, hoping David would concede. It would not be right to put him off. But could he truly give one more counseling session his full attention on an empty stomach?

David hesitated, but nodded.

"We can talk while we walk," Timothy offered, wanting to ease his urgency.

David took up step with the reverend, but did not speak. Was he unsure how to start? Timothy encountered this with some frequency. Not everyone was bursting at the seams to share their problems with him. Whereas he might wait and give David time to get more comfortable, he wanted to respect the brevity of their time together.

"David, I don't mind telling you I've seen a number of miners today. Is something happening I'm not aware of?"

David stopped walking and stared at Timothy. "What I say stays between us, right?"

Timothy paused and met David's eyes. "Of course. Always."

David quirked an eyebrow and let his gaze linger for a moment. Was he deciding how much he could trust Timothy? After a few moments, he shrugged and picked up his step again.

"It's no secret the mine owners announced a few days ago they would be extending our work day to ten hours, but paying us the same rate. Three dollars per day."

Timothy had not heard. And he did not like the sound of that, but he allowed David to continue.

"Several of us belong to a sort of union. We got together last night and decided to challenge that. I just think many of us are afraid for our jobs."

David fell quiet, but Timothy waited still. He had learned long ago that it was often best to listen first.

"I am not sure we're doing the right thing. I have this nervous sort of feeling. I'm just not at peace about it."

"And you seek peace," Timothy said slowly. It wasn't a question.

David nodded.

They arrived at the café. Timothy waved at the café's owner, Abigail. He slid his coat and scarf off. David did not. After greeting them, Abigail seated them in what she told David was the best table for her "best customer," the reverend. Timothy beamed at her. She was always particularly kind to him. He ordered meatloaf for himself, and David ordered a sandwich.

Their time was short, so Timothy decided to get right down to it. He pushed all pretenses and small talk to the side. There wasn't time to talk David into a realization. The man needed a straight answer.

"David, the only peace I can offer you is the peace that comes from being in God's will. And you can only know God's will through prayer."

David nodded. "Then I need you to pray for me. And pray for my job."

He didn't understand. "I can and I will, David. But you can only find peace as you seek the Lord yourself through prayer."

David examined his napkin, avoiding Timothy's eyes. "I ain't been much of a praying man in a long time, Preacher."

An old story. "That doesn't matter. All you have to do is speak your mind to God, and He will hear you. Ask what it is you want. Ask Him what it is He wants."

David looked up from his napkin, making a sound that was something like a laugh. "You make it sound so easy."

"Because it is that easy," Timothy insisted. Why did everyone try to complicate life with God?

Their food came, and David glanced at the clock. "I'd better eat this on my way. It's time for me to get back to work. Thank you for your time, Reverend." David stood, gathering his sandwich in his hands.

"Any time," Timothy said, watching David.

But as David turned to move off, he halted him.

"David."

David looked back toward Timothy.

"Please think about what I said."

David paused. "I will." And then he was off.

After David disappeared through the café doorway, Timothy paused and prayed over his friend's spiritual well being and over his job. He prayed that he would find true peace. Then he could delay no longer. He picked up his silverware and dug into his meatloaf, making a plan to visit Katherine and the patients at the schoolhouse on his way back to the church.

Katherine paced the schoolhouse floor. She hadn't dared look at her timepiece, but she had measured the day by the sunlight and shadows shifting on the floorboards under her feet. Things did not look good. Having worried after her friend Charlotte for a couple of days, she had neither eaten much nor slept more than snatches here and there.

As much as Katherine prayed and kept vigil over her friend, there had been no sign of a change for the better. Wyatt insisted that if there indeed were hope, there would be some semblance of improvement soon. Yet Katherine had seen nothing encouraging in these last two days. And she feared the worst.

Today Charlotte had finally been lucid, and Katherine got some of the medicine into her. But she knew better than to think this meant good things. Charlotte was quite lethargic. She just lay on her cot. Still. It was eerie. Katherine had seen this before. And it wasn't a good sign.

It seemed as if days had passed in the last hour before she heard footsteps on the stairs outside. Where had Wyatt been? He was late. The door had just opened when she was upon him.

"Please, come see Charlotte first," she insisted, tugging at his arm. "Something's not right." She was fooling herself to hide from what she knew to be true, to hope where there was none.

Wyatt put a hand on her arm and gave her a long look. His eyes seemed to peer deeper into hers than she liked. Why was he looking at her so intently? She dismissed it, turning away from his gaze and pulling him over to Charlotte's bedside.

As they approached the motionless form of her friend, Wyatt reached in his medical bag. He took Charlotte's vitals and hung his head.

She stirred under his ministrations.

"Wyatt!" Katherine motioned toward Charlotte, her eyes filling with moisture. Were they tears of defeat? Of hope? She did not know.

His eyes followed Katherine's.

"Dr. Sullivan," Charlotte said slowly, her speech slurred. "I'm . . . I'm not going to make it, am I?"

"I don't know that. And I'm not going to give up on you, yet." There was fight in his voice, but defeat in his eyes. This plague had taken more out of him than anyone.

Katherine put her head in her hands to hide her tears. But she could not look away from the exchange before her. So she forced her head to raise, her eyes to watch.

"Please, Doc. Please promise me . . . " Charlotte struggled to reach out to him.

He took her hand in his, stilling her effort as he sat on the edge of the cot. "Anything."

"Please take care of my children." Her words came out in gasps of air. And Katherine knew these were her final moments.

Wyatt nodded. "I will, Charlotte. I will."

Charlotte's lips formed a slow smile, a weak smile. She seemed satisfied. With some effort, she shifted her head so she was looking at Katherine. And Charlotte's other hand moved in Katherine's direction, a slight motion. Katherine came forward and took it.

"Charlotte," she said through her tears. Was Charlotte going to ask her the same thing?

Swallowing weakly, Charlotte closed her eyes, her breathing shallow. Her grip on Katherine's hand loosened.

Katherine's hands flew up to her mouth, sure that her friend had just slipped into death.

Wyatt checked for a pulse and looked up at Katherine, shaking his head.

Tears poured out of her eyes then. How much more of this could she take?

Wyatt stood, coming around the bed to stand next to her. And then his hands were on her arms, drawing her away from Charlotte.

"It's okay, Katie, she . . . "

She turned into his arms to face him. "No, it's not okay. All of this death! It's not right. I can't do this!" Katherine looked up into his eyes. "How can you stand it?"

"I . . . " he started, licking his lips as if searching for his words.

But the sound of the door opening drew their attention away from each other. Timothy's smiling face appeared. But it soon fell when his eyes met Katherine's.

"Timothy," Katherine said, fresh tears pouring from her as she brushed past Wyatt and moved into Timothy's arms.

He enveloped her in his embrace. "Katie, what happened?" His voice was soft.

She allowed her tears to flow. So many until she couldn't speak.

"Shhh," he soothed. "It will be all right."

Katherine didn't know if she could believe him. How could God allow all this pain and death? How could He allow the survivors to suffer such loss?

Wyatt stood and watched them for a few moments, unsure of what he should do. His hands balled into fists. He had lost another patient. Then there was the moment he and Katherine had, well, almost shared. But it passed him by, leaving him feeling cheated somehow.

Timothy's eyes were on him, shaking him from his trance. His eyebrows were furrowed, a question in his eyes. With hesitant hands, Wyatt pulled the sheet over Charlotte's face, and Timothy nodded.

"She's in God's hands now," Timothy offered, kissing the top of Katherine's head. "No more pain, remember?"

Katherine nodded into Timothy's shoulder, but his words seemed to do nothing to assuage her tears.

Wyatt needed some quiet. Moving past Timothy and Katherine in their moment he had no business overseeing, he stepped outside. His legs carried him farther away from the schoolhouse, from the sting of the recent loss, from the confusion of his interaction with Katherine.

He didn't stop until he reached the wooden bridge, which traversed the small stream that flowed between the schoolhouse and the town.

Looking out over the town he was charged with protecting, he slammed his fists on the wood of the bridge railing.

Yes, he was angry. Angry with this typhoid plague. Angry with himself for being unable to save so many of his patients. Angry with his inability to say the right thing to Katherine. Angry even, that it should bother him.

His anger dissolved into what was truly behind it all, grief. He felt his shoulders sag and his weight fell onto his arms, which now rested on the railing. What was he going to do?

CHAPTER 5

Loss

A ripple of news coursed through the mine. What was it? There was no way to know for sure. It was all murmurs and secrecy. And David was not in the know. When he asked his buddy, Jonas, all he had heard was that they were meeting again after work by the creek. The last thing David wanted was to be even later getting home because of one of these meetings. But it was important to his livelihood, so he would do what he must whether he liked it or not.

David had taken Timothy's suggestion and spent some time in prayer as he hacked at the stone. It seemed a bit silly, but he did it all the same. He spoke to this unseen God about his desire for peace, about his job, about his family's well being. Remembering Timothy's words, he did ask God what He wanted. And though God did not answer him, David had to admit it gave him some sense of peace to think his concerns were now in the hands of the Almighty God. Engaging his mind thusly had also helped his work go by faster.

As it was, the day came to a close. David wanted nothing more than to pack up and head home, but instead he packed up and headed for the creek. He sent up another awkward prayer as he neared the site where the miners were gathering. The voices became clearer as he drew near.

"What do you suppose we are doing here?" one man said louder than was necessary.

"Is this a good sign or bad sign?" another shouted to no one in particular.

"I think the talks did nothing," a disgusted miner grumbled.

"Since we didn't hear anything from the mine owners, they must have accomplished something," someone challenged him.

David, for his part, kept his mouth shut and ears open. Uneasiness crept into his being, but he attempted to push it down. There would be no use in working himself up. Several minutes later, he spotted their leader, whose name he still had not caught.

The man walked toward one end of the gathering and waved his arms, trying to get the group's attention. At length, the rumble of voices calmed and everyone turned toward him. Only then did he speak.

"I know you are all eager to hear about our negotiations with the mine owners. I will not make you wait any longer. They have agreed to keep the workday at eight hours."

Excited utterances sounded all around David. How could they have accomplished this? Did they truly overpower these larger-than-life men? It couldn't be that simple, could it?

"But, but, but . . . " The leader attempted to get everyone's attention again. "They will reduce our pay to $2.50 a day."

Another murmur went through the crowd, this time it was not so pleasant. These men, who seconds ago believed they had out-done their overseers, were now finding out they had been out-done themselves. And it did not sit well with them.

"Do not think this is the end, brothers. We have thought long and hard about this. Our power is great when we stand together, but we need the protection of greater numbers and assistance from those who know this path better. The Free Coinage Union proposes we join the Western Federation of Miners."

David did not know how this suggestion would help them. Their leader's confidence and assurances appeared to sway many votes. Maybe they felt there was nothing to lose. David, not so much. His thoughts kept shifting back to his wife and two little ones. Would they truly receive some manner of help from this so-called Federation, or were they stuck in this awful situation? Shrugging his shoulders, he was too discouraged to object to this man's plan.

It wasn't even that he had faith in the Western Federation of Miners. In the end, it seemed the Free Coinage Union had done all they could do. So why not ask for help from another larger, more experienced union? What could go wrong?

As the sun set, Wyatt dragged himself from the clinic and made his way over to the makeshift hospital. These long days and short nights had blurred together and he'd lost count. But he was confident in Katherine's ability to hold things together. She had proven herself more than capable of caring for the patients there, and most of them were recovering well. He did wonder if he might be avoiding the hospital . . . or Katherine. The more time he spent in her company, the more confused he became. She was tender and caring toward the patients. And she seemed to have developed a level of trust in him, but there was something more there, bubbling just under the surface. Something she held back.

She had not been the same since Charlotte's death weeks ago. Just as diligent with her patients, something in her step was lacking. Something about her affect had diminished. Would it ever return? Even as they had made some sort of turnaround with the plague and began to see more recoveries than deaths, she did not brighten.

Perhaps he made too much of it. She did have concerns about the patients under her care. Maybe that was all there was to it. Right now, Mr. Wilder's health had been giving her reason for worry. He exhibited many of the same signs so many patients did in their last days.

As Wyatt stepped through the door to the schoolhouse, he was not at all surprised when Katherine waved him over to Mr. Wilder's bedside. Beginning with his vitals, Wyatt found him to be more lucid than he had been and stronger.

"Have you been giving him the medicine?" Wyatt checked the man's abdomen for swelling.

"Yes." Her voice was strained.

Wyatt could understand. Even though Mr. Wilder showed improvement, so had Charlotte and many others before the end. After a thorough examination, Wyatt was rather pleased when he finally leaned back. He offered Katherine a smile.

"He's over the worst of it. He'll make it." Wyatt stood to his full height and placed a hand on Katherine's arm. "Good work, Katherine."

Though it was wholly unnecessary, he allowed his hand to remain on her arm, unsure himself just why he did so. At least she did not push him away.

Her face broke into a tired smile, and he thought he could see moisture touch her eyes. Each patient that pulled through was a miracle. She looked up at Wyatt and opened her mouth. His gaze was fixed on her every movement.

Whatever she intended to say was cut off as the schoolhouse door opened. They both turned to see Timothy walk in.

Wyatt dropped his hand from Katherine's arm and stifled a groan. But he noted Timothy bore with him a picnic basket, and Wyatt was glad for it. He had become concerned that Katherine expended all of her energy caring for these patients and not enough considering her own needs. At least Timothy looked after her.

Gathering his instruments and his bag, he prepared to leave as Timothy moved toward them. He would come later and check the remaining patients.

"Mr. Wilder is going to pull through," Katherine said, closing the distance between her and Timothy.

Wyatt could not miss the smile on her face for Timothy, who set the basket down and took her hands.

Wyatt felt as if he was intruding. Moving toward the door, he nodded at Timothy as he passed.

The two continued to speak softly to each other as Wyatt stepped out of the schoolhouse. Why did it cause his heart to constrict so?

No sooner had he shut the door than he heard Timothy's frantic cry.

"Wyatt! Wyatt!"

Wyatt rushed back into the makeshift hospital to see Timothy lifting Katherine's limp body. A trail of blood came from her nose, and he feared the worst.

"She complained of a slight headache, said she hadn't been feeling herself lately . . . " Timothy babbled. "Then she just collapsed."

Not caring that Timothy was there, Wyatt ripped at the front of Katherine's dress. He had to see the top of her chest. Sure enough, there were the telltale rose spots.

"Let's get her onto one of these beds," he commanded. His heart thumped louder in his chest than he imagined possible.

"Is it . . . ?" Timothy started.

Wyatt nodded. "She has the typhoid." He pulled out his stethoscope and listened for her heartbeat—steady, but slow.

Wyatt's breath quickened and his chest tightened. He needed a plan. "There is a room available at the clinic as soon as I can have it cleaned." He pulled out a handkerchief and dabbed at the blood streaking out of Katherine's nose, trying to ignore the fact that his hands were shaking.

Timothy's eyes were on him as he worked. "Who will tend to the patients here?"

"Most of the patients at the clinic and the hospital are well enough to return home. Enough that we can move those still sick here to the clinic. I'll need some help getting rooms cleaned and prepared." Now that her face was clean, Wyatt applied pressure to Katherine's nasal passage. "Keep pressure on this until it stops bleeding. And stay with her until I return."

Timothy nodded, turning his attention back to Katherine.

Wyatt moved to leave the schoolhouse, but turned at the door to look back at Katherine. Timothy stroked her hair and spoke to her. Of course, Wyatt could not hear what he was saying. Perhaps he prayed over her, maybe he spoke words of comfort. Either way, Wyatt felt a strange pang as he watched the scene.

Dismissing it as concern for Katherine's health, he became aware he was spying on an intimate moment once again. So he headed back toward the clinic to prepare a place for his newest patient.

Katherine had worked tirelessly, tending to patients these last several days. He should have seen this coming, should have insisted she rest more. But it was done now, and he was determined this was one patient he would not lose.

The Matthews' homestead was just as Lauren preferred it—full of fun and laughter. She bounced her grandson on her knee, listening as the small toddler squealed with joy. Was there a more beautiful sound in the world?

"Ride the horsey," she exclaimed to the chubby, smiling face.

She adored her grandchildren and couldn't get enough of them. Every time Mary brought them over for the day to visit, Lauren was grateful. They always had the best time together. Mary was a gift to their family.

But today, Lauren knew something weighed on Mary. Perhaps because David had a lot weighing on him. Tom told her some of what had been going on at the mine. Why wouldn't her son see reason and come back to work at the ranch with his father? Despite her wishes, he had to make his own decisions. And pushing him would do none of them any good.

"Grandma, look what I made!" Jessie's voice interrupted her thoughts. She glanced across the room toward the dining table to see her granddaughter beaming as she held up a drawing of a horse. It was a pitiful, scraggly, scrawny thing, but to Lauren, it was a work of art.

"That's nice, Jessie. Can you make Grandma another one?"

Jessie bobbed her pretty brown head and turned her attention to a fresh page. That should buy her and Mary another ten minutes of peace.

Leaning back in the armchair, Lauren shifted her attention back to Mary, who appeared to be deep in thought. Clearing her throat to break into the younger woman's thoughts, she tried to broach the subject they had been dancing around. "When does David start his longer shift?"

"He started this week," Mary said, eyebrows raised. She seemed surprised Lauren knew about it.

"David told Tom, and Tom mentioned it to me," Lauren explained. "I could see you were saddened and I figured . . . " She let her sentence trail. One day soon Mary would learn that not many secrets were kept well in this family.

Mary nodded, her whole body seeming to sigh in resignation. "It's been hard on him. All of this union talk. And then it came to nothing."

Lauren offered her a sympathetic look. What could she say or do that would give her daughter-in-law some comfort? There were no words, so she reached over and squeezed Mary's hand.

Mary's lips curled into a small smile. After a moment she opened her mouth to speak but stopped, tilting her head.

Lauren was about to ask her what gave her pause when she heard it too—the sound of a horse galloping at full speed. And it drew closer to the homestead.

"I wonder who that could be at this hour," Lauren said, looking over at Mary. Neither woman expected her husband. And whoever it was came in a big hurry.

Lauren passed Peter over to his mother and walked to the window to get a better view of their unexpected guest. She eyed the rifle Tom insisted she keep loaded in the house as she passed it. Once at the window, she was able to make out the form of the town's reverend and she breathed a sigh of relief.

Absentmindedly, she ran her hands over her dress, smoothing it out. She watched as the reverend tied up his horse and approached the porch. But he stopped several steps shy of the door. That didn't make sense. Why wouldn't he come in? Lauren stepped out on the porch.

"Reverend, please come in." She waved at him.

"No, ma'am, I dare not," Timothy said, out of breath from his ride. "I do not wish to spread the typhoid."

"Do you have typhoid, Timothy?" Lauren asked, concerned. But that would be silly. He wouldn't be riding about if he were sick.

"No, but one cannot be too careful."

Mary, with Peter in her arms, came up behind Lauren at the door. The two women shared a look. Why would Timothy now think he might have the typhoid? Lauren turned her attention back to Timothy.

"If you haven't come to call on us, what brings you out here?" Fear pricked at the edge of her consciousness.

"It's Katherine," Timothy said, starting to catch his breath.

Lauren's heart froze. "Katherine?"

"She has the typhoid."

Dread and determination battled for domination in her heart. But her desire after her child won over in a heartbeat. "Then I must go to her at once!" Lauren said, stepping back into the house and grabbing for her shawl.

"No!" He held up his hands as if to stop her. "You cannot risk yourself, Mrs. Matthews."

"I most certainly can!" What was he saying? No one would stop her from seeing her daughter. No one.

"Dr. Sullivan would never allow it. He has quarantined the clinic where he has the few remaining patients. And he refuses to let anyone in," Timothy explained.

Lauren leaned against the doorframe, eyes closed, thoughts swirling. She felt desperate to get to Katherine, but that was not the best course of action. Her heart fought her better judgment and, in the end, her will gained the upper hand.

Turning back to the reverend, she met his gaze. "You must tell me everything."

Mr. & Mrs. Matthews,

Greetings. I only wish our correspondence was under better circumstances. But I feel the burden is upon myself to keep you informed as to Katherine's condition. Dr. Sullivan wishes he had the time to write to you himself. Nonetheless, I feel it is my duty to continue to visit the clinic and communicate with Dr. Sullivan about the condition of the townspeople within.

There remain but a few patients in the clinic. I took my own case to Dr. Sullivan that I be allowed to assist in nursing these patients, including Katherine, back to health. He was unmoved by the force of my petition, however, and the quarantine holds. Dr. Sullivan sees to those in the clinic on his own. But he tells me all of the patients are in various stages of recovery. All, that is, except for Katherine.

It seems by the time we discovered she had become ill, she was well along into the second stage of the typhoid. I am sorry to tell you she spends little time each day lucid. Please take some comfort in knowing that her delirium is not violent. She is not at risk of harming herself or others. I wish I had more to share with you and that the news I bear is not of such nature as it is. But I promise to you I will send these reports to you daily until Katherine is fully recovered.

I write this with heavy hand, but I must admit I blame myself for not seeing the signs of her illness sooner. I was distracted. And I will have a hard time finding forgiveness for myself as she is in such a state. And so I leave you with this: not an hour goes by that I will not be in deep prayer for her return to full health.

Regards,

Reverend Timothy

Many days passed without many changes. Wyatt set a strict quarantine at the clinic. No one, not even the reverend, was permitted through the doors. Miss Abby would send food for Wyatt and fresh broth for the patients. It was left outside the door with a brisk knock before she scurried away. And Wyatt couldn't be more thankful. If not for the constant reminder, he probably would have stopped eating. Even so, his meals were never consumed at warm temperatures.

Wyatt prepared to take the bowls of broth to his patients. The stairs stretched before him, seemingly rising higher than they ever had. He had been relying on less and less sleep since Katherine had come to the clinic. Yes, even as his worn thoughts ran through the states of the patients within the rooms upstairs, he found his mind dwelling where it always did—on Katherine.

He spent the majority of his day with her. *Rightfully so*, he told himself. She was on the brink, at the edge. And that made him all the more determined. Intent that he would pull her through . . . somehow.

Now at the top of the stairs, he stepped into the first room. He forced himself to keep his mind on this patient, Mrs. Simmons. They all deserved his attention, but he also knew that once he entered Katherine's room, there he would remain. The rest of the clinic tenants were all but recovered and demanded less of his time.

"Dr. Sullivan," Mrs. Simmons greeted him, sitting up in her bed.

Wyatt balanced the tray of small bowls as he propped the door open and moved closer to the bed. He set the bowls on a stand near the door and brought one over to her. Instead of giving it to her, he placed it on the nightstand. Checking her pulse, heartbeat, and abdomen, he went through his routine. Everything seemed well enough.

"I know I keep asking this, Doc. But I'm rather anxious to get home," Mrs. Simmons managed to say as he moved his hands over her neck.

It wasn't just that he heard this from Mrs. Simmons every time he saw her, he heard this from every patient in the clinic. Almost every patient. Katherine wasn't in any condition to be asking such questions. Pushing her from his thoughts, he focused on Mrs. Simmons.

"It will be tomorrow." He leaned back and offered her a smile. "As long as you can manage to behave yourself."

The older woman grinned at his tease. "Good. I can't imagine my Otis is fairing well without me."

Wyatt patted her hand. "You won't have to worry about that much longer. Now, I'd like you to finish your broth." He stood and started toward the door.

The woman made an exasperated sound. "I'll be happy to get some biscuits and gravy when I get home."

Turning, Wyatt raised an eyebrow and one side of his mouth turned up. "Make sure you send me some." With that, he closed the door and left Mrs. Simmons in peace.

Patient after patient, the rest were much the same. Some would be released the next day, some over a couple of days. He wanted to be certain everyone had recovered before unleashing them on the general populace.

At last, he closed the door to the last patient's room and found himself standing in front of Katherine's door. Drawing in a breath, he felt a strange reluctance to enter. Why so, he could not discern. She was his patient, and he needed to care for her. He could not do that from the hallway. Neither could he deny he tired of fighting this unforgiving foe. And so he steeled himself against his warring emotions and opened the door.

Katherine lay in the same condition she had been for the last several days—still, in sleep on the bed. No one would ever know from this distance that anything was wrong. They could mistake her visage as that of a dreaming form. But a few steps into the room would break that presumption. She was covered in sweat from high fever and, every few minutes, muttered nonsensical things.

Wyatt moved to the bedside, setting a bowl of fresh, cool water on the nightstand. In his other hand, he bore the medicine she so desperately needed. He would go in a little while to get fresh broth for her on the off chance he could catch her in a lucid phase.

Would today be like the previous days? Unless one of the other patients called for him, his focus would be on Katherine. By her side, dabbing her with a cold, wet cloth and watching over her. Armed with the medicine, and soon the broth, he sat with patience, ready for whenever she became lucid, which was less and less often.

Still he sat in silent vigil. He was tired, but that did not stop his thoughts from dwelling on her and the sacrificial servanthood that landed her in this situation. It didn't seem right. Nothing about it seemed fair. And this was one of the problems he always had with the idea of an almighty deity, with God, who would make decisions like this at worst, or, at best, allow something like this to happen to such a selfless servant.

Wyatt didn't know when his questioning of God began. Maybe the day his father started hitting his mother. Maybe the day he stepped in to stop him and received a thrashing in return. How could a good God allow that to happen? He remembered how he had prayed then for God to change his father, that God would rescue him and his mother. But God never saw fit to hear Wyatt's prayer. So Wyatt didn't see fit to pray anymore.

Watching Katherine suffer drove him to greater resentment. Maybe in his dad's alcohol-infused brain, he and his mother deserved the beatings. But who would think that Katherine deserved this? Frustration is what came out. Frustration in his inability to help her, to bring her back from this darkness she found herself in. The emotion was so intense his eyes stung. So he sat, watching her, near tears at the thought that he might, in fact, lose this fight.

Her voice broke into these thoughts.

"Wyatt . . . Wyatt . . . " she slurred.

She called for him? Not Timothy. Him. But why? He moved his seat closer to the bed and leaned over to take her hand. "I'm right here, Katie."

Her voice was little more than a whisper; he had to lean in even closer to make out what she was saying. "No, Wyatt . . . we can't leave . . . Ellie . . . "

What? Leave Ellie? She wasn't calling for him. No, Katherine thought she was talking to him. And he knew what she was talking about. That day, that horrible day so long ago. The day that haunted him still. The day Ellie Mae died.

"No, no, no!" She began to twist and turn in her sleep.

How he wished he could pull her from it! But he could not. All that was left for him was a feeble attempt to soothe her.

"Shh, shh," he said, boldly stroking her hair. "It's all right. Everything is all right." His touch seemed to calm her, so he continued. After several minutes, she stilled and fell back into a deep sleep.

Some moments later, he pulled himself away and slipped down the stairs. He paced the wide space of the examination room. Katherine's condition continued to worsen. This had happened too often with the typhoid patients under his care.

Wyatt had to do something. He could not stand by and watch her die like so many others. So he gathered more of his medicinal water mixture and made his way upstairs, all the more determined. Stepping back into her room, he found her once again in a disturbed, fitful sleep. She spoke nonsense. Delirious. But that would not stop him. Not anymore. He sat on the bed beside her and gathered her into his arms. She was a furnace.

"Katie, I need you to come back," he insisted, speaking into her hair.

Her eyes opened halfway. She looked anywhere and everywhere but at him.

"Katie, listen to me. I need you to drink this." He held the glass up to her lips and poured some of the liquid into her mouth.

She spit it back out at him.

Not one to be deterred, he continued. "Katie, you must drink this!" He made several more attempts and got some of the liquid down her throat, at least a couple of tablespoons. Whether it was by chance or she had heard him somewhere through her delirium he wasn't sure. But he took comfort in it all the same.

The church was quiet. How could the small white building seem so dark and lifeless, eerie almost? Suitable, Timothy thought, as he returned from the latest funeral service. It was as if the ghosts of those who had passed awaited him there in the stillness, wanting a word with him. He lit a candle by the door and allowed the flame to bathe the church in its light, however dim, and push out any thoughts he had of lingering ghosts.

These funerals took so much out of him. How he hoped it would be the last! He was tired. No, not just tired . . . weary. All the happenings of the last weeks weighed on him—the loss of so many of the townsfolk, the fear and sadness that had rippled through this town, the uncertainty at the mines, and Katherine's illness. The latter of which he took on as personal guilt. Perhaps false guilt, but he could not convince his heart that he was blameless. He should have known, should have seen something in her demeanor.

She had been tired, too tired. And she'd complained of a headache in those last couple of days. He should have mentioned it to Wyatt. But she had shaken it off, so he did the same. Had he been in such deep denial? Not anymore.

His heart twisted in his chest as he passed the pews that once held so many people. He saw the faces of those he would not see again on this earth. Pausing at Old Man McCain's regular seat, he was struck. Mere moments ago, he had said a few words of comfort to his widow, friends, and family and laid the man to rest.

The thought flew into his mind, unbidden, that he might have to, one day soon, put Katherine's body to rest and say farewell to her for all of his earthly life. The thought left him breathless. He had to catch himself, gasping for air, and lower himself onto the dais's steps. Now his heart raced. And try as he might, he could not pull his thoughts from those that disturbed him so. What was there for him then? What would he tell a parishioner? To pray.

"God Almighty, I do not know how I should pray. You know my heart. You know how it beats furiously within me. And You know why. I fear for Katherine. I come before You pleading yet again, Father God, for a miracle, for the healing of her body. I'm not ready to let her go. This town is not ready to let her go. Her work here is not done. I pray You see fit to bring her back to us and allow her to complete that work. Bring her back to me."

Lauren sat at the dining table, head in her arms. David brought her a cup of coffee and sat in the seat next to her, but she barely acknowledged him. The most recent reports about Katherine were not good. Dr. Sullivan remained hopeful she would yet recover, but he could not give them a good prognosis based on her current condition. So many townspeople had been lost to the typhoid. Neighbors, friends, family, truly. And Lauren feared Katherine would join that number.

"Don't fret so, Ma." David put an arm around her. "Remember how stubborn Katherine is. She is a fighter. It's going to take a lot more than some plague to take her down."

Lauren smiled at him, patting his hand. She was thankful he and his family had come to keep her company this evening. What would she do without them?

"Katherine will pull through," Mary added, taking the seat on the other side of Lauren. "I just know she will."

Lauren appreciated their confident words, but they held no weight compared to those of Katherine's physician. Only he could say what was going on with her body. But only the Lord knows what will happen. So, she closed her eyes and sent up yet another silent prayer on her daughter's behalf. Would He see fit to answer her?

As she ended her prayer, she brought the cup to her lips and sipped the warm beverage, then nearly spit it back out. She made a move to get up. "I should put on some fresh coffee for us. This batch has gone stale."

Mary put her hand on Lauren's arm. "Let me do that."

Lauren nodded her thanks. She did not have the wherewithal to make coffee this evening. Not when her daughter might not make it through the night.

In a handful of minutes they were all seated with steaming cups, waiting, watching Jessie and Peter play on the carpet in front of the fireplace. It seemed an eternity before they heard the sounds of a horse outside.

David placed a hand on his mother's shoulder to still her as he got to his feet to look out the window. Only a few moments went by before he announced, "It's Pa!"

This is what they had been waiting for all day—Tom's return. He had braved going into town for provisions and for word about Katherine's condition.

Lauren wrung her hands. She only had to wait a few more minutes before Tom would be beside her, telling them what he had learned. It had seemed like days since they had heard from Dr. Sullivan. Though in reality it had just been two.

Mary walked to the stove and poured Tom a cup of coffee to set on the table. It wasn't long before he burst into the house.

"Grandpa!" Jessie said, jumping up to get a hug.

"Gra'pa!" Peter cooed.

How could she not suffer her grandchildren their hugs? But she felt as if she would burst if he didn't speak soon.

Once the hugs were distributed he came over to his seat. Mary scooted the cup of hot coffee closer to him.

He smiled his thanks and took a swig.

Lauren's eyes were glued to her husband, pleading with him to speak.

He did not hold out much longer. As he finished his long sip, he put the cup down and took off his gloves, sliding a hand over Lauren's. "Doc says she's made a turn for the better."

"Oh, thank God!" Lauren said, clasping her chest, nearly swooning.

"When can we see her?" David said.

"Doc wants us to give it a couple of days, make sure she's strong enough for visitors and the typhoid is out of her system."

Lauren was disappointed, but not disheartened. The worst was behind her. Katherine would recover. She met her husband's eyes, tears of joy in her own. Their daughter was safe.

The clock chimed noon. But Timothy hadn't needed the chime to tell him it was twelve o'clock. He had been pacing and watching the time-piece since early morning. News of Katherine's return to health had spread. And no one was more eager to see her than he.

Just earlier today, Wyatt had pronounced her well enough to receive visitors. As much as he wanted to rush to the clinic right then, he held back. Her parents would need time with her. So, he forced himself to stay away though everything in him screamed for him to go to her.

At dawn he decided that noon was the longest he could hold out. So he began his vigil at the clock. He attempted to distract himself with sermon writing, the piano, and cleaning the church, but nothing could keep him from the clock for long, as if that timepiece was his only connection to her. And he prized it greatly, watching the minutes tick by. But the waiting had finally come to an end.

No sooner had the long hand clicked over than he was out the door. In his enthusiasm, it became difficult to steady his walk. So, he found himself all but sprinting to the clinic. The walk from the church to the clinic on a good day took him about eight minutes. But it was only 12:02 when he was knocking on the clinic door.

Wyatt answered the door. "Yes?"

Timothy slid his hat off his head, feeling like a boy calling on a girl for the first time, speaking with Wyatt as if he were a disapproving father. "I'm here to see Katherine." He paused, and then thought to ask, "Are her parents still here?"

"Yes, but I'm sure they won't mind if you come up to see her for a few minutes," Wyatt said, his words hesitant. Did he not wish Timothy to see Katherine? Perhaps he simply protected her need for rest. Either way, Wyatt moved out of the way and allowed him to enter.

Once inside, Timothy climbed the stairs, tempted to take them by twos he was so eager to lay eyes on his Katherine again. As he came to her room, the only one occupied in the clinic, he knocked with light raps on the door.

It swung open, and Katherine's father greeted him.

"Reverend," he exclaimed. "Come on in."

"Yes, please do." Katherine sat in the bed, her voice a bit raspy.

Timothy shuffled his way into the room only to discover there wasn't much space for three visitors. So he stood by the door, his frame rather awkward in the small pocket. But that didn't matter to him. His gaze fell on Katherine. He again felt like a schoolboy with his wide grin and bright eyes.

Lauren spoke, but he didn't turn toward her. "We were thinking about going to the café for lunch. And we planned to bring something back for Katherine. Would you like something, Reverend?"

Hearing his title pulled Timothy out of his trance. "No, thank you. I just ate moments ago."

"All right, then," Tom said, a strange smile on his face as he glanced between Timothy and Katherine. "We best be on our way."

"Thank you, Ma, Pa, for the flowers," Katherine said, fingering the white lilies in a jar by her bedside.

Tom and Lauren looked at each other.

"It wasn't us, darling," Lauren said as she stood, stepping around the bed to her husband.

Katherine's eyes fell on Timothy.

He shook his head.

"Perhaps Wyatt brought them in," Tom suggested.

Katherine looked at the flowers for several moments, seemingly lost in thought.

Lauren moved to give Katherine a quick kiss on the forehead. "We'll be back soon."

And then Lauren and Tom made their way out of the room.

Timothy nodded at them as they left, but his eyes returned to Katherine's. Moving over to the chair Lauren had vacated, the one next to Katherine's bedside, he gave her a meaningful smile while he fiddled with the brim of his hat. After some time, he found his voice. "How are you? I mean, you look good."

"Thank you." Katherine offered him a weak smile. "I am much better. Wyatt says I'm over the worst of it."

"What a relief." He leaned forward, reaching for her hand.

She slid her smaller hand into his.

The contact invigorated him. It gave him courage and boldness. "I prayed for you constantly," he confessed.

"I know you did, Timothy. And I know your prayers pulled me through."

Timothy smiled, looking at their clasped hands. "I have missed you, Katie," he said, his voice serious as he raised his eyes again.

"And I you. But this is all behind us now, and we can get back to our picnics soon enough." Her eyes were bright as they met his.

"And our reptile hunts," he joked.

"And our reptile hunts." She smiled.

Silence fell between them, and he became lost in the joy of being with her. He would prefer it never end.

"Tell me news of Cripple Creek since the plague." The sadness in her eyes did not escape him.

Timothy drew in a breath, ragged with emotion. "The town is devastated by the many losses, but celebrating each recovery."

Katherine nodded.

"Katie," Timothy said as he leaned a little closer to her. "This is not the town you remember. There are hurts, scars. The people that remain have been changed by this plague."

She nodded again, looking down at her hands. Tears brimmed in her eyes. "What are we going to do?" she whispered.

He reached for her other hand, now encasing both of her hands in his, so delicate, so frail. "What we always do. Pull together. Look to God for guidance."

Katherine let her head hang for a moment.

Timothy could almost feel Katherine withdrawing. So, he decided to change the subject. "On the one hand, we were lucky. There are only two orphaned children."

"Charlotte's children." Katherine's head jerked up.

Timothy's nod was slow, trying to communicate his sorrow.

"What's happened to them?" Her question rushed out of her.

Timothy cleared his throat, not sure he liked where the conversation had turned. "The mayor and his wife are keeping them. We haven't been able to find any relations, so we'll have to see if anyone in town can make a home for them." He hoped that would satisfy her curiosity.

"What happens if no one in town volunteers?"

Why was she so interested? True, she was close to Charlotte and, of course, would be concerned after the children, but he didn't expect her to be so preoccupied. But he could no more deny Katherine whatever she asked of him than he could stop his heart from beating. "We'll send them on to Denver to an orphanage."

Katherine's expression became more thoughtful. But she did not question him further about the orphans. "Tell me, what news have you heard of my students?"

Smiling, Timothy squeezed her hands. He was pleased with her ability to focus on her students in the midst of all the unpleasantness. She was strong. Stronger than he anticipated.

CHAPTER 6

New Normal

The days that followed passed slowly for Katherine. Days in which she gained strength, but also had time to think on what might become of Charlotte's children. It occupied much of her thoughts. Her parents begged her to focus on her own recovery and allow God's will to take its course for the two children, but Katherine could not let it go. Charlotte had trusted her. Maybe not with her children, but with so many things. And she owed it to her friend to see that her children were cared for.

Even now, Katherine urged her legs to move faster as they carried her across the bridge toward the church grounds. She prayed she wouldn't be late for the meeting that would determine the fate of these two precious children. Sleep still clouded the edges of her mind. What she intended to be a simple rest had turned into an hour-and-a-half nap. When she realized her folly, she raced for the church as fast as her body would carry her. And though her body was still recovering from her illness, frustration pricked at her.

This meeting was too important to sleep through. So she had pulled on her shoes and rushed out of the room, not even taking the time to check her appearance. However, as she moved up the steps that took her into the small building, she ran her hands over her dress to smooth down the wrinkles and checked her hair with her hands, ensuring errant strands were pinned.

Stepping into the one-room building, Katherine glanced around. Not quite the turnout she hoped for. Other than the mayor, Timothy, and herself, only one couple came. A few years older than her, they seemed harder, roughened perhaps by years of hard work in the sun. They bore all the markings of a farming couple.

Timothy nodded to Katherine and stood to take his place on the dais. Had he been waiting on her?

Katherine chose a seat as Timothy stepped up to the pulpit.

"Thank you all for coming. We are here today concerning two children orphaned by the recent typhoid plague. Jack, age three, and Susie, who is not yet a year old. This meeting is to hear any interest from the town in adopting these precious children who are in need of a loving home."

Silence fell over the room for a few moments.

It was awful. Was the town not more open, more loving than this?

"Reverend," the man from the couple spoke up, standing.

"Yes, Mr. Jones?" Timothy addressed him as if he were one of several people volunteering.

The man spoke with frankness, not nearly as tactful as Katherine might have liked. "My wife and I don't have much use for the baby girl, but we think we might could take on the little boy."

Much use for the baby girl? How cold, how heartless, how . . .

Timothy's voice interrupted her thoughts. "I thank you for your willingness to open your home. We shall arrange a time for you to meet Jack and see if, in fact, he suits your family."

Mr. Jones bobbed his head and then he and his wife stood and walked out, nodding to Katherine and the mayor in turn as they passed.

The mayor, Timothy, and Katherine waited for a full half hour for anyone else that might come. And no matter how hard Katherine prayed, no one else did.

"I suppose we have our answer," the mayor said, clicking his pocket watch closed as the hour drew to an end. "At least we have a home for the boy. We just have to find a place for the girl or send her on to Denver."

Katherine's jaw dropped. Was everyone around here so callous?

Timothy nodded, avoiding Katherine's eyes. That was probably best.

"Let me know when you want to arrange a meeting for the Joneses and Jack. We'll do what we can on our end," the mayor said, standing.

"Certainly. And thank you for fostering the children."

Katherine bit her lip to keep from saying something she'd regret.

The mayor nodded. He then moved out of his pew, said a quick farewell to Katherine, and took his leave of them.

Once the mayor closed the door behind himself and they were alone, Katherine rushed over to Timothy. She felt as if she would burst, she could barely contain her emotion.

"Timothy, you cannot let the Joneses split those children up! They've already lost their parents, don't make them lose each other, too." Her words spilled out. He must see that she was right.

"You saw what I saw, Katie. There are no other families willing to take either of them. It might, in fact, be easier to find a home for Susie if she's alone. But, for now, at least there is a home for Jack."

Timothy's response surprised her. How could he not see things the way she did? "A home that will treat him as nothing more than a farm hand."

"That's not fair." Timothy's brow furrowed. Then his features softened and he reached out for Katherine's hand. "He'll be safe and cared for."

"But what about love?" She tried to pull free from his grasp.

He kept a firm hold on her hand. What was he thinking?

"Those children deserve to be loved!"

"I don't know if they can hope for that at this point," Timothy said with a gentle voice.

Timothy was just being the voice of reason. She should at least make an attempt to stem this idealistic streak within herself, but she couldn't stop the words that came. "I can give them love." Had she just said that?

"You?" Timothy's brows shot up and his hold on her loosened.

"Yes, me." Her voice firm, she continued, "I will take them."

"That's rather noble of you, Katie. It truly is. But I cannot, in good conscience, give two orphans to a single woman. How would you care for them? How would you support them? How can you be both mother and father?" His tone was soft, but his voice was firm.

Katherine looked to the ground. Deep down, she knew she asked the impossible. He had every right to treat her as if she were being ridiculous. She was. Yet, he spoke to her with such tenderness. Still, her heart ached for some way to help Jack and Susie.

"Your care for these children is admirable," Timothy said, his voice as gentle as ever. "But they are in God's hands now."

She raised her eyes to meet his. "At least do this, Timothy. Don't adopt Jack out to the Joneses yet."

Timothy became silent. He opened his mouth and closed it. His features softened and he raised a hand until his fingers grazed her cheek. "I can't wait too long. But I will give you one week to find another option for me." Then he withdrew his touch.

"Thank you, Timothy." A part of her wanted to draw closer to him, but she thought better of it and pulled away, preparing to take her leave.

As she turned to gather her shawl, she felt Timothy's gaze still intent upon her. Looking back over her shoulder, she offered him a smile and a quick wave before heading toward the back of the church.

Only then did she notice Wyatt had slipped into the church and sat, staring, in the last pew. It gave her pause. How long had he been here? What could be his reason for being here at all? What possible consideration could he have for two orphaned children?

To say things had been awkward between Wyatt and Katherine since she had been discharged from his care would be putting it mildly. She still harbored resentment toward him, but something had changed. Something in the way he looked at her was . . . different somehow. Still, as she found her footing, she held her head up and walked past him and out of the church without so much as another glance in his direction.

The day began like so many others. David Matthews awoke and breathed in the freshness of a new day. But it weighed on him. He went about his morning routine, preparing himself for the day ahead, despite the fact he was a bundle of nerves. As he kissed his wife good-bye, he allowed himself to linger in that moment for a couple of seconds longer, taking what comfort he could from her presence.

Because today, instead of taking his place in line at the mine, David grabbed his picket sign and marched off after the other miners. Today was the big day. The day everything had come down to. They would stand up to the mine owners. Even now, as David marched behind his fellow miners, John Calderwood's words from their last meeting rang in his ears.

"We must stand together. We must stand firm. We will not tolerate this treatment. We will stand against it and say 'not here, not now, not our mine.'"

This new man on the scene, Calderwood, was the president of the Western Federation of Miners and a former miner himself. He had already sent notice to the mine owners of their demands: that they go back to the eight-hour workday for the full three-dollar wage. Apparently, the mine bosses had not responded well.

The memories of that prior meeting plagued David. He remembered Calderwood's message about their next course of action. In David's opinion, the man sounded a bit preachy. It left David feeling more than a little unsure if this was the right thing to do.

But the decision had been made. He joined this union for a purpose, and his place was with the rest of the miners, his "brethren" as Calderwood called them. David would stand with them, not against them. Looking at the others around him, he knew he was no strikebreaker; no one would be calling him a scab.

As he and the small group arrived at the entrance to the mine, they saw others gathering as well. He continued replaying Calderwood's pitch, "We must stand together. We must stand firm." When he spotted some of his work buddies, he raised a hand in greeting. They congregated together not far from the larger group crowding the mine entrance. His gaze rested on each of his "brethren." Could he find something reassuring in their features, their posture, their commitment? It strangely seemed to be lacking. Perhaps they were thinking the same thing, each looking at him in the same way.

And then Calderwood arrived. He seemed more upbeat than any of them, making rounds, shaking hands, and patting miners on the shoulder. For a brief moment, David wondered whether this man was a union leader or a politician. Was there a difference?

As Calderwood approached David, he reached out his hand. When he took David's hand, it was warm and solid. Confident. "Glad to see you here, David. How are the kids and the wife?"

Surprised the man remembered that much, David's reply came out slow and stumbled, "They're all right. The wife is a bit nervous."

"Hang in there." Calderwood winked at him. "We'll get through this together."

In that moment, he knew he was on the right side. He felt a strong sense of commitment and realized that if it weren't for this man, no one would be here. Calderwood continued on his path of welcoming everyone, though David realized it was more than that. The man encouraged the miners in their decision to follow him. And they were going to need it.

He remembered the man's words from the earlier meeting, "We won't let them intimidate us. It won't be easy, but we will prevail!" And he distinctly remembered the cheering after. Strange, but as he searched the crowd this morning, nobody was cheering. The excitement of the other night didn't seem to be here today. But it did not escape David's notice that everyone's mood lifted with Calderwood's presence. If there was one person that could rally them to victory, it was he.

And with that, David proceeded into position to form their strike line.

Life in Cripple Creek returned to some semblance of normal. While the trouble at the mine kept the town in an uneasy state, people still went about their days much as they did before the plague. School had resumed, but there were empty seats. And that devastated Katherine. It served as a daily reminder to the students that their town had been touched by something tragic. Katherine rearranged seating, hoping to lessen the sting of the absent students.

Still, as Katherine sat at her desk grading papers after her students were dismissed, the words on the papers blurred. She could not move on. How could she expect any of her students to? It seemed as if her chest could not expand it was so tight. And it ached. Not only did she mourn the loss of the missing students, she had not come up with any solution for Charlotte's two young children. And she only had a week! How she wished she could take them on herself. But she understood Timothy's wisdom in not letting her have them. Even though she was certain she could provide a better life for them than the Joneses.

Rubbing her eyes to clear them, she glared at the handwriting in front of her. It was no use. The lines were still blurred. So she gave up and rested her head in her hands.

Moments later, she heard the door open and close. She straightened herself and worked to stack the papers, looking toward the intrusion.

"Dr. Sullivan," she clipped as politely as she could, making every attempt to disguise her surprise. "Is there something I can do for you?" Katherine tried to hide the emotion that was, without a doubt, displayed on her face. She rose and started to erase the chalkboard, turning her back to him. What did he want? There were far more important things on her mind than to suffer his imposition.

"I came to speak with you about something of importance," Wyatt said, his voice hesitant.

"Oh?" She half-turned to face him. Biting at her lip to contain her earlier emotions.

But there was none of the smugness in him today she always associated with Wyatt. Come to think of it, since the plague hit, she had not seen it. No, there seemed to have been a change in him.

"It's something that I think involves both of us." He looked at her, his eyes glistening with emotion, wide and sincere.

Was this it? Were they going to have it out about Ellie? Not quite the time and place for it, but she would prepare herself to face off with her greatest enemy now if need be. So, she put down the eraser and turned her whole body to face him, trying to exude confidence she didn't feel.

"Go ahead." She crossed her arms in front of her body. A shield.

"It's about the orphans." He licked his lips as if he struggled to find the right words.

Never would she have expected anything of the kind to come out of his mouth. Even though Charlotte had asked him to look after her children, he had not made any move to do so. What could he want to say about them now? Her arms slackened and fell to her sides. She supposed her expression begged for him to continue because he did so as he walked toward her.

"I don't want to see those children separated or mistreated any more than you do. Their mother did ask me on her deathbed, after all, to look after their well-being." Wyatt's voice broke with emotion.

Katherine looked down. The memories of so many sick and dying townspeople came back to her. It all played in her mind's eye, the most striking memory that of Charlotte's death. That scene replayed over and over until Wyatt's voice cut into her thoughts.

"The thing is," he said, shifting, no longer meeting her eyes. "I heard you talking with Timothy and . . . "

Wyatt seemed quite tense. More so than she had ever seen him. She didn't even know it was possible for him to be nervous.

"And I thought . . . if you were married, you would be able to take on those children."

Katherine remained quiet, in part because she didn't know what to say or where he was going, but mostly because she enjoyed watching him squirm.

"And I bet you'd be good for those children," he met her eyes at last.

Surprised at his compliment, she didn't notice for a few moments that a silence had fallen between them.

"I would like to try. I would. But there is the problem that I am not married," she said, her voice quiet.

"What if you married me?" Wyatt held her eyes.

"What if . . . what?" Her mouth fell agape. Did she hear him correctly?

He took a breath and let it out. "What if we got married?"

That was the most ridiculous thing she had ever heard. Marry him? Her worst enemy? The man who had left her best friend behind? No, no, no, no, no! She looked up, prepared to throw him out of her schoolhouse.

"Just think about it," he said, backing up toward the door. Then he was gone.

And she was alone with her thoughts.

It had been a beautiful day despite everything in it. The birds sang as if it were a day like any other. And the house chores needed tending to all the same. All in all, everything threatened to lock Mary into believing it truly was no different. But it was. Mary's mind remained busy throughout this otherwise normal day, reminding her what set this day apart. Today was the big day. The day of the strike.

Once Jessie returned home from school, Mary set her down with her homework at the kitchen table while Peter napped. Then she continued to do what she had been doing all day—wondering about her husband and how he fared. He had never been involved in a strike. And he was nervous. She was nervous for him.

Much of their time together the previous evening had been spent in silence. But as they were getting ready for bed, David requested something she had never known him to ask—for her to pray for him and for the strike. She obliged and was surprised when he prayed, too.

That morning, she had risen with him. There were so many chores she needed to attend to, so much to manage, especially with a family. But today had been different. David wanted to pray together again and, once he rode off, she'd been left to suffer the worry and fears that threatened to overtake her. She had wished one of the kids would wake early, so she would have someone to spend the time with.

But not today. This day, the kids slept, nestled comfortably in their beds long after David left, leaving Mary to face this struggle by herself. She did the only thing she knew how to—she prayed even more. As she prayed, she tried to turn her husband over to God. But it wasn't easy. Her mind kept playing out scenarios where David was hurt, or fired, or other terrible thoughts.

When David had first started working in the mines, she used to worry about him being injured or trapped, but as the months went by, she had worried less and less. Not that those thoughts didn't visit her each day, but they no longer plagued her every waking moment.

Today was different. She'd heard rumors from other wives that strikes could get out of control. When she asked David about it the night before, he reassured her the stories were hogwash, and suggested perhaps she needed to stop listening to so much gossip. But she couldn't help but hear those words, rumors though they may be, play back in her mind. When the kids did wake, she was grateful for the company. And she shifted her focus to dressing them and preparing for breakfast.

Now, as Mary watched Jessie doing her homework in silence, those haunting thoughts returned. Glancing out the window, she wondered how long they would stay at the mine. Would David be home late tonight? Would all be well? Or would something have happened during the day? Would he be hurt perhaps and have no way to contact her? She stilled her anxious mind. That was not likely. If he were injured, they would take him to Dr. Sullivan. And the good doctor would make sure she was notified.

"Ma," Jessie called to her from the table.

"Mmm?" she answered from her post by the window.

"I need some help subtracting these numbers," Jessie said, her frustration coming through in her tone.

"I'm coming," Mary said, tearing herself away from the window, thankful yet again for the distraction.

"Reverend!" Mrs. Abby said as she approached the table where Katherine and Timothy seated themselves in the café. "So good to see you! We don't see enough of you around here," she admonished him. "You know you can stop in any time you're hankering for some home cooking."

Katherine glanced between Mrs. Abby and Timothy. The woman's concern over him was almost motherly. Didn't his mother live just two miles outside of town?

"Yes, you've been so gracious as to extended that offer on many occasions. Don't I take you up on it enough?" Timothy gave her a broad smile. Did he enjoy this kind of attention? It was difficult to discern.

"No, not nearly enough." Mrs. Abby put a hand on her full hip and held a coffee pot in the air.

"Well then, I shall do my best to remedy that." Timothy interlaced his fingers in front of himself and drew his attention back to Katherine.

She offered him a simple smile, only somewhat amused by the interchange.

"I can't help but wonder about the Valentine's Dance in a couple weeks. Will you be going?" Mrs. Abby looked between the two of them.

Katherine's face warmed under her scrutiny. Timothy had not yet asked her.

"Oh," Mrs. Abby said, putting a hand to her mouth. "I see."

Chancing a glance at Timothy, Katherine saw that he smiled at her. Perhaps he intended to ask her at this meal.

"I guess I need to learn to keep my big mouth closed." Mrs. Abby smiled as she wiped a hand on her apron.

That would be nice.

"Now, let's talk about what you're here for. Lunch. Any thoughts?"

"I think we both want the meatloaf." Timothy glanced at Katherine.

She nodded in agreement.

"Two meatloaves coming up," Mrs. Abby called out louder than was necessary. Giving them another meaningful glance, she turned and moved on to the next table.

As she walked away, a brief silence fell between them. Katherine's mind filled with the things that lay before her to say. She worked the edge of her napkin with her fingers. And she hoped Timothy wouldn't see her nervousness. Or perhaps mistake it for something connected to the Valentine's Dance exchange.

She broke the silence. "I enjoyed your sermon Sunday."

"Oh?" He leaned forward on his elbows. "What was it you liked?"

"I had never thought about the parable of the prodigal son that way. You know, from the point of view of the older brother. And the fact he was separated as well by his own pride."

"Ah. Yes, it was a new twist for me as well. All week, it seemed God was leading me to tackle this particular passage. But I thought 'everyone has heard this story a million times.' So, I knew I had to approach it from a different angle. The more I thought and prayed about it, the more God opened my eyes to the plight of the older son."

Katherine nodded. How could she admit she felt as if part of her was the elder brother and part of her was the prodigal when it came to her relationship with God? Some days she was a rebellious child, struggling to trust, and other days, she was reconciled to God, but caught up in her pride and self-righteousness.

"You've been rather quiet today." Timothy lowered his voice.

Katherine shook her head, not ready to push farther yet. "Just thinking about some of the points you made in the sermon. I haven't stopped mulling over it."

"Anything you want to talk about?" His eyes softened. And though he spoke as a minister, his gaze was that of a man looking at a woman. Not altogether innocent.

"Not just yet. I'd like to get a handle on my own thoughts first." She hoped that would satisfy him on the subject.

He nodded, pressing her no further.

Mrs. Abby came by and set their plates in front of them, beaming. "Enjoy!"

They nodded their thanks.

"Shall I bless our meal?" Timothy's brown eyes met hers again. They calmed her.

"Yes, thank you." She found it difficult to tear her eyes away from Timothy's and bow her head, but she did so.

Timothy returned a quick blessing, praying over their meal and their conversation. And he even remembered Charlotte's children in his prayer. Katherine had to fight back a sniffle at his thoughtfulness.

Once he closed the prayer, she took a moment before looking up, gathering her emotions. Her mission remembered, her hands began to shake. She caught them in her lap to still them, but she still shook inside. Why was she so nervous? It was the right thing to do. Timothy was so kind, so caring, a godly man. And he cared for her.

Lifting her head, she watched him pick up his fork and turn his plate clockwise to better access his meatloaf. She was comfortable with him. It would be wise to not take that for granted.

"Have you found anyone else willing to take the Peterson orphans?" he said before taking his first bite.

"No." Katherine played with the food on her plate. "It's only been a couple of days, though."

"I promised you a week. But that's all I can give you. I can't keep Mr. and Mrs. Jones waiting forever." Timothy's voice was gentle, but serious.

"I know," she said, moving her meatloaf over with her fork. This was the best opening she would get. "If only there was a perfect, newly married young couple who were willing to take on those precious children."

"If only," he agreed, taking another bite of his meatloaf.

She set down her fork and looked across the table at him. Her eyes searching for his. "Maybe there could be," she started.

"I thought you said you hadn't found anyone else." One of his eyebrows went up.

Reaching for her water glass, she then ran a finger along the rim. Why was this so hard? "I haven't. Not exactly. The thing is, perhaps it's a couple that would be just married."

Now his brows became furrowed, creasing his forehead. "I don't understand where you're going with this."

Katherine cleared her throat. Where was her courage? She needed it now. Her eyes were on his again as she summoned every ounce of determination within herself. "What if we were to marry?"

Timothy all but choked on his food.

She rose from her chair to assist him.

He held up his hand to stop her as he got control of himself.

Not the reaction she hoped for. Should she explain? "I apologize for being so forward, but we could make a good home for those children."

Having recovered himself, he took a gulp of his water. Once he set the cup down, he stared at her, but did not speak. His silence tortured her.

"Timothy, say something," she pleaded.

"I don't know what to say, Katie," he said with a gentle tone. "I'm surprised."

He was quiet for a few moments, still staring at her.

Katherine prayed his answer would be "yes." Marrying Timothy would give her a way out of having to accept Wyatt. An out she needed so desperately. Wyatt's offer had started making sense to her.

After some moments, Timothy reached across the table, holding his hand open.

She slid her trembling hand into his larger one and prepared herself for his answer.

"I am flattered, Katie. And I do care for you. So much. But I don't think we are ready yet. If we got married just for the sake of those children, noble as it would be, it would be wrong."

Her shoulders slumped as everything in her body seemed to drop. His rejection was delivered in his kind, caring way and, even though her heart wasn't truly in her proposal, it still stung. Sad and dejected, she wanted to run from him. But a part of her sparked, indignant at his refusal.

"What do you mean? Those children deserve every good thing. They deserve a good solid home with people who will love them. How can it be wrong to want to provide that?" She tried to pull her hand away.

He covered it with his other hand. "It's not wrong to want to give them that, Katie. It's admirable. But your thinking is not clear right now. Marriage is a big step between two people. Many things must anchor those people to each other for a marriage to hope to be successful. Not just the rather noble, yes, but quite temporary circumstances of two children."

She looked away. Something in her knew he was right. An image of Jack, being put to work on a farm as soon as he was old enough to hold a shovel, appeared in her mind. It made her feel sick. And what if Susie, being shipped away to Denver, never saw or even knew of her brother again?

What if Katherine had never known David? Or had they been split up? She couldn't imagine it. Her life would be incomplete. Torn from her family, her brother, never to feel secure in anything. It would be almost like it was when she lost Ellie Mae. Grief washed over her anew.

Perhaps that was why she could not let this go. Katherine understood what it was to lose someone and she would do anything to prevent these two small children from experiencing any further loss. The only way they could recover being orphaned would be their adoption by caring parents, people who would pour love into them, nurture them. Not sacrifice them on the altar of convenience. Determination filled her.

Katherine had to do everything in her power to prevent their further suffering. Didn't Wyatt say that he, too, didn't want to see the children mistreated? That he only wanted to see them cared for? But could she marry Wyatt? The boy who had left her best friend behind? Could she trust him? Did she have a choice?

Katherine shifted to look at Timothy. "I understand. Thank you for being so gentle and yet so honest with me."

He nodded. "Of course." A warm smile spread across his face.

Unsure of what else to say, she was grateful Mrs. Abby came by their table.

Timothy released her hand.

"Everything all right?" Mrs. Abby's brows were furrowed as she looked down at the two of them.

Katherine nodded, but turned away as a wave of regret filled her. Nothing about her choice would be easy. Turning her back on Timothy. Allying herself with Wyatt.

"Sure is, ma'am." Timothy picked up his fork and started back into his lunch.

"I noticed y'all hadn't touched your meatloaf."

"We just got caught up in conversation," Timothy said. "Can't a man get swept away by a lovely young lady anymore?"

His compliment stung her just as much now as his rejection had earlier.

Mrs. Abby gave them a knowing smile. "Just don't let your lunch get cold now, ya' hear?" Then she moved on to check the next table.

Timothy looked at Katherine with a mock serious face, getting a bite of meatloaf on his fork. "I guess we'd best get to it then."

She pressed a smile to her face that she didn't feel. But Katherine was glad her proposal hadn't made things more awkward between her and Timothy. It was in his nature to put people at ease. So she took up her fork and dove into her meatloaf, potatoes, and green beans.

The streets of Cripple Creek were more lively than usual for this time of day. Perhaps it stemmed from the miners being out of work as the strike was still on. David had to be careful as he maneuvered his horse through the city streets with so many people milling about. He made his way to the General Store to pick up a few items for Mary, but his mind remained on the strike. Seemed his mind was always on the strike.

Their strike had served one of its intended purposes—the mines shut down. At least, the mines that refused to comply. Some of the smaller mines had been quick to agree to the demands of the Western Federation of Miners. This had given them hope for a short strike at first, but the larger mines held out. What would happen, and when it would happen, was anyone's guess. It had become a waiting game.

Nearing the store, he pulled back on the reins to slow his horse. As he tied off the reins, he checked his mental list. It would not serve him well to return without something Mary needed. She seemed particularly on edge of late. He stepped into the store.

"Good afternoon, David," Mr. Yerby called out from behind the counter. The man greeted every customer without fail.

David smiled. "Good afternoon to you, sir."

"Anything I can help you with?" Mr. Yerby put his hands on the counter and leaned over.

"No, sir. I'm here to pick up a couple of things for Mary, but I know where everything is."

"Just holler if you need anything," Mr. Yerby said, returning to his ledger book.

"Will do." David moved further into the store. Scouring the shelves for the few items he needed, he found them all with ease: coffee, apples, sugar, and oats. He couldn't help but grab a piece of licorice for Jessie and one for Peter. Taking his wares to the counter and laying them out for purchase, he smiled at Mr. Yerby.

"That'll be 75 cents," he said, tallying it in his ledger.

David reached in his pocket and pulled out the money. Money. That was another thing he was concerned would become a problem if this strike didn't end soon. How was he supposed to provide for his family? He and Mary had been wise, saving as much money as they could for such an occasion as this, but it would only last so long.

"How's that strike of yours going?" Mr. Yerby asked, his words coming slow, his voice hesitant.

David shrugged. "There's not much to tell."

"I hear tell that a judge is coming from Denver soon and the mine owners have asked to get on his docket."

"Oh?" One of David's eyebrows went up.

"That's what I hear," Mr. Yerby said, looking past David as his next customer walked in. "Good afternoon, Dr. Sullivan!"

David looked over his shoulder at Doc. He tipped his head in greeting. Doc did the same as he moved past him and toward the side of the counter where the newspapers were stacked.

Turning his attention back toward Mr. Yerby, he nodded to the man as he gathered his things off the counter. "I'll keep my ears open. Thank you kindly."

What could the mine owners want with a federal judge's time? This news troubled him the entire ride home.

CHAPTER 7

Prospects

These past three days had been the craziest of Katherine's life. Two proposals . . . one delivered by her, nonetheless. What would her parents think? She took a deep breath as she walked. They would soon find out exactly what she had been up to. And her plans for the future. Her heart beat faster as she thought about her mother's face in reaction to her news. Or what her father might say. Closing her eyes, she forced air in and out of her lungs. This was not about her.

The ranch loomed ahead of her. The time for plotting and planning had come and gone. This was it. Katherine opened the door to her family home slowly, knocking as she did so.

"Ma," she called out, glancing around the room.

"Back here, Katie." It was her mother's voice. The sound came from the back bedroom she and Katherine's father shared. Not long after, Ma emerged, meeting Katherine in the family room.

"Good to see you, darling. Glad you could make it for dinner." Then, as she drew closer to Katherine, her tone changed. "Oh my, Katie, you're looking thin. Are you eating enough?"

"Yes." Katherine smiled. No matter what happened, her mother always found something to fuss over. That was just her way of loving Katherine.

Ma moved over to the kitchen, tied her apron on, and began washing vegetables.

"Anything I can do to help?" Katherine moved toward the sink.

"You can set the table." Ma nodded toward the cupboard.

Instead of moving toward the cabinet, Katherine continued to shuffle over to where her mother was. She watched her mother for a few moments before Ma looked up from her work.

"Did you forget where the dishes were?" Ma smiled at her. It eased her a little.

"No, ma'am. I, um, had something I needed to ask you." Katherine clasped her hands behind her back to keep them from shaking.

"Spit it out, child, I haven't got all evening!" Another smile played across her mother's lips.

"I hoped it would be all right if I, um, sort of invited someone to join us for dinner."

Ma didn't miss a beat, but shifted to cutting the vegetables. "I wish you would have mentioned it sooner, but there will be plenty of food. Who is it we have the pleasure of hosting this evening? Timothy?"

Katherine grimaced. If only she could nod and let it be, but her mother would find out sooner or later. There was no use dodging the question.

"No. I invited Wyatt to join us."

Ma's hands paused but for a moment before she continued her work. "Oh?"

Everyone in the house knew how Katherine felt about Wyatt. Her parents had always tried to help her see things differently. As if Wyatt wasn't to blame for what happened to Ellie Mae. But Katherine had been deaf to their words. And since Wyatt's return after medical school to fill a much-needed role in their town, Katherine's parents had come to respect the man. That was hard for her to swallow.

"Yes." Katherine watched her mother's features. "He'll be along closer to suppertime."

"All right." Her cutting finished and her eyes flickered to Katherine's. "Now, can you set the table then, dear?"

"Yes, ma'am." Katherine feigned a salute and headed over to complete the chore levied upon her.

Within the hour, the table was set, including fresh flowers, and the kitchen was filled with the aroma of a well-deserved dinner. Katherine and her mother found themselves chatting about school and Katherine's students.

A sound at the front door interrupted their brief reverie. Katherine held her breath. She glanced at the case clock. This was still a little early for Wyatt. But she prepared herself all the same, stepping out of the kitchen to receive her guest.

"Stop playing with your hair," Ma admonished. "You'll pull it out of that bun. It looks fine."

Dropping her hands as if jabbed by a pin, Katherine clasped them in front of her. She hadn't even realized she was doing that.

Ma moved to rid herself of her apron to prepare for her company, but the intruder opened the door without waiting to be welcomed into the house. It was Pa who appeared. Katherine let out her breath. She had almost forgotten it was past time for him to be home.

"Pa!" She crossed the room to embrace her father.

"Katie, my dear." He enveloped her in his arms. "I can't wait to see what you two have scrounged up for dinner." After he released Katherine, he walked over to his wife and kissed the side of her face.

Katherine enjoyed watching her parents together. If only she could be so well matched. But, she realized, she had made a decision to hitch herself to Wyatt already. There would be no such hope for her. She turned away from her parents, an ache in her chest.

"It will wait until you've washed up," Ma teased her husband.

"All right, all right."

Katherine heard the pump sink working as Pa tried to wash the day off his hands. She picked up a book from an end table and attempted to focus on the cover.

"It seems we will have the special honor of an added dinner guest this evening." Ma spoke to Pa, but Katherine felt that Ma's eyes were on her.

"Timothy decided to join us?" The pump stopped.

Katherine's face warmed.

Was it Katherine's imagination, or did Ma's words come slowly?

They tortured Katherine. "No, not the Reverend. This evening we will be host to Dr. Sullivan."

Katherine set the book down and turned to face her father. She would not hide from this.

"Doc? Well, I'll be," he declared. He looked over at Katherine, a question in his eyes.

She was wrong. The look in his eyes became too much. Katherine turned her head toward the clock. "He should be here any moment now. I can't imagine what could keep him."

Right on cue and right on schedule, there was a knock at the door. Katherine froze. This dinner would be necessary before they made any more steps in their plan. Still, her stomach rolled, and she wished time would speed up and it could be done already. She dreaded the idea of spending any extended amount of time with Wyatt. So why did she think she could marry him? Sucking in a deep breath, she forced it out slowly and pictured the faces of Charlotte's children. They needed her.

Looking over at her parents, a wave of nausea overcame her at the idea of involving them in her horrid plan. But they deserved to get to know the man she was to marry a little better, and they should hear first from her before anything else was done. Still, she feared they would look at her choices the way Timothy had looked at her when she had proposed.

"Well, Katie, are you going to stand there all night, or are you going to open the door?" Ma's firm voice interrupted her thoughts.

She all but jumped at the abrupt halt to her train of thought. But she soon recovered and moved toward the door. Hand on the latch, she closed her eyes and opened the door.

Wyatt stood on the porch with a bouquet of fresh flowers. He had dressed well for the occasion. A church suit. And he had combed his blonde hair back out of his face. It brought out the strength of his jaw. "Good evening, Katherine. You are looking well-rested."

Well-rested. Was that the best he could do? She resisted the urge to roll her eyes as she reached for the flowers. "These are lovely, thank you."

"Ah." He pulled them just out of her reach. "Thank you, but they are for your mother."

Ma appeared behind Katherine. "Won't you come in?" She gave Katherine a nudge.

"Yes, please do." Katherine managed through clenched teeth. She backed up to make space for him to enter the home.

"Dinner smells wonderful," Wyatt said, flashing one of those charming smiles of his. "Here," he held out the flowers toward Ma. "These are for you."

"Thank you, Dr. Sullivan." She gathered them and moved off to find a vase while Wyatt took off his winter things.

Yes, he could charm the fleas right off a dog, couldn't he?

"Doc," Katherine's father said as he came over, putting his hand out to grasp Wyatt's in a hearty handshake.

"Mr. Matthews."

"You know better than that. It's always been just 'Tom.'"

Katherine didn't like all this friendliness between them. But it would be for the best. She just had to keep telling herself that.

Wyatt nodded and took his hand back.

"Dinner is ready," Ma interjected, motioning toward the table.

Katherine watched as Wyatt held back a moment. He waited as the Matthews stood behind their seats. Then he took the empty chair. That put him next to Katherine. Without further ceremony, everyone sat.

Joining hands, Katherine's parents bowed their heads. Wyatt held his hand out toward her. With some hesitancy, she slid her hand into his. As her father said grace, she found it difficult to follow along no matter how hard she tried. Why was Wyatt's hand so warm? So fit for hers? Before she knew it, Pa closed his prayer with an "amen."

Katherine and Ma chimed in a chorus of "amens" as well. And Katherine drew her hand back from Wyatt's, rubbing it as if he'd stung her.

It took a moment for her to realize her parents had begun passing the food around and asking Wyatt about his practice. He shared vague details about his work, but kept most things private. And conversation soon turned toward the ranch.

"I'm working on training a horse, but he has a lot of spirit in him," Pa was saying.

"I'd love a chance to take a look at your horses." Wyatt speared a piece of squash with his fork.

Wyatt had never seemed interested in ranch life before. Or horses. Except that scraggly gelding he rode.

"I don't see why we can't do that after dinner."

Wyatt smiled and gave Katherine a quick nod.

She ignored him.

After some moments, the focus shifted to Katherine and the school. She didn't want to say too much in front of Wyatt. Why should he care? But she shared how her students were progressing in their academics and highlighted some of the more promising individuals in her class. There, if he were to gossip about her, he wouldn't have anything to condemn her with.

After dinner drew to a close, Wyatt and Pa made their way over to the barn. Katherine looked after them through the window, wishing she could go, too. She didn't like this idea of Wyatt and her father being alone together.

"Katie, can you bring me those plates?" Ma worked on filling her dish bin with water.

"Yes, Ma," Katherine said, tearing herself away from the window to do so. She worked to help her mother clean up, but couldn't help but worry what transpired between her father and Wyatt. What was Wyatt saying to him?

She didn't have to wonder for too long. They returned in short order. Her father's face was dark. His features contorted in a mixture of confusion and aggravation. What had happened?

"Doc, I hope you don't mind making yourself at home for a few minutes. I think my wife, my daughter, and I need to talk."

"Of course," Wyatt said, moving toward the sitting area in the living room.

Katherine's eyes sought out Wyatt's. He looked calm and innocent enough as he shrugged in her direction. She didn't believe it. What had he done? Her hands curled into fists at her sides.

Pa didn't so much as glance back to ensure his wife and daughter followed him as he headed further back in the house toward his bedroom. Katherine shared a look with her mother before they took up step after him.

As soon as they entered the bedroom and Pa closed the door, Ma spoke, "Tom, that was rude. I hope you . . . "

He held his hand up. "It seems Doc Sullivan has some pretty serious ideas about Katherine."

Katherine's heart beat so hard she was sure her parents could see it thumping out of her chest.

"What do you mean?" Ma's eyebrows furrowed across her forehead.

"He has asked for Katherine's hand in marriage." Pa's words were slow, each word emphasized.

Katherine sat on the bed to keep from fainting. Why would he do that? She wanted to be the one to tell her parents about their arrangement! And now Wyatt had spoiled everything. Her heart squeezed and she saw red.

"Is there something you need to tell us?" Ma turned her eyes on Katherine, her voice rising a couple of pitches.

Katherine laid her head in her hands. "I wanted to tell you first," she started. "I never expected Wyatt to say anything to you, Pa." She looked up, meeting their gazes.

They crossed their arms almost in unison, watching her and waiting for her to continue.

Where to begin? "Wyatt and I have come to . . . an arrangement. We want to provide a home for the Peterson orphans. So, Wyatt thought if we got married, we would be the ideal candidates."

Katherine's parents exchanged a look. Were they gauging who should speak first? She took advantage of it.

"I'm sorry it came out this way. Truly, I am. This was not how I planned it."

"Katie," her mother said, sitting down next to her and putting an arm around her. "Are you sure this is what you want? Because I will tell you that marriage is hard work when you love each other and don't have children. You and Wyatt have . . . well, you don't have a good history with each other. It's not the ideal basis for a lasting marriage."

Just as she feared. It was Timothy's speech again. "I know all of that, Ma. But I can't turn my back on these children."

"And what of Timothy?" Ma rubbed Katherine's arm.

"He didn't want me." Katherine met her mother's eyes. Her lip quivered at admitting the truth of it. Was she ready to give up hope? All their times together flashed across her mind. The looks, the touches . . . He was the kind of man she could be happy with. But it wasn't to be. And his words, his rejection still stung.

"That can't be true . . . " Ma looked over at Pa.

Katherine sighed. "It is. I asked him to marry me to help save the orphans and he said, while it is a noble reason to marry, marriages have to be based on more than that." She looked at the floor. His words rang in her ears. And they sounded reasonable.

"He has a point." Pa took a step closer to where Katherine sat and laid a hand on her shoulder. "A marriage is an enormous commitment. It takes a lot of work. Even when you love each other."

Katherine nodded. She had heard it all from Timothy. Would her parents dissuade her? It was as if she were on the edge of reason. But Charlotte's face came back to her in those moments. Jack's and Susie's faces haunted her.

"But your mind is made up?" Her father's tone was soft, but flat. It wasn't a question.

She looked at her mother then father, and nodded.

Pa let out a long, somewhat ragged breath.

"We will be here for you every step of the way," Ma assured her.

"I gave him permission," Pa said. "I could find no reason to deny him other than my concern for you."

"Thank you." Katherine bit her lip to keep from crying. Was she disappointing her parents? A heaviness settled in her chest. "Please know that I hear your concerns. I just have to do this."

Ma nodded, taking Katherine's hand in hers. The touch comforted her.

"As you can imagine, we cannot ask Timothy to marry us. So Wyatt has suggested we find a judge or reverend in a nearby town, or even Denver if we have to."

"When will you go?" Ma's voice was quiet.

"Saturday. Timothy gave me a week. He will only hold off on giving Jack to the Joneses and sending Susie away to Denver for that long. So we have to do it in two days if we are to return as husband and wife in time to meet the deadline."

Ma looked at Pa. There was sadness in her eyes. What was the matter?

"We cannot be there with you," Pa said as Ma looked down at her hand, interlaced with Katherine's.

Couldn't go? Her parents wouldn't be able to go?

"One of the ranch hands is off with his ailing mother. Took off today. And it's calving season. Several due any day now." Pa spoke with authority, but his eyes reflected the same sadness she saw in Ma's.

"At least you must let us host a reception for you when you get back." Ma squeezed her hand. "To show our support."

Katherine nodded. Fresh tears pricked at her eyes. This time it was too hard to fight them.

Her mother embraced her, rubbing her back as only she ever did.

When Katherine pulled back, she looked over at her father. His lips formed a straight line across his face and his eyes remained serious. He wasn't quite as ready to throw in his support, but she trusted a few days with her mother and he would be.

"I think we've kept Doc waiting long enough," Ma said, standing. "Shall we?"

Katherine wiped her eyes and they returned to the family room to find Wyatt leafing through a book. Standing there as if he had no part in what had happened.

"Our apologies," Ma said. She was ever the gracious hostess.

He set the book aside. "Not at all. But it is getting late and I know Katherine has to teach in the morning."

Though she burned toward him still, Katherine nodded. She would be pleasant in front of her parents. No need to give them more reason to doubt her. "Thank you for coming to dinner."

"And thank you for having me, Tom, Lauren. I had a wonderful evening."

"Then you must come again," Pa spoke up.

Katherine offered her father a grateful smile. Yes, he would come around.

Wyatt nodded. "I will." Then he turned to Katherine. "Shall I escort you back into town?"

As hard as she tried, she could find no reason to say "no," so she nodded. It didn't take long to wrap her winter shawl around herself and say her farewells to her parents. Then they left the house, closing the door behind them.

Wyatt offered his arm to help her down the stairs.

Still full of anger, she ignored his help and made her way down on her own.

However, when they reached his buggy, she had to let him help her up into the seat. As much as she tried to ignore his hands on her, she could not. Why was she reacting this way? He hoisted himself up and took the seat beside her. She drew her shawl more tightly around herself, but not from the chill in the air. Being this close to Wyatt had warmed her. There was silence between them, giving her space to dwell on her thoughts.

How she regretted that this was her only path. That this was where her future lay. In this man's hands. Was there any other way? If so, she could not see it. He had already crossed her by speaking out of turn to her father. She would have to watch her back.

"Are you going to say anything?" he asked after several moments, breaking the silence.

She took a long breath. Katherine wanted to say "no," then thought perhaps to yell at him. But neither of those reactions would get her anywhere. Maybe she should just tell him what was on her mind.

"I wish you would have let me share the news of our arrangement with my parents in my own way, in my own time."

"How was I to know you hadn't already?"

She was silent. He had a point. Not that she would concede that.

"If we're planning to do this in a couple of days, I needed to do the honorable thing and square it with your father. Can you understand that?"

Katherine watched his jaw muscles clench. She could understand, but she didn't want to give any ground. Wasn't she justified in being angry with him? Maybe what he had done was out of respect for her and for her father. It wasn't something he had to do considering their strange circumstances, but he had all the same. He had done what he believed was right by her.

Letting out a deep breath, she admitted, "Yes, I can."

Feeling his eyes on her, Katherine turned to face him. Their eyes met and held for a handful of seconds. The wall around her heart crumbled a little. Would it continue to do so? She looked away and he turned back toward the horses.

"So," she said, breaking into the silence. "We're going to do this."

"I'm prepared to."

"So am I," she said with more confidence than she felt. If one of them were to back out, it wasn't going to be her.

"Then I'll meet you at the coach station on Saturday?" he said as he slowed the horses. They neared the boarding house.

She nodded. "Saturday."

He jumped down and walked around the cart to assist her. Reaching out to set her foot on the step down, she hit the side of her still-weak ankle on a bar and twisted her foot, causing it to give way underneath her. Wyatt reacted quickly, holding out his arms to catch her. It almost knocked him off-balance when she fell into his waiting arms, but he held his ground.

And then she was in Wyatt's arms, her arms wrapped around his shoulders to steady herself, their faces so close together. She became overwhelmed by the heat between them. But it made her uneasy.

"Are you all right?" Wyatt asked, his words deep and slowed, his eyes on hers.

"It's, um, it's that ankle you checked out a while back. Guess it's not quite healed," she said, her voice just above a whisper.

"Do I need to check it out again?" She felt his voice vibrate in his broad chest as he held her.

It mesmerized her. Where was her voice? "No, I thank you. I'm sure it's fine. I'll just need to be more careful about putting all of my weight on it."

"Probably so."

She needed to be out of his arms. Now. "Can you, um, put me down?"

He stared at her but did not move. Was he as affected as she? Her words seemed to shake him free of his trance.

"Yes." With great tenderness, he set her on her feet, careful to support her weight until he was sure her ankle could support her.

"Thank you," she said, stepping away from him as soon as she could. "And thank you for the ride back to town."

"Of course." His eyes were still on hers. Was it her imagination or did those hard steel-blue eyes appear softer tonight?

With that, she turned and walked into the boarding house without looking back. Once inside, she rushed up to her room and looked out the window, watching him get back into his buggy and drive off. Only then did she catch the smile on her face.

Wyatt stepped out of the General Store, newspaper in hand, readying himself to board the coach. He had dressed in his traveling suit, a rather practical brown jacket and pants. And he bore with him a simple bag containing what he would need for the overnight trip. Never mind that he had tried not to dwell on the gravity of what he was about to do as he gathered his things that morning. No, he made his decision and he would abide by his word. After all, this was about the children. The children he promised to look after. And this was the only way.

They were what this was all about. It had nothing to do with the strange sensations that crept into his being at the sight of Miss Katherine Matthews. She had always been a rather curious sort of girl, never fit in with the other girls quite right. No, she was her own person. And smart. Maybe that was why she had always intrigued him so. He stopped himself. This manner of thinking could not lead to good things.

Pulling out his pocket watch, he wondered where Katherine could be. He glanced in the direction of the boarding house for perhaps the hundredth time since he'd arrived in town early that morning. Had she changed her mind? Did that disappoint him? Or was he relieved?

While he did want to provide a loving, stable home for those two children, he had an uneasy feeling when it came to thoughts of marrying

Katherine. Only not in the way he would have thought. It was a nervous, excited sort of uneasiness. He wondered if he made the right decision or if he was being too hasty with his future. But the thought of marrying Katherine didn't scare him like he imagined it would have. His emotions were too mixed on this subject.

Their elopement should be their biggest obstacle. To overcome their trepidations, and probably better judgment, to say "I do," would be the hardest of it.

In his musings, he hadn't realized he was staring at the door to the boarding house until it opened and Katherine walked through, suitcase in hand. He glanced at his watch again. She cut it close, but was still within their time window.

Katherine kept her head down as she approached the coach, looking up only as she handed off her bag to the stagecoach hand.

Wyatt moved over to where she stood. "I was beginning to think you had changed your mind."

She jumped a bit, almost knocking herself off balance.

Wyatt took a step back but held out his arms to catch her.

Katherine righted herself, planting her feet on the dirt road. "No, it just . . . took a little while to get myself together," she said a little sheepishly. She fidgeted with the folds of her jacket.

Wyatt took in her appearance. He could have kicked himself for his comment. His first words should have been about how she looked. She must have struggled over what to wear for her wedding day, knowing it need also be appropriate for travel. A white dress would be altogether impractical with the coach ride, the dirt being kicked up. Was she wearing her best church dress under her travel jacket? All he saw of her wedding attire was the long pink skirt.

His eyes flashed over her face. He had given little thought to his apparel for the civil ceremony. But it was different for her. This was her wedding day, the only one she would have. And though this was a marriage arranged for reasons such as they were, that did not detract from the fact today was special to her.

"That dress is lovely on you, Katherine."

Looking up at him, her eyes searched his face as if seeking something hidden behind his compliment. He hoped she could not see too much of the emotions stirring within him.

At last, she offered a simple, "Thank you."

Moving around her, he reached up and opened the door to the coach. Wyatt then offered his hand to help her up. She accepted his assistance, placing her soft hand in his. Though her hand was cool, it caused his skin to warm several degrees. Once she stepped inside the coach and settled inside, he climbed in and sat on the bench opposite her.

His eyes were on her face, but her focus was on her gloves as she pulled them onto her hands. He couldn't help but stare at her slender fingers as they worked their way into the fabric. So fine, so delicate. Having held one of those hands at her parent's dinner table, he knew for a fact the way they fit in his. Small and perfect.

It wasn't long before another man boarded the small coach, taking a seat next to Wyatt. And his focus was shattered. Soon after they were all settled, the coachman glanced into the car. He gave them a nod and closed the door. Then they were off.

"Here it is," Wyatt said as they arrived at the building that boasted a sign indicating it was the city courthouse. Dark clouds loomed overhead. The sky looked as if it might open up any minute and pour down upon them.

Katherine nodded, eager to get indoors before it started raining.

Wyatt reached for Katherine's hand as they walked up the few steps that would take them to the front doors. Why did it seem like a strange gesture to her? He was only being a gentleman. But it struck her all the same. Perhaps because of the way it chipped at her long held opinion of him, perhaps because of the warmth of his hand, even through her cotton glove.

As Wyatt held the door open, Katherine entered the building swiftly, grateful to be able to slip her hand away from his. A middle-aged woman with graying hair sat at a desk just inside the large entry. She rummaged through paperwork as they moved farther into the courthouse and closer to her.

"May I help you?" The woman looked up from her papers, her brown eyes warm in their greeting. It calmed Katherine's nerves, if only just slightly.

"Yes, ma'am. My name is Wyatt Sullivan. I telegraphed the judge about a civil ceremony this afternoon."

"Ah, yes. Dr. Sullivan. We've been expecting you. Please have a seat, and I'll let Judge Dougan know you are here."

Wyatt nodded and led Katherine to a bench nearby. She was so nervous that she shook. What could she do to distract herself? Shifting in her seat, she began maneuvering out of her travel jacket. Wyatt's hands were on her sleeves then, assisting her to pull her arms out. It was not helping calm her to have him so close.

Still, she glanced over at him, thanking him, before setting the jacket to the side. Then she worked to smooth over the front of her dress, wishing she could release the wrinkles from the long trip. The dress had a sweetheart neckline trimmed in lace, and the bodice hugged her figure before meeting the waist. Her sleeves had a slight puff before they, too, hung close to her skin. As much as she loved her favorite church dress, she never imagined it would also be her wedding dress. Her childhood fantasies had put her in a flowing white gown that was not at all practical for any human being to wear on any occasion. But her dream was not to be.

Katherine caught herself. This was neither the time nor the place to break down. She had made her decision. Her eyes slid closed as she attempted, yet again, to still the emotions within herself and prepare for what was ahead. Her wedding.

They were going to do this. She was going to marry Wyatt Sullivan. Never could she have imagined agreeing to any manner of regular acquaintance with him, and now she would be pledging to live with him, raise children with him.

Realization slammed into her. She would live with him. What would that entail? Katherine had not thought that far ahead. Where did he live? Was there room for her and two small children? Would Wyatt expect she share his room? His bed?

Her time for contemplation came to an end when the judge's clerk came out of his office and bid them follow.

"Judge Dougan is ready for you."

Katherine tried to swallow past the lump in her throat. Was it too late to call this off? She had too many questions that needed to be answered.

Wyatt stood and stepped in the direction of the judge's office. He then seemed to notice Katherine wasn't with him. Turning, he met her eyes.

Her breaths were coming in gasps. Not now.

He glanced back over to the clerk and held up a finger.

She nodded.

Wyatt closed the gap between them, taking his seat beside her again. Only this time, he took her hands in his.

"What is it?"

"I . . . I . . . " She couldn't speak. Trying to breathe, she shook her head.

"We don't have to do this." His voice was gentle.

Katherine looked over at him. His eyes were sincere. And so deep. Had she never looked into his eyes before? They hypnotized her. She couldn't look away. "What about the children?"

He turned away. The break in eye contact was too abrupt. "This is the only way I know," he said, turning to face her again.

She searched his eyes again. Something there made her feel as if warm broth were being poured into her whole being. Her breathing normalized. "Then this is what we must do."

His expression changed. No longer did she read his concern for her, but she saw hope there. Squeezing her hand, he got to his feet and gently tugged at her to help her stand. She rose onto no longer shaky legs and allowed him to lead her toward the judge's office.

They stepped into his chambers to find him sitting at his desk. The judge was an older man with a receding hairline and a kind face. His smile invited them closer, indicating they should sit in the vacant seats in front of his desk.

"It is always a pleasure to take part in the joining of two people in matrimony. Especially with cause such as you have."

Katherine glanced over at Wyatt. How much had he shared?

"I thought it only fair to fill you in on the details," he said, although Katherine guessed it was more for her benefit than for the judge's. "Seeing as we were asking you to fill your office on an uncommon day."

"Ah, yes. With a story such as yours, how could I not?"

Katherine smiled and nodded. Was she to play the part of a doting fiancée?

"I am only too happy to oblige and marry you."

Wyatt smiled at him. "Thank you, sir."

"Now, these civil ceremonies are quite simple unless you are looking for something in particular?"

Wyatt looked to Katherine. Was that a glint of sadness in his eyes? Was he regretting the elopement as much as she?

There was no need to make this more difficult. Shaking her head, she said, "Whatever is usual is fine."

Wyatt turned back to the judge and nodded his assent as well.

"Then I shall retrieve our witness, and we'll get started." Judge Dougan walked over to the door and called his clerk back into his chambers.

The clerk helped him put on his robe and then he beckoned Wyatt and Katherine to join him across the room. They did so, standing before Judge Dougan with his clerk off to the side. Then he began.

"The step which you are about to take is the most important into which human beings can come. It is a union of two people founded upon mutual respect and affection. Your lives will change, your responsibilities will increase, but your joy will be multiplied if you are sincere and earnest with your pledge to one another.

"Wyatt, will you have this woman to be your wedded wife, to love her, comfort her, honor and keep her, and forsaking all others, keep you only unto her, for so long as you both shall live?"

"I will," he said.

Was it Katherine's imagination, or was there a softness in his voice? She didn't have long to think on it as the judge was asking her next.

"Katherine, will you have this man to be your wedded husband, to love him, comfort him, honor and keep him, and forsaking all others, keep you only unto him, for so long as you both shall live?"

"I . . . I will," she said, wanting to hide from the mix of emotions swirling through her. It seemed as if every emotion available to man was present in her at that moment—anger, bitterness, sadness, some form of happiness, determination—they were all there and more.

"Join hands and repeat after me," the judge said.

Turning to face her, Wyatt reached for her hands. She slid them into his, trying yet again to ignore how securely and perfectly her hands fit into his.

Wyatt said his vows after the judge, never taking his eyes off Katherine. The intensity of his gaze caused a tingle to go down her spine. And then the judge turned to her.

Katherine met Wyatt's gaze as she repeated after the judge. She would have him know she was not afraid of him.

"Are there rings?"

Wyatt once again surprised her when he produced two rings from his pocket. He truly had taken care of the details. She hadn't even thought of rings.

"Please place the ring on your bride's finger and say, 'With this ring, I thee wed.'"

As he took her hand, she saw that she had slight tremors throughout her limbs. She wished there were a way to hide it from him. But he slid the ring on her finger. A perfect fit. How did he do that? Then he clasped her hand in his, rubbing her fingers. Was he attempting to still her shaking?

"Katherine, please place the ring on Mr. Sullivan's finger and say, 'With this ring, I thee wed.'"

Pulling her hand from his hold on her, she grasped his hand firmly through her trembling and managed to get the ring on his finger without much trouble. Wyatt's fingers came around hers once again.

"In as much as you have consented together in wedlock and have been witnessed by this company, pledging your vows to each other, by the authority vested in my by the State of Colorado, I now pronounce you husband and wife. You may now kiss your bride."

Katherine hoped their awkwardness wasn't too obvious as Wyatt pulled her closer and leaned over, pressing his lips to hers. The moment their lips met, she became lost to the world around her. There was only him and the feeling of the soft pressure his lips created on hers. But it was over soon enough, and he drew back. She looked into his eyes. Had he, too, been affected by their brief contact? Quickly averting her gaze, she tried to pretend as if it was nothing.

The judge leaned forward to shake Wyatt's hand.

"Congratulations, Dr. Sullivan."

"Thank you, Judge." Wyatt returned the man's hearty shake, but his voice sounded distant.

"My clerk will get your papers in order. I wish you both the best of luck."

Katherine nodded her thanks, and they both followed the clerk out of the judge's chambers.

As they stayed on for their marriage license to be filled out and signed, Wyatt did not release her hand for the entirety of the exchange.

CHAPTER 8

Confrontation

Rain drizzled onto the streets of Denver. Katherine shivered as she moved behind Wyatt. His pace picked up as neither had thought to bring proper protection. Ducking under an overhang, Wyatt pulled her along with him. They found themselves at the General Store. Wyatt stepped inside and Katherine was strung along behind.

"Sorry to trouble you, sir," he said to the shopkeeper. "But I hoped you could point me in the direction of the hotel."

The rain had cooled the late winter air even further, causing Katherine's wet clothes to cling to her uncomfortably. Even the slightest breeze brought on an unwanted chill.

"Not far," the man said, offering them no more than a glance as he assisted a customer. "Three doors down, that way." The man pointed to his left.

Wyatt thanked him and took Katherine's hand. They braved the rain again for the short sprint to the hotel. Was the rain coming down harder? Once they stepped inside the spacious lobby, Wyatt released her. Quite relieved to be out of the rain and indoors where they could remain for the duration of the storm, Katherine said a silent prayer of thanks.

"Why don't you have a seat while I arrange for our accommodations?" Wyatt suggested.

Katherine didn't argue, taking the few steps over to a bench nearby. But she hesitated as she looked down at her well-weathered dress and jacket. The rain had taken its toll on them. Should she risk sitting in the finely decorated lobby and soaking this bench? She decided against it, instead leaning against a nearby column.

Her eyes wandered over the area while she waited on Wyatt. This appeared to be a rather nice hotel. That must mean expensive. Frowning, she turned her attention back to her attire. A couple of people stared in her direction. Her face flushed. Oh, that she could hide! She was only too eager to be rid of her wet things and in dry clothing. Against her better judgment, she prayed they would be able to stay here, regardless of the price, and not have to venture back out into the storm for other lodgings.

She made quick work of removing her gloves. There, at least her hands would be drying. The glint of metal on her once bare finger caught her attention. Splaying her fingers, she examined the simple wedding band. Her mind drifted back to the ceremony. And to the brief kiss they shared at its conclusion. Why should she dwell on that? Yet she found herself unable to pull her thoughts away, so she permitted herself to explore it.

It was a fact she hadn't much experience in these matters. She could count on one hand the number of beaus she'd had in her adult life. Her studies always came first. That kiss had, in fact, been her first. And that must be why it caused such a reaction in her.

"Hey." Wyatt came up behind her.

She straightened her posture, trying to hide what she had been thinking.

"They only have one room left." His voice was apologetic.

Still, she stared at him. How was she supposed to share a room with him? Then again, it would be silly for them not to now that they were committed to share their lives for so long as they both shall live.

All she could do was nod. Between the traveling, the emotions of the wedding, and being caught in the storm, all the fight had gone out of her.

"This way." He indicated the stairway with an outstretched arm.

Katherine picked up her bag and moved in that direction. They took the stairs up one level. Wyatt then moved around her, leading the way to a door with the number 21 inscribed on it. Sliding the key into the door's lock, he opened it with ease. He pushed on the door, holding it open for her to enter.

Spacious enough, the room had a large window that faced the street. She took in a deep breath—it smelled like fresh flowers. Not surprising as there were two bouquets in the room, one on the nightstand and one on the vanity. Dressed in a quilt of mint green, mauve, and tan, the bed in its sturdy oak frame became the main feature of the room. The vanity and nightstand were the only other pieces of furniture. Were she and Wyatt to share this bed? Did he expect to exercise his husbandly prerogative?

Katherine set her bag on the floor by the bed and moved her arms to cross in front of herself.

"Well, it's dry," Wyatt offered.

"No, it's nice," Katherine said, still uneasy.

Wyatt moved farther into the room, setting his bag by the vanity. He walked over to the window and looked down on the street below.

All Katherine wanted to do was put on something dry and crawl into bed. They had another big day tomorrow.

"Are you hungry?" Wyatt turned, his eyes on her.

Katherine's stomach churned at the thought of food. She hadn't eaten since the quick bite they grabbed by the train station.

He drew close to her. Perhaps a little too close for her comfort. "You look tired," his voice was gentle. "And cold. I'll go find something to eat while you get into dry clothes. I think I spotted a café downstairs. We can have a picnic up here before you get tucked in."

Katherine had to admit that sounded wonderful. "Thank you."

Wyatt had to squeeze by her to get to the door, crossing quite closely to her body. The warmth emanating from him threatened to draw her in. But then she remembered who it was and moved out of his way, all but scurrying across the room.

Wyatt's eyebrows furrowed for just a moment before he stepped out into the hallway.

Katherine closed and locked the door behind him. The last thing she wanted was for Wyatt to walk in on her while she undressed. Eager for dry clothes, it was mere moments before Katherine had divested herself of her wet garments and pulled on her nightclothes. She located a robe in her suitcase as well, for which she was thankful. It would give her an added layer of modesty. Laying out her dress and chemise to dry, her thoughts again began to drift.

Today had been a blur. And now she was married. Married to Wyatt Sullivan. All for a good cause, she told herself. Tomorrow they would see it come together. They would go to the church and present themselves as the best candidates to take the orphaned children. Would the mayor and Timothy see it their way?

Timothy . . .

What would he think when he discovered what she had done? Katherine wished she had told him. She did not relish the idea of his reaction. How she wished she could avoid hurting him! But she had been a coward. And so there was nothing left but for him to find out this way.

A knock on the door echoed in the room. Katherine pulled her robe tighter around herself and moved to answer it. "Yes?"

"It's Wyatt."

Katherine unlocked the door and opened it just enough to peer out. It was indeed Wyatt and he had plates of food. She swung the door open the rest of the way to admit him.

"I hope you don't mind. I took the liberty of ordering you pot roast."

"Mind? It's my favorite meal." How did he know?

"Is it?" He flashed her a smile.

She settled in the bed, pulled the covers over her lap, and reached for the plate.

Wyatt sat on the edge of the bed with his plate of chicken and dumplings.

All was silent for a few moments as each enjoyed their warm dinner. But her eyes drifted to Wyatt. What was he thinking? Was he relieved? Or full of regret?

"What a day, huh?" Wyatt spoke at last.

She nodded, taking another bite of potato.

"How are you . . . that is, are you . . . what's on your mind?" he managed.

She looked at him, gauging his question against her own mixed thoughts and emotions. "I have been thinking on many things. Mostly about tomorrow. And the next day. I'm afraid we haven't planned that far ahead," she said, her appetite waning. "I don't even know where we will live."

"With me, of course." Wyatt's face was blank.

"What is . . . I mean, how big is . . . that is, where is your house?" Katherine hid her warming features by examining her food.

"It's not far outside of town. I need to be close in case of late-night emergencies."

She nodded her understanding.

"It's the old Womack homestead," he offered.

That didn't help. Katherine had never been to Bob Womack's home.

"There will be a room for me and for you and for Jack. I'm afraid Susie may have to stay with you until I can commission an extra room be added."

Katherine nodded again, relieved he did not anticipate that the two of them share a room.

"You look as though you can barely keep your eyes open." He laughed a little.

"I guess I am quite tired after everything today." The understatement of the year.

"It has been a long, rather eventful day," he agreed. He reached out to take her plate. "I promised I'd take these back downstairs."

As he took her plate, she settled against a pillow and pulled the covers up to her chin.

"I'll be back soon."

With that, he was gone. Katherine turned down the lamp and rolled over so her back was to the door. She closed her eyes and attempted to quiet herself to sleep. Moments later, when Wyatt came back, she pretended to be more asleep than she truly was.

He leaned over her and must have decided she was indeed asleep as he went about changing his clothes.

Katherine tried not to look as she heard the rustle of clothing, but something in her was too curious. So, she peered through eyelid slits at his form, silhouetted against the moonlight as he dressed in his sleepwear. He must have felt her eyes on him as he jerked his head back around to look in her direction. She closed her eyes.

It wasn't long before she heard him moving around the room and then she felt him leaning over her again. Was he going to slip in the bed beside her? Her heart stopped and she prayed he would not be so bold.

The unused pillow swished from beside her. And the chest at the foot of the bed creaked. She guessed he pulled out extra coverings. Was he preparing a makeshift bed on the floor?

Letting out the breath she didn't realize she was holding, she said a prayer of thanks for his gentlemanly sensitivities. It wasn't long before she heard his deep, even breathing. Then, and only then, did she fall into sleep.

Katherine clawed at the walls of the mineshaft, trying to escape. Her air was running out. At last, the wall started to crumble and she saw a pinprick of light. Continuing to pull at the rocks, her heart leapt; she made progress.

Amidst the sound of the rubble, she heard a voice crying out. She stopped moving. And stopped breathing.

"Katie!"

It was Ellie Mae!

"Ellie Mae, where are you?" she hopped down and stepped back toward the darkness, unable to see anything beyond the step in front of her.

"Katie, help me!"

"I'm coming!" Katherine picked up her pace, now running back into the tunnel. The rumbling sounds grew louder, surrounding her. Filled with fear, Katherine was tempted to turn around, but she trudged onward, into the darkness, determined to help her friend.

"Katie, don't leave me!"

"I won't, Ellie! Where are you? I can't find you!" Katherine followed the voice into the pitch darkness. Then it seemed her cries would come from another direction. Was she becoming disoriented? The sounds of the quaking around her became paralyzing, but she was desperate to find Ellie. She couldn't leave her. No, not again.

The thundering of the tunnel became so loud she couldn't hear Ellie anymore.

"Ellie!" she screamed, "Ellie! Ellie!"

"Katie!" Someone shook her, rubbing her face. "Katie!"

Her eyes opened. There was no tunnel, no Ellie Mae. She was in the hotel room in Denver with Wyatt. He leaned over her, hands on her arms, shaking her awake. Ellie was dead and had been for many years. Katherine lay covered in a layer of sweat as tears flowed down her face.

"Katie, are you all right?" Wyatt asked, his voice now gentle as he pushed her hair out of her face. He sat on the edge of the bed and pulled her into his embrace. "That must have been some nightmare. But you're safe."

Katherine did feel safe in his arms, but the memory of what happened to Ellie was fresh in her mind, in her heart, and she couldn't let herself remain in Wyatt Sullivan's embrace. She pushed at him to create some distance between them.

She smacked at her face, wiping the tears away. "I'm fine," she lied.

His eyes darkened. Who cared if he didn't believe her?

But she would have none of his comforting. The wound was fresh. He had left Ellie Mae behind. If it weren't for him, she wouldn't be having these nightmares.

"Very well," he said, getting up.

Immediately, she wished she had let him calm her. But she would not have it. Heart racing a million miles a minute, she panted.

He walked over to his pallet on the floor. Moving as if to lie back down, he paused, then turned toward her and said flatly, "Just so you know, Katherine, I, too, have nightmares about that day." Then he dropped onto his mat.

She stared after him. Wyatt? Nightmares? It couldn't be true. No, he was cold and uncaring about what had happened that day. That's how she'd always imagined him, so that's how he had to be. Right?

Tom and Lauren Matthews stepped out of the church and into the bright sunlight. Lauren raised a hand to shield her eyes as they prepared to say their farewells to the reverend who, as usual, stood at the exit. He always shook hands with each of the church members, sharing a few words with them, and then sent them on their way with a quick blessing. Now their turn, Tom and Lauren each took a turn clasping Timothy's hand.

"Lovely sermon, Reverend," Lauren said, a smile on her face.

Tom nodded in agreement.

"Thank you," Timothy responded. But he hesitated. There seemed to be something more he wanted to say. "I didn't see Katherine today. Is she well?"

Lauren and Tom exchanged a look. Had Katherine not said anything to Timothy after all? If that was the case, Lauren was certain neither she nor Tom were at liberty to share Katherine's plan. But she didn't want to lie about her daughter's whereabouts either.

It was Tom who ended up speaking. "Thank you, Reverend, she is quite well. Found herself on an errand in Denver this weekend."

"Denver?" Timothy's voice betrayed his surprise. "When . . . " He cleared his throat. "When will we have the pleasure of her company again?"

"We expect her back this afternoon," Lauren said, slipping a hand into the crook of her husband's arm.

Timothy smiled at that. "I look forward to it."

Lauren sensed he wanted to ask something further, but held back.

Instead, he straightened himself and returned to his pastoral posture. "May the Lord bless you this week. Go in peace."

Nodding her thanks, Lauren allowed Tom to lead her down the few steps off the church's porch and onto the lawn. There they waited for David and his family. It wasn't long before they, too, made their way out of the church and into the churchyard.

There was no mistaking her David anywhere, but he looked different today. His features were drawn, and his eyes had lines under them. And his skin, it appeared almost a sickly pale. It tugged at her mother's heart.

But the rest of the clan looked well enough. Gazing over at Mary, her bright eyes and liveliness brought a smile to Lauren's face. And little Jessie. A picture of everything a girl should be in her gingham dress and matching bows holding her twin braids. Mary carried the wiggling Peter in her arms, his light brown curls bouncing in the sunlight.

Lauren and Tom moved to intercept them.

Leaning down to meet her granddaughter's eyes, Lauren said, "You are so pretty today, Jessie."

Jessie did a little curtsy and twirl for her grandmother.

They all laughed, even David. It did Lauren's heart good to see him laugh.

"I heard you mention to the reverend that Katherine is in Denver?" David's question rushed out of him.

Lauren paused, straightening to her full height again. "That's a bit of a long story," she said, her words slow, chosen carefully. "But one that we can share over lunch. Y'all still coming over?"

"Of course." David's eyes darkened with concern, but he turned to Mary, who nodded.

"Then, shall we?" Tom offered his arm to Lauren, indicating they should move on to their carts.

"We shall," David agreed, mimicking his father and offering his arm to his wife.

They loaded their carts and maneuvered the horses toward the Matthews' homestead. Soon after, they were all gathered around the lunch table, enjoying the fruits of Lauren's hard work preparing the Sunday meal. Their conversation touched on many things, but Tom and Lauren had not yet shared anything about Katherine.

"How are things on your front, son?" Tom ventured to ask.

David shook his head. "About the same. Nothing much to say. We're still on strike."

Lauren sensed he didn't want to say anything more about it. It weighed on him. And that bothered her. She was glad Tom steered clear of the subject for the rest of lunch. It became easy enough when Mary brought up the subject of Katherine.

"What were you going to tell us about Katherine?" Mary asked.

Lauren and Tom exchanged a look. Who was going to tell them?

Tom shrugged.

And so, Lauren decided it was up to her. Glancing over to ensure the children were happily distracted with their toys in the family room just beyond, she lowered her voice as she related the tale of what Katherine had decided to do.

"And you let her go?" David asked, incredulous. "You let her carry on with this crazy plan?"

"It's not our place to stop her," Lauren said, blinking in surprise at David's comment. "No matter how much we may or may not disagree with our children's decisions, we can only give our advice. Then we must do our best to support them."

David looked down at his food. Was he realizing his own hypocrisy?

"It's not been an easy decision for Katherine, but she's doing what she thinks is best by those kids. I'm sure she will need your support, too," Tom added.

David nodded.

"Of course," Mary said, "We'll do whatever we can to ease her transition. I can't imagine how her life will change in such a short amount of time . . . from single and childless to working wife and mother of two. That is, if the town council will even let her continue teaching."

"I don't know if she's considered that." Tom wrapped his hands around his coffee cup.

Lauren nodded. "There will be many questions to be answered when she returns. Things she will have to face. And issues she will have to resolve. It won't be easy. And if they allow her to teach for the remainder of her contract at the school, I'll be watching the little ones during the school day. That is if she and Wyatt are awarded the children. We're not even sure they will be."

"I hope you're not putting yourself out," Mary said, leaning toward Lauren.

"What other choice does Katherine have? She has a contract at the school for the remainder of the semester. The town needs a teacher. And Wyatt can't close his practice during the day to watch the children. I'm happy to help any way I can."

"And we will, too," David's voice was now firm, resolute.

"Yes, I'll come over at least a couple of days a week to help you," Mary offered.

Lauren smiled. "Thank you, I'll enjoy the company." Her heart swelled to see her family working as a unit, helping each other out, and supporting each other through tough things. This, after all, is what family was all about.

A cloud of dust surrounded the telegraph office as the coach came to a stop. Pressed against the inside of the door, Katherine barely waited for someone to open it and offer her a hand in her hurry to get to the ground. Her feet touched the solid surface of the dirt road and she breathed a sigh of relief. They made it. But there wasn't a moment to lose. Lifting her skirts, she pushed off, racing toward the church.

"Katherine, wait," Wyatt called after her.

She didn't so much as pause.

Wyatt gave the driver instructions as to their bags, but she was soon too far away to hear anything more.

As she pushed onward, Katherine's lungs begged for her to slow down, muscles burning from the exertion. But she dare not. They might already be too late. And once again she cursed their bad fortune to have been delayed at the train station.

Nearing the church, she heard Timothy's robust voice through the open windows. "If there are no other volunteers, it seems Mr. and Mrs. Jones are the only family to step forward to take in one of these precious souls."

Her heart pounded, jumping into her throat. She prayed Timothy would listen.

The door to the church rushed toward her and Katherine held up her hands to push it out of her way. Then she burst into the church.

"Wait," she cried out, breathless. Vision blurred, she leaned forward, hand on her stomach, her breathing uneven.

"Katherine?" Timothy's voice rose above the din of whispers around her.

Rising to her full height, she met his gaze. She had never seen his eyes so wide. And as she took in the space, she noticed that everyone in the church stared at her with gaped mouths. The Joneses, the mayor and his wife, even a small boy she guessed to be Jack. The intensity of their eyes threatened to silence her, but she forced herself to swallow past the lump in her throat and push her trepidations to the side.

"I . . . wish . . . to . . . take . . . both . . . of . . . the . . . children."

Timothy's features shifted, becoming set and stern. His gaze moved across the room. Was there something he hesitated to say in front of this small crowd?

At last he spoke, lowering his voice as if that prevented others from hearing. "Katherine, we talked about this. It is not possible for a single woman to take on orphans."

"How about a newly married couple?" Wyatt came up behind her, startling her. He grabbed for her hand that now bore her wedding ring, raising it to eye level, displaying it next to his.

Timothy's mouth fell open. His eyes betrayed the shock and hurt Katherine knew he must feel.

It pained Katherine to have caused him such grief. Regret cut through her.

A thick silence fell over the room. Katherine pulled her hand free of Wyatt's grasp. She wished it were possible for her to just disappear. Though she turned her face away, she felt everyone's gazes still on her, judging her.

Her salvation came minutes later when Mayor Jacobs stepped forward, drawing the attention from her when he addressed the group. "It seems the Reverend and I need to confer for a moment."

Taking the preacher's arm, Mayor Jacobs pulled Timothy to the far side of the dais. They spoke for several moments. Were they deciding which couple was most suited for the children?

Katherine watched, her eyes glued to Timothy. His posture was stiff as his head bobbed and shook. But it seemed as if the mayor did most of the talking. As she looked on, she felt nothing, numbed by Timothy's reaction. She hadn't expected anything different, but the reality of it stung.

At length, the mayor returned to the pulpit. Timothy remained where he was, in the background, and he seemed to be avoiding Katherine's eyes. Perhaps it was for the best. Could she truly face him right now if he did look at her?

"After much consideration," Mayor Jacobs said from his position on the dais. "We have determined it would be best for the children to remain together. So, we have decided to award custody to Dr. and Mrs. Sullivan." The last words came out of his mouth with some hesitation.

All else flew from Katherine's mind. Filled with joy and relief, she whirled around, throwing her arms around Wyatt's neck. They had done it! Wyatt's arms slid around her back and held her in a warm embrace.

Only for a second, Katherine became lost. But then the flush of heat came. Though her body longed for more, she was surprised she would allow herself even a moment in Wyatt's arms. She pulled away, her movements awkward. But her embarrassment was covered by the sudden appearance of the mayor's wife.

Katherine turned, moving away from Wyatt. Alma carried a wiggling baby girl in her arms and urged the small boy to step forward even while she held his hand. So these were the orphans. And they would soon be hers to care for. What did she know of raising children?

"Congratulations!" Alma said, smiling. It deepened the lines around her face. "They are both precious angels. If John and I were even a few years younger, we would have considered taking them ourselves. As it is, these old bones would be no good chasing these little ones around."

She held out the tiny bundle toward Katherine. Should she accept the child? Her stomach dropped. This, too, was something she hadn't considered. Her goal had been keeping the children together. But what did she know about babies or toddlers?

Still, she opened her arms to receive the small package, hoping Alma wouldn't notice her slight shaking or that she held her breath.

Little Susie felt so light in Katherine's arms, weighing almost nothing. Her eyes were a bright shade of blue. The cutest chubby cheeks reminded Katherine of a baby doll, and the child's blonde curls peeked out from underneath her bonnet. She waved her arms at Katherine's face as she gurgled and cooed. Something stirred in Katherine's chest.

Alma crouched down with careful movements until she was at eye level with the young boy. "Jack, you're going to go with Dr. Sullivan and Mrs. Matth—Mrs. Sullivan. They're going to take good care of you."

Jack looked at her with large blue eyes set below shaggy brown hair. Mrs. Jacobs pulled him toward her for a hug. He complied, snuggling into her embrace at first, but soon squirmed to be set free.

She stood again, her eyes meeting Katherine's. "I'll send John over with their clothes, bottles, and the cradle."

Katherine nodded, swallowing hard. She couldn't let anyone know how overwhelmed she felt.

"And I have just the place for this little guy," Wyatt said as he swung Jack up into the air and into his arms. The boy beamed.

Good. Wyatt had some semblance of a plan. Katherine relaxed for the first time in weeks. But only slightly. The hairs on her arms prickled. An odd sensation. Glancing around the room, she spotted Timothy, still behind the dais, his eyes boring into her.

What must this be like for him? Watching this scene play out? It could not be pleasant. The intensity of his gaze told her that much. As her eyes met his, she wished for a moment for the two of them. Perhaps she could explain. But no explanation would fix this, and she knew it.

Wyatt stepped up beside her. So close. Too close. The familiar heat from his body emanated through her travel jacket and dress sleeves. How did he always radiate such warmth? She wanted to step away, but his hand was on her arm. Her eyes moved from Timothy's face to Wyatt's only to find that Wyatt watched Timothy as well.

"We'd best get these children home. By the time we get settled, it'll be time to put them to bed." Wyatt shifted his focus to Katherine.

She no longer felt comfortable looking at either man, so she turned her attention to the wriggling baby in her arms. The tiny face blurred. No, she would not cry.

Mayor Jacobs and Alma moved toward the exit. Katherine raised her head to their backs. It would not be wise for her and Wyatt to be in the church alone with Timothy. So, she nodded.

His features softened. Did he see the unshed tears in her eyes? Did he care? How could he? Either way, he became distracted when Jack started playing with his nose.

"Did you get my nose?" Wyatt faced Jack.

The boy giggled.

Wyatt took a couple of steps in the direction the mayor and his wife had gone.

But Katherine hesitated, inexplicably torn.

Turning back toward her, Wyatt shot a look in Timothy's direction before holding out a hand to Katherine. "It's time, Katie."

Katherine chanced one more apologetic glance toward Timothy before she moved to join Wyatt.

He placed his free hand at her elbow and escorted her outside.

CHAPTER 9

Settling In

A couple of hours later, they were at Wyatt's homestead with Katherine's things from the boarding house and the children's things from the Jacobs' home. Everything had been stacked in the great room. Yet another daunting task for Katherine—unpacking. Staring at the mountain of work in front of her, it was all she could do not to break down. All she wanted to do was bathe to clean up from her long trip, eat, and climb into bed. That was not possible. There were other responsibilities now.

The door banged open. Wyatt and Mayor Jacobs shuffled in carrying a rather large cradle.

"Let me help you get this to the room Susie will be sleeping in," Jacobs said.

"This way." Wyatt indicated they should go down a short hallway.

Susie started to fuss and Katherine bounced her a little. She had been examining her new home. It appeared to have been originally built as a one-room homestead and since updated. Perhaps by the Womacks and then again by Wyatt. But she couldn't be certain. Bedrooms had been added and the kitchen had been updated with a sink and pump. The space that used to serve as the dining room, family room, and bedroom was now one large open dining room and family room with a large fireplace.

It could use a woman's touch. Still, Wyatt had done a good job making a nice home. One bedroom was situated directly off the great room and then a short hallway carved out where the other two bedrooms were built.

At that moment, Wyatt and the mayor came back into the large room.

"Thank you," Wyatt said, gazing over the trunks and boxes that littered his living area.

"Not a problem." Jacobs looked between Wyatt and Katherine.

An awkward silence fell over the room.

The mayor pulled out his pocket watch and noted the time. "I best be getting along. Good luck to y'all."

Katherine smiled her thanks.

Wyatt clapped him on the back and walked him out.

"I'm hungry," Jack said, looking up at Katherine.

"Hungry? We'll see about getting you something to eat then, okay?"

"Okay," he said, his manner trusting.

Katherine had no idea what they were going to do. She was relieved to see Wyatt when he returned.

"Jack is hungry," she said simply, trying not to panic, hoping he had a solution. "And I think Susie is, too."

"Sure," he said. "Let's see to some dinner, then." He came over and crouched down on Jack's level. "What say you help me make sister's bottle? Can you be a big boy and help me out?"

Jack nodded; it was apparent he liked being called a "big boy."

"What can I do to help?" Katherine asked.

"Just keep doing what you're doing," Wyatt called over his shoulder. "Keep that little angel occupied."

Katherine nodded, not that he could see her. She walked around the room and continued bouncing the fussing baby while Wyatt and Jack worked in the kitchen. What were they doing? Wyatt seemed to have some sort of plan. It wasn't long before Wyatt brought her a contraption filled with milk. He handed it over to her, warm to the touch.

"How do I . . . ? That is . . . I've never . . . "

"Let me show you." Wyatt took her elbow and led her over to the rocking chair. Once she was seated, he adjusted Susie in her arms so that she was reclined on Katherine's arm. "Try to angle the bottle so she doesn't swallow any air."

Katherine put the bottle's tip in Susie's mouth.

Wyatt went back to the kitchen and grabbed a towel. Bringing it to Katherine, he laid it over her shoulder.

"Now, take the bottle out."

Katherine obeyed.

Susie protested with a cry. What did Katherine do wrong?

"Yeah, she's not going to like that," Wyatt explained. "Turn her so her tummy is against your shoulder and pat her back."

Katherine followed his instructions, unsure how much she truly trusted him. She didn't like the unhappy sounds Susie made.

After some time, Susie let out a burp.

"Good. Now, let her have some more milk. And stop every few minutes and burp her like that again."

Katherine looked up at him, this time with a grateful smile.

"I'll get to work on some dinner for the rest of us." He shifted his attention to the young boy who had watched the whole exchange rather curiously. "If my friend Jack over here can help me."

Jack nodded, a broad smile across his features.

Katherine found herself once again thankful for Wyatt. He seemed to know what to do when she didn't. How was that possible? He was a valuable partner indeed.

Lauren Matthews placed the last cleaned and dried dish on its shelf in the cupboard. Moving her hands over her apron, she took in the stillness around her. Tom sat in the great room, enjoying the crackling fire. But, peaceful as it might seem, the Matthews' home was too quiet for Lauren's liking. She was used to the noises of grandchildren in these rooms and the laughter of her now-grown children bouncing off these walls. The loss of it seemed even more poignant this evening knowing her youngest child had moved in with her new husband. Things would never be the same.

Hanging her apron on its nail, she took a moment to gaze out the window. And she wondered just how Katherine fared with her new situation—new house, new children, new husband.

I should be there for her.

Lauren turned toward the great room; all she could see of her husband was the back of his head. "Tom, don't you think we should check on Katherine and Wyatt?"

"Whatever for?" He leaned over the side of the chair, turning sideways so he could look back at his wife.

Lauren fidgeted with her hands. "To make sure she's settling in all right."

Tom settled back into his chair. "She knows just well how to move into a place."

Taking a step toward him, she said, "Surely I should go over and help her set up the children's things . . . "

"Katherine is quite capable." Tom's voice was firm.

Lauren searched for a reason, any reason Tom would agree to. "Should we go over and take something for them to eat?"

"I'm sure they will be just fine."

She set her hands on her hips. "Should I . . . "

He rotated in his seat again to catch her eyes. "I think, my dear, that the best thing we can do for them is to let them be. They need to figure it all out on their own."

Lauren didn't like that answer, but her husband was right.

"Now, come here." He patted the arm of the chair next to his. "Come sit by my side for a while. Let the fire warm you."

Lauren took slow steps toward the room and sat in her chair. She watched the flames flicker and dance. She couldn't help but reflect on their early days as a married couple. They were just kids. But they learned how to manage without their parents' help.

Turning toward her husband, she reached out a hand for his. "Tom, remember our first night together?"

He grasped her hand. "I sure do. How can I forget having to round up all those horses because I forgot to latch the gate? Must have taken me an hour."

Lauren's shoulders shook with barely contained laughter.

Tom was not one to let sleeping dogs lie, however. "Hey now, I wasn't the only one that goofed that night." He gave her a sideways glance. "You know, I could use a piece of corn bread."

Lauren's eyes opened wide. She had waited on the front porch for him to return, and ended up burning her corn bread.

"Now hold on," she protested, dropping his hand. "We promised to never speak about that ever again."

He smiled back at her, broadly enough to show teeth.

"And I told you that was the best corn bread I ever ate. My conscience is clear," he said as a laugh escaped his lips.

"Those were good times," Lauren said, leaning back and putting her hand in his again. "Things were simple then. We didn't have two children to feed yet." She enjoyed reminiscing but bit at her lip, still finding herself worried about Katherine. "Are you sure they're all right?"

Tom met her eyes again. This time, his voice was gentle and loving. "We had our own ups and downs, and we made out just fine. Katherine and Wyatt may be dealing with some things we never did, like raising a couple orphans, but they have to figure it out on their own. If they ever need us, they know where to find us."

"You know, that's the fifty-eighth reason I married you. You seem to know when to help and when to let go." Lauren began to relax, letting the warmth of the fire pervade her body and drive away her uneasy thoughts.

Tom nodded. "Only the fifty-eighth?"

She squeezed his hand. "Yes, dear. But, trust me, there are more."

And they continued the rest of the evening staring at the fire, enjoying each other's presence. In silence.

Katherine paced with Susie, bouncing her with gentle movements while she listened to Wyatt weave together a tall tale for Jack's bedtime story. As he recounted the story of The Three Little Pigs, Jack sat, wide-eyed, enamored with Wyatt's interactive storytelling technique. She, too, found herself drawn into this old tale as if hearing it for the first time. All too soon, the story came to a close. His droopy eyelids and slackened body told Katherine that Jack was indeed ready for bed.

Wyatt must have noticed too. He took Jack in his arms as he recited the closing lines of the story. His voice faded as he carried the young toddler to one of the back bedrooms. Katherine couldn't help but smile after them as they went. As awkward as the events of the evening may have been, this already began to feel more like the interactions of a family. How she hoped Jack could sense that and find security in it. This little boy deserved it after everything he had been through.

"I think she's asleep."

Katherine startled.

Wyatt's soft voice was behind her, perhaps a little too close.

"Oh?" Katherine tried not to react lest she stir the baby.

"She's off to dreamland," he said, peering over Katherine's shoulder and down at Susie's face. His breath warmed her ear and neck, his lips so close. It made her dizzy. He must have spoken again, for when she gathered herself, he watched her expectantly.

"What?" She turned to create some distance between them.

"I think we should put her down." Wyatt motioned down the hallway toward the bedroom she would share with Susie.

Katherine nodded, taking a deep breath. Her body protested her movements, longing for the respite of sleep.

Taking a small lamp, Wyatt led her down the short hallway and through the doorway of the bedroom to the left. It was a fairly large room with a dresser, bed, her trunk, Susie's trunk, and Susie's cradle. The bed, covered with a red and blue quilt, looked rather inviting. Her muscles ached to release her weight onto the comfort of the cushion. But she and Wyatt had some work yet to do before she retired for the night.

Moving over to the cradle, Katherine laid Susie down, covering her with a small blanket. Working to tuck the blanket around Susie, she watched the sleeping child. Part of her did not want to leave this peaceful moment and part of her just did not want to be alone with Wyatt. Things with Wyatt were . . . complicated. Why shouldn't they be? Her head and emotions were a jumbled mess on the matter.

After some moments, a hand on her shoulder drew her attention away from the small form. Wyatt gestured toward the door. They should leave Susie to her rest. Sighing, Katherine followed him out of the room though everything in her protested.

Wyatt turned to face her as they stepped into the great room. He stopped so abruptly, she almost bumped into him. His hands were at her elbows to steady her, but she pulled away.

An eyebrow quirked, he said, "You look tired. Let me show you how to make a bottle for Susie and then you need to get yourself to bed."

"What about all those dishes?" Her voice sounded weak. Even she could hear it.

He glanced over at the sink. "I'll take care of them."

But she could hear in his voice that he was just as tired as she. With two sets of hands, the work would go quicker and get them both to bed at a more reasonable hour. So, she squared her shoulders and garnered what strength she could muster.

"Come now, you made dinner. The least I can do is help with the dishes."

Opening his mouth, he appeared as if he might argue. But she moved over to the sink and started washing without waiting for his response. It wasn't long before he joined her. Side by side they worked until the dinner dishes were washed, dried, and put way. Then Wyatt showed her how to assemble the bottle and encouraged her to turn in while he checked the barn and horses once more. It was her turn to concede.

Katherine went through the motions of putting on her night-clothes, not giving it much thought. All she knew was the comfort of the bed and the warmth of the covers as she slipped between them. And then she was out.

The house was dark and still. Its inhabitants had long since given up consciousness to the sweet release of sleep. All, that is, except one. For the longest time, David lay in bed wide awake, holding his wife as she drifted off. She was precious to him. He promised to provide for her and their family, and never had that promise been threatened like it was now. After some time of not being able to sleep, he eased out of the bed and made his way into the family room, hoping to not disturb his wife's restful night.

David tried to shut his mind down but could not relax. What kind of effect would this strike have on his innocent family? Already it made him less the man he wanted to be for them. Picketing every day was not the job he signed up for, nor did it get him excited about going to work each day. Not that mining had done that either.

And what of their finances? Their savings? How long would their money hold out? They had expected this strike to be over and done with by now. David had started feeling restless since the strike began. The longer it lasted, the harder it was to shake off the feelings of dread.

There was the other option. He could always work at the ranch. That would be an honest job that wouldn't involve negotiations, unions, or anything. But he couldn't get over his desire to make it on his own. The thought of working for his father kept coming up, and he kept knocking it down, reassuring himself all this nonsense with the mines would get sorted out soon enough. Why should he eat from his father's hand when he could earn his own living? At least that's what he told himself.

"David? What are you doing all alone in here?" Mary's voice startled him out of his thoughts.

He looked back at her, standing in the doorway to their room. "What? Oh, honey, you shouldn't be up. I just . . . I couldn't sleep."

"What's the matter?" She came over to where he stood, putting her arms around him as he gazed out the window.

"Nothing." The last thing he wanted was to burden Mary with his problems.

"Talk to me," she pleaded with him. "Don't keep it all inside." She turned his face so he had to look into her eyes.

A peace existed there he could find nowhere else. How could he protect that peace? He couldn't.

David decided to trust her with his thoughts. "My mind is on this strike."

Mary nodded, but remained silent.

"I wonder how long it will go on. I . . . I wonder how long we can go on, with the way things are." His eyes shifted toward the floor. He couldn't look her in the eye anymore.

Her soothing voice spoke then, not much more than a whisper. "You know, if you've had enough of it, your father would always have a place for you at the ranch."

David took a few steps away from her. How could she not understand?

The hurt was evident in her features.

He let out a long breath. "I've got to make my own way. Can't you see that?"

"I do, darling. I do," she said, closing the gap between them again and cupping his face in her hands. "I just hate to see you worry so."

"It's not your fault. I wish it was that easy, to go work for my father. All of this worry and striking and our troubles would go away. But . . . " David hesitated, turning away from her to gaze out the window again. "It doesn't feel right to just go work for my father. I would feel as if I can't pull my own weight."

Mary reached up and hugged him from behind.

He turned to face her again.

As they held each other closer, she said, "I understand. We'll do what we need to make it. And we'll do it together."

"I love you," David whispered.

"I love you, too. Now let's see if we can get some sleep." Mary laced her fingers in his and pulled him toward the bedroom, but he held back.

"Before we go, could we pray?"

Mary smiled. "Of course."

Katherine roused herself from sleep. Susie's cries pierced through the peacefulness of the night. How long had it been since the last time she'd fed the tiny one? Surely she had just lain back down. Groggy and groaning, she pulled herself out of bed, rubbing her eyes to clear her sleep-blurred vision. Only a few moments passed before she stumbled over to the cradle and lifted the small screaming bundle. Noting the wet diaper, she did her best to soothe Susie's protests while she put on a fresh cloth.

A little more cognizant, Katherine turned toward the door. Could she make it to the kitchen without waking Wyatt and Jack? The silhouette of a masculine figure stood in her open doorway. Immediately on guard, she bit at her lip to keep from screaming. Wyatt. It was only Wyatt. She let out a long breath.

"I'm sorry." She shifted Susie in her arms, feeling out of place in naught but her nightclothes. "I tried to keep her quiet so she wouldn't wake anyone. She's just so impatient." Katherine's face warmed at the picture she was certain she made—hair disheveled, eyes rimmed with sleepiness.

"What? Oh, no," Wyatt said, rubbing sleep from his face. "I came to take her off your hands."

"What?" Did she hear him right?

"You have school early in the morning. You've been up for one feeding already tonight. Let me take this one." He stepped into the room.

Why was he being so thoughtful? Hadn't he shown her how to make the bottles so he wouldn't be disturbed? Yet here he was, no more than two feet in front of her, arms outstretched, eyes sincere.

So she handed Susie over to him, trying to maintain some appropriate distance between them. "Thank you. I moved the bottles to . . . " she began.

"I know where everything is," he cut her off. "If not, I'll find it. I want you to get some rest."

With that, he turned and walked toward the kitchen with the fussing Susie. And Katherine had nothing to do but to curl back under the covers and, out of respect for what Wyatt did for her, try to get back to sleep. It wasn't as easy as she would have thought, with her mind replaying the scene that had just occurred. But after some moments of calm, she drifted into a peaceful sleep. Although her dreams for the remainder of that night would be filled with one Mr. Wyatt Sullivan.

The miners made their way to the mines again, David among them. He heard the complaints every day, but more and more the miners were silent. And he knew why. The daily grind of the strike wore thin on the men. They had been at it for a month and many of them were depleting their financial reserves. Just as David wondered what he was going to do if this strike didn't end soon, those around him must have the same concerns.

If he had nothing else, David could always ask his father for a job, though that was something he didn't want to resort to. So, he, like his mining brethren, wanted to be able to see this thing through.

John Calderwood had continued to move among the men daily, encouraging them, standing with them, telling them they were doing the right thing and that the mine owners couldn't hold out forever. When he spoke, it all sounded so good, so reasonable to David. And many began to believe the owners were nearing their breaking point. Calderwood's words sounded so confident, so sure. But soon even his speeches, too, started to lose traction with the men.

Just then they arrived at the mine with their signs. A few of them with the energy tried to rile the others up. It worked to some extent. But as the mine owners approached with their own mob, the miners stirred to action.

Something different was in the air. Even David sensed it. For one, the mine owners arrived with a group of sheriff's deputies and an air of confidence about them. One of the men walked straight to Calderwood and handed him some papers. David strained to hear what was being said.

"We have an injunction to keep your striking miners from interfering with our mine operations," the largest of the three owners, Hagerman, said.

A hush fell over the crowd as Calderwood took a moment to read over the paper.

"You'd best get your people to move out of the way, or we can have the deputies do it for you," Hagerman continued.

"That won't be necessary," Calderwood spoke up. "Just give me a few minutes here."

"You have two," Hagerman said, chest filled to bursting as he rose to his full five feet and eight inches. He wasn't all that intimidating next to

Calderwood's taller frame, but he seemed to think he presented quite the frightening display.

"Men, we have to clear the way to the mine," Calderwood said, his face a mask of neutrality. "Split the line to make a path."

David, along with the other miners around him, was confused, but they all did as they were instructed, some going right, some going left; creating an opening to the mine.

Then a puffed up Hagerman led the line of deputies and strike-breakers down the path.

Watching the strikebreakers walk by toward the mine devastated David. His heart dropped at the thought that their fight was over. They had lost. And he wasn't the only one. The miners around him went through the motions of protesting the scabs, but they all knew this was trouble.

The next morning, Katherine found it difficult to leave the two children behind at her mother's house. More so than she'd expected. Shouldn't she be ready for some relief? But when she closed the door behind herself, she longed to rush back inside and gather Susie to herself for one last embrace. Katherine trusted her mother. That wasn't the issue. Then what was it? Had she become so attached? And so quickly?

But there was nothing for it. Katherine made her way to the school, duty-bound to teach for at least the remainder of her contract. And that's what she wanted, wasn't it? She'd never imagined herself being the kind of woman who enjoyed sitting around the house, minding the children, waiting for her husband to return. Certainly not waiting around for Wyatt like some lovesick wife. Never.

Katherine left her horse and cart at the town livery and, cutting through the General Store's alley, headed to the schoolhouse. Despite the additional things in her morning, getting the children ready and dropping them off, she would still arrive before her students. Yawning, Katherine was reminded of her difficulties rising that morning. But Susie made for the cutest little alarm, waking her just as the sun tipped over the horizon. They'd had several sweet moments together this morning during the first feeding of the day.

And then Wyatt had joined them, dressed and ready. Was he always such an early riser? Relieving Katherine of her task, he insisted she prepare herself. By the time she washed her face, dressed, and pulled her hair up, Wyatt had Jack up and eating breakfast. How did he manage so much? Thanks to him, the morning went more smoothly than she could ever have hoped. Still, she longed for those hours of missed sleep.

As she approached the schoolhouse, reaching for the door, she heard movement within. It concerned her. She doubted any student would go into the closed building without permission. If they arrived, they should have waited in the schoolyard.

Katherine put her ear closer to the door. Sure enough, sounds of shuffling feet came from within. What should she do? Was she to confront some stranger in her schoolhouse? Perhaps a miner who had chosen to sleep there? Maybe someone dangerous? Her heart pounded in her ears. She should get Timothy, but that would be awkward. Could she run to town to get Wyatt? That seemed just as awkward.

Taking a deep breath, she prayed for protection and opened the door.

Timothy's surprised brown eyes met hers.

Her mouth opened, but she couldn't make any words come out.

"Katherine," he said, setting a piece of chalk down. The blackboard was filled with sentences. A grammar assignment?

"What?" Her voice squeaked as she pushed out the one word she could form.

He straightened his black jacket, looking at the floor. "I didn't . . . that is, I wasn't expecting to see you this morning."

Katherine stared at him, unable to speak. Why wouldn't she be here? She was the teacher, after all.

Timothy met her eyes and a thick silence filled the room. After several moments, he spoke. "Mayor Jacobs came to visit me last night. He asked if I would teach the students for a couple of days until the town council has a chance to decide what to do."

Her brows furrowed. She tried to swallow, but her mouth was dry. What was he talking about? Decide what to do? All of a sudden, she needed to be doing something with her hands. Glancing for an object to grab, anything as a refuge for her nervous fingers, her eyes darted this way and that. But there was nothing. So she clasped them in front of her stomach, which started to feel uneasy.

"I . . ." she cleared her throat. "I don't understand."

Timothy's brows shot up. "Katherine, you knew you wouldn't be able to teach once you got married. That is simply not proper. And the fact that you now have children . . ."

Katherine's knees turned to liquid. She leaned on a nearby student desk but found sliding into the chair more helpful. This had not occurred to her. How could it not? Married women weren't allowed to be schoolteachers. In all their planning and rushing, she and Wyatt hadn't considered it.

And, knowing that this was only proper, she still felt it was wrong. What would happen to the students? Timothy couldn't take on the schoolhouse and maintain his duties at the church for more than a few days. The town council must know that. She was the only qualified teacher within reach of this town, married or not. Surely, they had to think of the children and what was best for them.

Timothy shifted his weight from one foot to another, drawing her attention.

"I . . ." She struggled for the right words. "I'll be going."

Standing with slow movements, she stepped toward the schoolhouse door.

"Katie, wait, it's . . ." Timothy called after her, but she ignored it.

Now outside, she gained momentum as she stepped down the stairs. Then she all but ran across the schoolyard toward town, tears stinging her eyes.

Never had she felt so unwanted.

CHAPTER 10

Reactions

Two days.

Two days had passed since Wyatt came home to discover that Katherine had been pushed out of her teaching position. It had taken much coaxing and maneuvering from him, but, in the end, she told him the whole story. And though it sounded as if Timothy was only following the direction of the mayor, Wyatt couldn't help but suspect the reverend played a bigger part in all of this.

When Wyatt inquired with Mayor Jacobs, he learned that the town council would meet to decide whether to allow Katherine to keep teaching, find another teacher, or suspend school for the remainder of the semester. Wyatt had not anticipated this. And he didn't like it.

All the more so because of the sadness in Katherine's eyes when she relayed the story to him. Her obvious pain brought out an intense anger in him. And that baffled him as well. He wanted to protect her somehow, but he hadn't been able to.

That was about to change. Phillip Yerby let it slip earlier in the day that the town council would be meeting this evening at the church to discuss and vote on the situation. As it would seem, Wyatt missed the invitation. Or did he? While Mr. Yerby seemed surprised Wyatt did not know about it, Wyatt became more and more suspicious that he'd been kept in the dark on purpose.

Nearing the church, he knew he would be the last to arrive. Nothing new there. But this meeting was about to take a drastic turn.

Wyatt stepped to the door and, taking a deep breath, opened it. As the room became visible to him, the shocked faces of the other members of the town council and the confused townspeople appeared before him as well. Timothy recovered the quickest. His eyes narrowed.

"Dr. Sullivan," Mayor Jacobs said as he stood. "We, ah, weren't expecting you."

"Weren't you? I thought this was a town council meeting. And, last I checked, I'm a member of the town council."

"That's true." The mayor looked down at the table before meeting Wyatt's eyes again. "But this matter we're discussing. Well, it didn't seem right you should be voting on it."

Wyatt's jaw clenched. He didn't trust himself to say anything.

Mr. Hammond shook his head. "Let us hear him speak then." He turned back toward Wyatt. "If that is why you have come."

Several in the congregation voiced similarly their desire to hear him speak.

"It is." Wyatt let a breath out through clenched teeth.

Mayor Jacobs took his seat and watched Wyatt as he would any dangerous animal. They all did.

Wyatt took several steps forward.

"I don't know how you suppose to find a suitable teacher in a matter of days. Is there some unmarried, childless woman in the town that I am unaware of who carries the kind of qualifications Katherine has?"

The men blinked back at him, and the townsfolk fell silent, staring at the councilmembers on the dais.

"We are not presuming to find someone with equal qualifications." Timothy spoke up. "But we must respect propriety. Especially for our children. It is not appropriate for a married woman, much less a mother, to be filling such a position."

Some of the townsfolk agreed with Timothy.

"And unnecessary," Mr. Hammond rumbled. "When the preacher can fill in for the rest of the semester."

"The preacher? How do you expect him to carry his load and hers?"

Wyatt balked. "Doesn't he already have a position that demands his full attention?"

Everyone looked at Timothy.

The reverend's now steely gaze rested on Wyatt. And he felt it.

"It is true. I cannot cover the teaching post for more than a few more days."

The collective gasp of the congregation could not be missed.

"Then we must consider allowing her to finish out the school year." It was Philip Yerby who spoke up. "That makes the most sense."

Wyatt breathed a sign of relief. He had one friend here. Someone who saw reason.

"No," Timothy said, his voice harsher than Wyatt ever remembered. "We must suspend school for the remainder of the year."

"How does that make anything better? The children robbed of their education? Don't forget the time they've already lost because of the typhoid. Suspending school cannot be the answer." Wyatt flung his hands in the air. This had to be the most frustrating interchange he'd had with these men.

"If we hadn't been able to hire Miss Matth . . . I mean, Mrs. Sullivan to begin with, were we not going to ask Mrs. Jacobs to step in for the year?" Yerby leaned forward and looked across the table.

Jacobs and Hammond nodded. Timothy looked forward, eyes trained on Wyatt. Again, Wyatt felt the intensity of Timothy's gaze on him. But he refused to back down. He now had the majority of the town council on his side.

"Are we prepared to vote then?" The mayor shifted in his seat.

Could the others feel the tension in the room between Wyatt and Timothy?

There came a round of agreement.

"I still think Dr. Sullivan should recuse himself from this vote since it involves his . . . Mrs. Sullivan." Timothy's words were firm and resolute.

His basis was sound. Wyatt would not be able to convince the members otherwise.

"That seems fair enough." Mayor Jacobs met Wyatt's gaze. "If you don't mind, Doc, would you step outside?"

"Step outside?" Wyatt looked over the entire collection of towns-folk. "Is this not a public assembly? Am I not a member of this town? Would you take away my right to watch the vote?"

Mayor Jacobs glanced over the room. Was he sweating? "Please, Dr. Sullivan, don't make this harder than it has to be. I only ask you step outside so that the members of the town council may vote without intimidation."

Wyatt held the mayor's eyes for a moment before he nodded. He only hoped that there would be no further discussion after he left. If Timothy tried to further convince them without him there to respond . . . But he had no choice.

So, he turned and stepped out of the church.

The minutes slipped into hours while he waited. Or so it seemed. Had Timothy seized the opportunity to share what arguments he could make? Had it worked? Was he able to convince them?

Wyatt sat on the top step and did what he could to distract himself, working his finger joints, popping them, clasping them. But it did not make the time go by any faster.

After what felt like more than two hours, but in reality was only a few minutes, Mayor Jacobs opened the door and invited Wyatt back inside. Why would the man not just tell him their decision? But the mayor simply led Wyatt back in and took his seat.

Wyatt didn't need anyone to tell him, though. One look at Timo-thy's downcast features and he knew. They were going to let Katherine stay on for the remainder of the year. Smiling to himself, he fought the urge to beat at the air in triumph. He couldn't wait to tell her.

So it had come. The day of the Valentine's Dance. Katherine turned over in her bed as she realized what day it was. And, as it turned out, it was a good thing Timothy never got around to asking her to go with him. Katherine could not imagine that Wyatt would want to go. Did she even want to? She would have to face the town council, the townspeo-ple, and Timothy. And she would spend the whole time chasing Jack while trying to soothe Susie. No, it was best they stay home.

How long had she slept? Wyatt had sent her to her room to catch up on some sleep while he watched the kids. The morning had passed with the same busyness as usual. Perhaps that was why she had not realized until now what day it was.

Shifting to a sitting position, she rubbed sleep from her eyes. And then slowly she forced herself from the bed. Her hair must be a mess. She pulled the remaining pins out and let it fall, running a brush through the gentle waves to clear any tangles.

Once certain her appearance wouldn't scare anyone, she stepped out into the hall. There were no sounds. Were the children in bed? No, Susie wasn't in her crib. Moving out into the family room, she continued to search for any sign of life. Where was everyone? She found Wyatt, sitting in his chair, facing the fire, reading.

"Wyatt?"

He turned. His face was a mask.

"Where are the children?" Her heartbeat thundered in her ears.

Wyatt stood up and walked toward her. "I took them over to your parents' house. I didn't think you would want to take them with us to the Valentine's Dance."

"You didn't what?" Surely she hadn't heard him.

He had closed the distance between them. His eyes were soft on hers. "The Valentine's Dance. You did want to go, didn't you? Seems I remember you liked that sort of thing."

Her heart warmed. Of course she wanted to go, but she didn't see how. Could she go with Wyatt? They were man and wife now, so they would be expected to appear at these things together. Why shouldn't they go? She looked up at him, but his eyes were not on hers, but on her hair.

"I like your hair down." His voice was husky. "Would you wear it down for me?"

Something foreign to her flushed through her body. Not unpleasant, quite the opposite. She didn't think she would be able to speak with this thing coursing through her.

"I need to get ready, I suppose." Wyatt smiled and his eyes caught hers again.

He moved past her, his shoulder brushing against hers. She closed her eyes until she heard the door to his room close. What was she going to do?

Wyatt worked to get the cart ready. He couldn't help but smile as he remembered the look on Katherine's face but an hour ago. It was nice to know he could have that kind of effect on her. But it was not funny. For it was she that drew him to it. Why could he not control himself around that woman?

He finished hitching the tan mare to the cart when he heard the front door shut. And there was Katherine in the gentle light of the late day's sun. Her dress was covered with her long wrap. And he frowned as his eyes traveled upward. She had pinned her hair up. Not in an unattractive way, but she had not left it down.

As she walked toward him, the corners of his mouth turned up. There was no sense in letting it ruin his evening. Why let her get the best of him? She was still likely to be the prettiest woman at the dance. He hoped she wasn't wearing a shredded garment under her wrap.

"You are lovely tonight," he said as she came closer.

She tipped her head to one side and searched his eyes. He forced a smile onto his face.

"Thank you." With her shorter strides, she soon closed the distance between them.

He reached out and took her hand. Should he pull her against him? Would that prove that the nearness affected her as it did him? Looking away from her, he moved toward the cart. This was not a game.

Once he helped her into her seat and got into his, he urged the horses onward. Why did she even agree to go with him this evening if only to taunt him? There was a bitter taste in his mouth. Perhaps he should turn around and forget the whole thing. Would that serve his purposes? No, he must do his best to give her a good evening.

They arrived on the main street in short order. Parking the cart was little trouble. Helping Katherine down was another matter. She placed her hands on his shoulders as she hopped down in front of him.

He removed his hands from her waist as quickly as he could and turned to ensure the horse was tied off. Her small hand on his arm stopped him. His eyes met hers.

"Wyatt, I do thank you for bringing me tonight. I do enjoy these things."

Her eyes were bright and glassy. Had that been difficult for her to say? It seemed so.

He smiled and nodded. "My pleasure." But he did not break eye contact. Instead, he lost himself in the depths of her eyes for several breaths. Then his eyes shifted to her lips.

She pressed her hands against his chest then, creating distance between them.

What was she doing to him? Baiting him?

He narrowed his eyes as he watched her walk toward the boarding house café. He secured the horse's reins and then trudged after her.

Katherine stood just outside the café doors when he caught up to her. Why hadn't she gone in? She couldn't be waiting for him.

"What's the matter?" His tone was harsher than he'd intended.

She turned toward him. Her face drained of color. Had she even caught his words? "I . . . I'm not sure I want to go in. Can we just go home?"

"Go home? Why?" He couldn't imagine any reason she wouldn't go in. They were right here. And he had worked to arrange this evening for them. Of course they were going to go in.

Katherine glanced between the door and his face. She looked like a rabbit caught between a shotgun and a hound dog. At last, she nodded.

Wyatt stepped forward to open the door for her, and she slipped an arm around his. The contact surprised him. Why would she lean on him now?

They stepped into the café, already filled with townspeople making merry. And though the music continued to play, there was no mistaking the collective stares they got as they entered. Or the whispers.

Katherine gripped his arm tighter and pulled closer to him. He looked over at her face, now coloring. Was she embarrassed? Why? Because of some town gossip? And why should the townspeople concern themselves with their elopement. It wasn't that scandalous.

The crowd opened up, and Timothy stood across the room, staring them down. And Wyatt realized what he had done. He had made Katherine a public spectacle. Perhaps their elopement was not newsworthy, but the broken courtship followed immediately by a marriage to another man was. It was clear on the faces of the people around him. They scorned her for what she had done.

Wyatt drew Katherine over to a corner, blocking the piercing eyes with his body. What could he say? I'm sorry? That seemed weak. He hunted for the right words.

She looked down, her face flushed and her arms crossed in front of her chest.

Using a finger to tip her face up so he could look at her eyes, he said, "I would like, more than anything, to dance with my wife tonight."

Katherine sniffled and a small smile marked her face.

He shrugged off his winter coat and worked on her outer cape. Once he had relieved her of it, he was surprised to see the same dress she had worn to their wedding. That was one dress he would not forget. His heart expanded.

"May I?" He put forth his hand, hoping she would accept it.

"Of course." She slid her hand into his and allowed him to lead her onto the dance floor.

He did not miss the jabs, the whispers, the pointing, but he also did not want to miss this opportunity to just hold Katherine in his arms for the entirety of a song. And so he put a hand on her waist, held her close, led with their clasped hands, and moved about the open floor. No matter what anyone would say about that night or about Katherine, it was the first time he danced with his wife.

David paced the floor of his family room. He could scarcely believe what he had become party to in the last week. After that day when the strikers were brought face-to-face with the strikebreakers, Calderwood had told them not to give up, that all was not lost. Their next job had been to try to persuade the strikebreakers to join the union. This became an altogether unsuccessful venture. So the miners resorted to threats and violence against the scabs. In the end, their tactics worked to keep many nonunion miners away from the mines. Though the things that had transpired led to a win for the miners' strike, it had come at a price. Was it a price David was willing to pay?

Even now, David waited to leave on another mission "for the cause." The clock chimed. Time to go. What awaited him, he did not know. So far, he had been able to keep his hands clean, but he feared the longer he remained part of this strike, the more likely that would change. All the more with the tactics they were taking on. He said a quick prayer for God's protection against any involvement in anything he would later regret.

He mounted his horse and made his way to the meeting site. A group of miners were already gathered. Once he arrived, the older man who had first led the Free Coinage Union walked over to him.

"Glad you could make it, son. Did you bring your firearm?" The man's voice was even and calm, as if he asked David what he'd had for lunch.

David did not like it. "No, sir, no one told me to. I don't usually carry my gun to the mines."

"That's all right. We have a few extra." He motioned for a man to bring him a gun. Handing the rifle supplied over to David, he nodded.

Should he take it? There didn't seem to be an option. The man held it out to him, arms outstretched. David opened his hands to receive the weapon, but held it at arm's length, ready to pass it back.

"What do I need this for?"

The older man patted David's shoulder. "Oh, it's just for intimidation."

That did not reassure David. "So, I won't be in a situation to use it?"

"No, it's just a precaution."

David wasn't sure he trusted the man. He already wished he hadn't come.

"Pretty exciting, huh?" A voice said from behind him.

David turned to see his friend, Jonas.

"Do you know what's going on here?" David's eyes returned to the rifle, still held loosely in his grasp.

"No." Jonas shook his head, but that didn't seem to bother him. How could it not?

It made David feel even more unsettled. He trusted this situation less and less.

But before David could hand over his weapon and ride off, the older leader stepped forward and began speaking. "Men, for those of you who don't know, we are going to prevent those same deputies from doing to another mine what they did to us—protecting strikebreakers. Your firearms are for intimidation only. You are not, and I repeat not, to fire on the deputies, no matter what happens."

That eased David's mind . . . somewhat.

As the last student left the schoolhouse, Katherine deflated into her chair. She shuffled papers around on her desk. Many things needed to be done in order to prepare for the next day. Still, Katherine made stacks with the papers and slates. She should work through some of them, but she needed to relieve her mother of the two children. Which was more important? These things would be here later, and she could always come back to finish them. So she gathered what could be done at home and headed out to collect her cart and horse from the livery.

The ride to her parents' homestead went by quicker than usual. Perhaps because she was deep in thought about the recent happenings with the town council. She had won back her place at the school. But by how much? Did she truly still have their support? Or was it by a slim majority? And what about Timothy? How did he vote? All of these questions swirled in her head.

And Wyatt, she wasn't even sure how he felt. That first day back, when she had been pushed out of the school, she came home in such a state. When she shared what happened, Wyatt had become quiet, stand-offish almost. Would he prefer she stay at home with the children? She didn't know. Had he voted against her?

And just like that, the Matthews' homestead loomed in front of her. Would there ever be answers to her questions? As she entered the house, shrieks of laughter filled her ears. Susie squealed and wriggled on the floor as Ma leaned over her, making faces. Jack, too, laughed as he watched the interchange.

Katherine twisted an errant hair behind her ear as a burning sensation settled between her shoulder blades. She forced a breath out between clenched teeth. It all seemed to come so naturally to her mother . . . and to Wyatt. Was she even cut out to be a mother? Pushing those thoughts to the side, she stepped further into the room. It would do no good to think like that.

"Am I interrupting something important?" she said, painting a smile on her face. Her presence broke the spell Ma had wrapped the children in.

Ma moved to stand, gathering Susie in her arms. "Of course not. How was school?"

Katherine shrugged her shoulders. "It was a day."

Jack slid over to the blocks on the floor.

"Come," Ma said, waving a hand toward the dining table. "Sit for a minute."

Katherine obeyed and took a chair next to her mother's seat. When Ma sat, she adjusted Susie to a more comfortable position and looked over at Katherine.

"You look tired, honey."

Who wouldn't be? "I am. My sleep has been interrupted every night by little missy here."

A knowing smile lit her mother's face. "Is that all that wears on you?"

Katherine became silent for a moment. Should she share her heart's concerns with her mother? The last thing she wanted to be was a burden or cause her mother to worry.

"No, there's more." Katherine's words came slowly as she examined her hands, clasped together on the table. "I'm not . . . that is, I don't seem to be . . . I just think that . . . I'm not good with the children."

Ma reached out and laid a hand on top of Katherine's, her features pained. "Oh, sweetie. I'm sure that's not true."

"It is." Katherine met her mother's gaze, a tightness in her throat giving way to tears. "Wyatt knew exactly what to do and when and how and . . ."

Ma's features softened as she squeezed Katherine's hand. "He does have the advantage of experience. Don't forget, he sees babies and small children in the clinic. And received training on their medical needs."

Katherine nodded. Her mother spoke the truth, but she wasn't satisfied. "It was more than that. He seemed so comfortable, so at ease with the children. Even you, you're a natural, Ma."

"Don't forget that I, too, have experience to lean on."

She wasn't even sharing her thoughts well. Katherine looked down at her hands.

"Katie, mothering doesn't happen overnight. It's a skill that's honed and perfected over time and many, many mistakes. You will learn to be a mother to these two precious children. I know you will. Just be patient with yourself."

Her mother was only trying to make her feel better. Or could it be true? After all, Wyatt didn't need time to adjust.

Ma seemed to read her mind. "I bet Wyatt had his own nerves to deal with. You were just too caught up with your own self-doubt to see it."

Turning her hand to clasp her mother's, Katherine's voice grew stronger. "Thanks, Ma. You always know just what to say."

"That, too, is a result of time and acquired wisdom."

Katherine's face widened in a smile. "I best get these children home. I'm planning on making dinner tonight."

"You're planning to cook?" Ma's eyes widened.

"Yeah," Katherine said, stepping over to where Jack sat on the rug. "Wyatt made dinner last night, and I wanted to make sure I did it tonight." She helped him put the blocks away.

"Have you ever cooked a family dinner by yourself?"

What did her mother mean? Of course she hadn't. Ma knew as much. She had attempted to train Katherine in the tasks of homemaking, but Katherine's mind had always been on other things. By the time she left for finishing school, the family had not yet had an edible meal by her hands. But that was different.

"No, but I watched you plenty of times. And I wasn't serious before. I am now. How hard can a simple meal be?" With the blocks put back in their box, Katherine stood and faced her mother again.

Ma's eyes returned to normal and a slow smile broke out on her face. "We'll talk tomorrow."

Now that Katherine had Jack's hand, she came toward her mother and collected Susie.

"Yes," she said, her eyebrow quirked at her mother's odd expression. "I'm sure we will."

And with that, she and the children were off.

Wyatt finished with his last patient of the day, an arthritis checkup. His patient had been doing well on the latest medicinal regimen he had put her on, and he encouraged her to continue her daily exercises. As he ushered her out the door, a horse galloping down the main street caught his attention. The rider drew closer and it became clear that whoever tore through the town was headed for the clinic.

He pulled the elderly patient back into the building for her own safety and watched as the rider approached. Once the horse drew closer, Wyatt saw it was David Matthews in the saddle. His immediate thoughts were of Katherine. Was she hurt? That gave his heart pause within him.

Moments later, David pulled the horse to a halt just short of the clinic doors and hopped off. "Dr. Sullivan, there's trouble at the mine. We need your help!"

Relief washed over him, but Wyatt had no time to take it in. "What's happened?" Had there been a cave in?

"It's the strike." David's face fell. "A group of strikers were armed and they . . .well, they ambushed and captured some deputies who were trying to protect strikebreakers."

Wyatt's eyebrows shot up. Why would David be involved in something like this?

David raised his arms in an apologetic shrug. "Somehow shots were fired. No one knows which side they came from, but it led to a fistfight. And, needless to say, there are some injured men out there now."

Wyatt did his best to belay his judgment and instead stepped back into the clinic to grab his medical bag and go after his horse. He was a healer first. No matter what. Then, once both men were mounted and ready, he allowed David to lead him to the men that needed his attention.

Hours later, Wyatt made his way home. Today had been particularly grueling to say the least. His body ached, and he was worn. One patient after the next kept him busy at the clinic all day and then he'd had to clean up the fallout from the miners' ill-laid plan. Had he even the chance to sit down today? Filled anew with an eagerness for home, he pushed his horse into a faster trot.

What would be waiting for him at home? One thing he did know— it wouldn't be empty. Katherine would be there. Comforted by that thought, he urged the horse to pick up his step. She had been adjusting to her new role quite well, but she still leaned on him. Not that he minded. They were partners in this, after all. And she had to learn a lot rather quickly. He'd had some experience to draw from.

But nothing in his experience had prepared him for dealing with the emotions she stirred in him. Yes, he'd had a schoolboy crush on her years ago. Had that not faded when she'd begun to treat him as if he'd forced Ellie Mae into the mine? That it was somehow his fault?

When he stepped foot in the schoolhouse the day she returned to Cripple Creek, when he saw her face, he knew then there might be trouble. For the same feelings stirred in his chest then that filled him now as he thought about her. Feelings difficult to describe. A tightening, painful almost, constricting of his heart.

He should have married Betsy long ago and been done with this foolishness. Yet something had always kept him from moving forward with her. Could that something have been Katherine? That thought made the ache inside him sharpen.

All in all, each time he came home to her, he feared, he wondered, what would this evening bring?

But the time for all speculation came to an end as the house now stood in front of him. The lights burned, and movement within drew his attention. He made quick work of closing his horse in the barn stall. Stopping for a moment, he steeled himself for what lay ahead.

As he opened the door to the house, he was assaulted with a burst of smoke. Coughing, he flapped his arm to clear the air. The house was filled with it. Was his home on fire? Adrenaline coursed through him, and every muscle in his body went on alert. Where was Katherine? The children? He had to get them out. But as he stood at the ready, the smoke cleared, escaping through the open door, and he took stock of the house. There was no fire. The remaining smoke poured from the kitchen stove.

The kitchen was a disaster. But Katherine still scurried about, trying to save whatever dish she had burned. Jack bounced up and down, running around the great room, and Susie cried from her high chair.

Wyatt leaped into action, opening the windows to continue airing out the house. He picked up Susie and bounced her with gentle movements to soothe her.

"What happened?" he asked Katherine.

She whirled toward him, her face registering surprise. Clad in an apron splattered from her hard work preparing whatever she had made, the marks of dinner were on her face and in her hair. The sleeves of her top were rolled up, and she had a sopping wet towel in her hand that dripped on the floor. And her eyes, her once sharp eyes, were now dull and watering with unshed tears. Her lip trembled, and she seemed afraid to speak, as if fearful everything would spill out, tears and all.

And so he remained silent, not sure how to proceed.

"I . . . I was trying to make dinner," she managed.

"All this?" He waved his free arm. "Is from dinner?"

She nodded, a few tears escaping. "Chicken and dumplings."

Wyatt looked at her, touched by her efforts and moved by her tears. He couldn't be mad at her. Especially since she had been preparing his favorite meal. But how did she know? Was it just a coincidence? No. That night in Denver, after their wedding. She must have remembered he'd ordered chicken and dumplings. His heart melted a little more.

"It's all right, Katie," he said, longing to reach out to her, but timid at the same time. "Why don't you get Susie a bottle, and I'll get this cleaned up. I'll make dinner tonight."

She wiped at a tear and her shoulders slumped. Taking Susie from his arms without any other acknowledgement, she moved off toward the family room.

He hated how defeated she was in that moment. But there wasn't much he could do about it. Still, it gave him an idea.

Another long day at school came to an end. Katherine's days dragged more and more, and her nights were abbreviated. Her evenings were filled with the schoolwork she used to do in the afternoons. No more. Now that was time she spent with the children. Then the leftover papers. Susie interrupted what sleep she did get, though Wyatt still took his share of feedings. All of this combined made for one tired schoolteacher. Did her students know? How could they not?

Katherine went through the motions of packing up and gathering the children from her parents' house. She did it all as if in a daze. Then she made her way home. It intrigued her how, in such a short time, she began to think of Wyatt's house as "home." That's where her things were. And where her small family gathered at the end of the day. A smile graced her lips.

They were a mismatched family indeed, but a family all the same. A warmth spread through her body, soothing her. Her little family. Glancing over at Jack and Susie in the back of the wagon, she sighed. She wanted to be so much more for them, for Wyatt. And she would be.

Pushing past the weariness, she became determined anew. Tonight she would attempt to make dinner again. Only this time she'd prepared herself, having had a long conversation with her mother and received some tips from the expert. This time would be different. Her expectations were more realistic. They would be having something a bit more simple—breakfast. So what if it was odd. It would be made by her, and she would be proud of it.

Katherine pictured Wyatt's surprised face when he would walk in and discover she had completed an entire meal. He would be impressed, wouldn't he? A rush of tingled excitement spread from the center of her chest, expanding outward. Why did she care so much to please him?

They approached the homestead and Katherine busied herself

putting the horse and cart up. Then she gathered Susie in her arms and took Jack's hand, leading them to the house. But as they drew near the door, she heard movement within and froze. She hadn't noticed Wyatt's horse in the barn. Could it be he returned early and started dinner already? Her heart dropped. No surprise. No proud moment. It all vanished.

She opened the door and stepped into the family room. While the house was indeed abuzz with the smells and sounds of dinner cooking, Wyatt was not to be found. There, in her kitchen, was none other than Betsy Callaway.

What could be her business here? Katherine opened her mouth to speak, but nothing came out. Then she licked her lips. Her mouth had become rather dry. She was dumbstruck by the sight before her. Betsy, however, continued to cook, oblivious to Katherine's presence. After some moments, Katherine found her tongue.

"What are you doing here?"

Betsy jumped, nearly upending the pot of boiling water she stirred, but soon regained her composure. Wiping her hands on the apron that belonged to Katherine, she said, "Oh, Wyatt asked me to come over and make dinner."

"What?" Something in Katherine's chest squeezed painfully.

"Wyatt asked me to make dinner." Betsy met her gaze, staring back with cold eyes.

Once again, Katherine didn't know what to say. She couldn't dispute Betsy's claim . . . yet. So, she closed the door behind herself and went about taking care of the children. After she changed Susie's diaper, she saw to it that Jack was occupied with some toys before turning her attention back to the intruder in her home.

She stepped into the kitchen, balancing Susie on one arm, and put her other hand on her hip. "Betsy, are you certain you understood Wyatt?"

"Yes," Betsy spoke as if she were explaining something to a small child. "He asked me to come over, cook, and have dinner ready for him. There aren't many ways to misunderstand that."

Katherine supposed not. She looked at the floor, the clamp squeezed tighter around her heart. What could she do but take Susie back to the family room? So, she and Susie joined Jack on the floor to play. Watching the case clock, she counted the moments until Wyatt came home and watched Betsy move around the kitchen as if nothing came more naturally to her.

It seemed as if hours passed before hoofbeats, the sound growing louder by the second, came closer to the homestead. Should she go outside to meet him? No, it was best she wait with the children. At last, Wyatt walked through the door. Relief washed over her. Finally, he would put an end to this craziness. Rising to her feet, she opened her mouth.

"Betsy, so glad you could make it," he said, acknowledging her before he even looked toward Katherine.

A coldness swept through her. What could she say? Betsy had spoken the truth. He had no problem inviting Betsy to come into their, well his, house and cook for them without so much as asking Katherine.

Wyatt moved into the great room.

Katherine held her breath.

But he moved past her and crouched on the floor next to the small boy, giving him a hug. "How's my Jack-boy?"

"I got to brush a horse today!"

"That's great. You're such a big boy." He released Jack so the small hands could go back to playing. Then Wyatt turned his attention to Susie, who lay in Katherine's arms. Letting her grab his finger, he shook his hand, smiling down at her.

Katherine remained as still as she could. A curious pain shooting through her chest. Her eyes glued to his face.

"What is it that smells so good?" he called to Betsy while meeting Katherine's eyes at last.

"Pot roast," Betsy announced, a broad smile breaking out across her face. "One of your favorites, if memory serves."

"Yes, that is correct." Wyatt's eyes moved over to Betsy.

Katherine frowned.

Betsy let out a light laugh. "It's almost done. Shall we gather everyone to the table?"

Katherine longed to disappear, to shut herself up in her room, but she knew the children needed to eat. So she passed Susie over to Wyatt and worked to set the table. Though, in her anger, she could think of better uses for the knives than setting them next to the plates.

By then, Wyatt had the children settled at the table. And so Katherine sat, trying not to scowl while Betsy served the meal. It did not escape her notice that Betsy made sure Wyatt got an extra helping. Why that should bother her, she didn't know. But it did.

Betsy sat and the meal commenced.

Everyone dug in, everyone except Katherine. She was none too eager to partake of the meal. Instead she pushed the vegetables around on her plate.

"Mm, mm, mm. This meat is so tender," Wyatt complimented.

Betsy smiled and spooned more onto his plate.

"And these potatoes, cooked to perfection."

Heat warmed Katherine's face. How could he treat her this way?

Betsy dared to look over at Katherine with a wicked sort of grin. In her own home, Katherine was supposed to endure this in her own home?

"And this gravy . . . " he started.

Katherine shot to her feet. "Wyatt, may I speak with you?"

Wyatt raised a brow, but stood at Katherine's request. "Betsy, if you'll excuse us."

Katherine didn't so much as glance over her shoulder as she walked toward her bedroom. She trusted that Wyatt followed her. Once she found herself in the safety of her room, she spun on him.

"Why did you invite her to come? To teach me a lesson?" She all but spit out.

"Exactly." Wyatt's voice was kind, as if it was part of some plan Katherine and Wyatt had come up with together.

"What?" Katherine's eyebrows shot up. Her shoulders slumped.

"To give you a cooking lesson." His gentle tone still confused her.

"How can she give me a cooking lesson when she's finished dinner before I arrive?"

"She what?" Now it was his turn to be confused, and his wide eyes showed it.

"Yes," Katherine said flatly, arms folded. "She was in this house cooking when I got here today."

"She was supposed to come after you got home." He appeared deflated.

And Katherine began to put the pieces together. The way he had carried on about the meal . . . It had been his intention to compliment Katherine on her cooking. Yet, because of Betsy's maneuvering, he had insulted Katherine without knowing it. It almost made her laugh. Almost.

Katherine kept her voice softer, but not kinder. "That doesn't make me feel better."

"Look," Wyatt voice was pleading. "She wasn't supposed to come over and cook for us. She was supposed to help you learn how to cook."

"Wait. You told Betsy I can't cook?" Her eyes widened, and all of the color drained from her face.

"When you say it like that, it doesn't sound good."

"I'm so embarrassed. It'll be all over town. How can I ever face anyone?" Katherine's hand was on her forehead. She imagined the talk, the looks, and the comments behind her back. Added to what folks were already saying.

Wyatt reached out to touch her arm. "Come now, you can't think Betsy would . . . "

Katherine jerked her arm back. "How can you think she wouldn't?"

Wyatt shifted uncomfortably.

"You must know Betsy made this meal to impress you. To . . . to . . . to show me up." Katherine wasn't sure why she cared so much. What did it matter to her what Wyatt thought of her? Or of Betsy Callaway?

"Now, that's not true."

"No? No? Then why?" She knew she sounded a bit high strung.

"I don't know why." Wyatt's voice came out conflicted, exasperated.

"Exactly."

They stared at each other. They were at an impasse.

"Look," Wyatt said, his voice calmed once again. "Let's just go out there and try to finish dinner."

"I'm not going while she's out there." Katherine looked to the side, determined that Wyatt would not change her mind. It was Katherine or Betsy. Wyatt had to choose.

She sensed Wyatt's eyes on her, but she wouldn't look at him.

After some moments, he threw his hands up in the air. "Very well. Have it your way." Wyatt turned and walked out of the bedroom.

Not long after, Katherine heard their voices. But she couldn't discern what they were saying. Closing her eyes, she prayed Wyatt was telling Betsy to leave. When she heard the front door open, Katherine peered out her doorway. Wyatt's back became visible as he stepped outside.

Katherine came out of her room, but could not escape the feelings swirling through her knowing Wyatt was outside with Betsy. Alone.

Giving the children a once over, she assured herself they were fine. Just covered in potatoes and mashed up carrots. She moved to the kitchen window, unable to stop herself from peeking out onto the front porch.

They were conversing. Betsy reached over and placed a hand on Wyatt's arm. She appeared sympathetic enough, but Katherine knew she was just trying to find a reason to touch Wyatt, to make some kind of move on him. It angered Katherine so much she had to look away.

Why should it matter to her what Wyatt did? This wasn't a real marriage after all. And she already knew what kind of man Wyatt Sullivan was. He was vain and cold and . . . A tear escaped from her eye. Slapping it away, she became determined that she would not shed another tear on the man's behalf.

CHAPTER 11

Tempers

Another day of striking. David did not know what it would all come to, but he had to do what he could. Even though he felt less and less sure as the days went by, he became more and more committed. Whether he wanted to or not.

Maintaining his place in line, he held his sign up. That was all he could do, wasn't it? The men around him did much the same, some were vocal; more were subdued as he was. But they all kept things calm.

Hoofbeats thundered in the distance. His head turned. A sea of blue dotted the horizon. Soldiers. How many were there? At least a couple hundred. David's heart dropped. What could be the meaning of this? Would their strike be put to an end? Would they be attacked?

As they neared, David became more nervous. He saw that the sheriff led the large group. Was that a good thing or a bad thing?

The soldiers came to a stop just short of where the miners were. David eyed the weapons they wielded. This could go wrong rather quickly. He hoped no one did anything stupid.

Calderwood did not seem the slightest bit concerned as he stepped out of line toward the man in the lead, next to the sheriff.

"Excuse me, Officer, I am John Calderwood. I speak for these men. Is there something unlawful about our peaceful assembly?"

"Adjutant General T.J. Tarsney." The man nodded as he introduced himself. "I have come to investigate reports of an out of control mob."

Who had sent for the general? This appeared to be a state militia of sorts. Why were they summoned? Had the mine bosses gone so far as to report them to the governor? Was the sheriff in with them?

"I can assure you that the union members will cooperate with your operation fully. We'll even surrender for arrest if you can find that we have done anything unlawful."

Tarsney looked over at the sheriff. The man had red creeping up into his face. Sliding off his horse, Tarsney walked over to the sheriff and pulled him to the side.

They spoke in hushed tones, but soon the sheriff's voice rose. Though David still could not discern what was being said. When the two men parted, the sheriff was red-faced and appeared to shake. Tarsney's mood seemed no better.

"My apologies, Mr. Calderwood. If I need anything further, where can I find you?"

"I'm at the boarding house in Cripple Creek."

Tarsney nodded before he mounted his steed. "Good day to you, sir. Please, go about your business."

And then he turned his horse and the troops with their guns just left.

But David felt no better about the situation. In fact, the sick feeling in his stomach began to grow.

Katherine stood by a steaming pot. But as hot as the water got, it couldn't match the heat she felt inside. The tightness in her chest had not let up since the night Betsy made dinner. It was horrible, carrying this weight around. Still, she hadn't been able to relieve it. Her hands worked to cut vegetables to add to the stewing mixture.

This was only the second Saturday they'd had together as a family. It had been both draining and elating at the same time. Katherine found she rather enjoyed interacting with the children, not having to worry about the many things that took up their evenings. But it required more energy than she was accustomed to, and Wyatt's presence had put a damper on the whole event.

Currently, Wyatt was putting both of the children down for their naps, and then it would just be the two of them. She filled anew with a rush of anger for his behavior the previous evening. How could he even think what he had done was appropriate? Just then, she heard him moving about in the great room. A glance over her shoulder confirmed that he had indeed returned. What was he doing?

"Ouch!" she said as stinging pain shot through her from her finger. Looking down, she saw blood drizzling. She had managed to make a clean cut with the knife.

"What happened?" Wyatt called out.

"Nothing," she held up her wounded finger to examine how deep the knife had cut. She heard Wyatt come up behind her.

"Let me look at it." Wyatt reached for her hand.

She pushed him back with her shoulder, holding her finger close to herself.

"What is the matter, Katie? Let me see what happened." He attempted to walk around her until he was in front of her, facing her.

"I can take care of it on my own!" She glared up at him, still trying to hide her injury.

"I'm sure you can, but I'm a doctor. This is what I do." He held his hands out again.

Her anger flared. "That's not all you do."

"What is that supposed to mean?"

She grabbed for a nearby kitchen towel and wrapped her hand. Why had she said that? Was she ready to get into all of this?

"Just stop trying to be so perfect. I know you're not." Then she looked down at her hand, unable to meet his eyes.

"Hey, if anyone knows I'm not perfect, it's me."

Her eyes narrowed as she met his gaze again.

"You seem to have this anger toward me for some sin I've committed."

"How can you not know?" She applied pressure to her finger, which still stung.

"Because I don't." His voice was firm.

"It's . . . it's because of Ellie." There, she'd said it.

"Ellie?" His brows came together, his mouth drawn. But his voice was quiet, resigned almost.

Katherine felt a prickling sensation behind her eyes, but held her ground. "You left her behind."

"To save our lives. To save your life." Was it her imagination or did Wyatt raise his voice?

"No." Katherine shook her head, refusing to hear it.

"So, you hold this against me," he said, his voice on edge.

Now the tears were undeniable, but still she fought them. "Why couldn't you help me get Ellie out?"

"Because there was nothing anyone could do for her. Can't you see that?" His voice held a hint of anger. "We escaped with our lives. You should be thanking me!"

"Ha!" was all she could manage.

He took a breath through clenched teeth. "You must believe me that I would never have left Ellie Mae if there had been any hope."

Katherine bit her lip. She wanted to be angry, wanted to fight forgiving him, but her heart told her he spoke the truth.

"And then . . . then . . . " Her voice rose, but she couldn't find the right words, the next grievance.

"Then what, Katie? What?" he challenged.

"And then you invite her into our house." Katherine met his eyes again, raising her chin.

"And you just can't let that go, can you?" He moved closer to her. "What is it? Are you jealous?"

"Certainly not!" She tried to step back, but found the counter was directly behind her.

He stepped even closer, pinning her. "Feel threatened by her?"

She felt more than a little threatened by him in that moment. His body was right up against hers. Her heartbeat quickened, it thundered in her ears. Surely he could hear it.

He looked her over and then met her gaze. "You're trembling. I must've hit pretty close to the mark."

"No," she protested, looking into his eyes, trying to stare him down, wanting to show him she wasn't afraid. But as their eyes locked and their gaze intensified, she felt the fire between them. The burning of their anger and the heat of their unstated attraction.

His lips came down on hers.

Everything in her wanted to resist him, but her body melted into his. Then Wyatt's arms surrounded her, pulling her tightly against him. Her own arms moved as if independent of her will. They wrapped around his strong shoulders, her injured hand resting there and her other hand twisting up into his thick hair. He leaned over her to deepen the kiss.

As much as her body remained caught up in his kisses, something in her mind screamed for her to stop. She had to stop this. Now. She pushed on his shoulders, attempting to move him away from her.

He, too, seemed caught up in the moment. And he resisted at first, continuing to hold her firmly to himself.

But as she continued to push against him, he did pull back, disentangling his limbs from hers.

They both breathed heavily. Katherine leaned against the counter, her knees little more solid than the stew in the pot.

Wyatt backed across the kitchen, running a hand through his hair. "Katie, I . . ."

Still leaning on the counter, she ran her hands over her dress, smoothing the fabric. She found herself unable to meet his eyes.

"I shouldn't have done that," he said, his voice uneven.

She nodded, eyes still on the floor as she hugged her arms close to her chest. Her mind reeled from the rush of emotion and adrenaline coursing through her body. The towel, now only somewhat covering her cut, fell away. And she remembered the wound, still bleeding, still stinging.

Wyatt, too, seemed to return to his senses and remember her injury. Closing the gap between them, he took her hand. Moving her finger this way and that, applying pressure to the sides of the cut, he examined it.

"I don't think it is deep enough to warrant stitches. But, you'll need to keep pressure on it. I'll finish dinner."

"Just wrap it. I can finish up here."

"Please." His eyes softened as they met hers. "Let me help you."

Something changed in her as she searched his eyes. Something had been softening in her since she had come to live with him. Perhaps he was not the man she thought he was. The "vain Wyatt Sullivan" she had imagined him to be. He had proven to be rather kind, considerate, and selfless.

Realizing they had been standing in silence for several moments, she swallowed against a parched throat.

"Perhaps you can wrap it, and we can both work on dinner."

The corners of his mouth turned up and he nodded. "My bandages are just over here." He held up an arm to indicate they should move toward the family room.

Katherine obeyed, all the while wondering what she had just opened the door to.

General Tarsney and his troops had left town. David could breathe much easier. Even though they had found the striking to be lawful that day, he had feared the militia being in town the entirety of their strike. Would the mine owners sway the general with their money? Evidently, they found no reason to stay and had told the governor as much. And no one in town was sad to see them go. Well, almost no one. With the removal of the militia, the mine owners decided to close the mines. It seemed a victory won for the miners.

David and his fellow miners did not have time to celebrate, however, before the sheriff placed Calderwood and eighteen of the miners involved in the assault on his deputies under arrest. What a blow to their movement! To lose their leadership and a number of their fellowship was devastating. What were they to do? The miners were left without a compass, it seemed.

But this was not the day to think on these things. Today was Sunday and the Matthews family joined together for lunch just as they had every weekend. Only this Sunday was different. There were new family members among them.

Jessie huddled close to Mary's skirt, as if nervous about the new man among them. Peter, for his part, didn't act as if anything was different. Jack, having already gotten used to being at the Matthews' homestead, took it upon himself to play his version of host. David found that to be most amusing. The small boy would babble on to anyone who would listen. And Susie seemed content in Katherine's arms.

Meeting his sister's eyes, he noted that she sat off to the side in the great room. Alone. Where had Doc gone? Glancing around the downstairs, he could not spot Doc anywhere. No matter. This would be a great opportunity to share a few words with Katie.

Taking the seat beside her, he nudged her shoulder. She nudged him back.

"How's motherhood treating you?" He looked over at her.

"Fair." She met his gaze, a small smile on her lips.

"And what about Doc?" He raised an eyebrow.

Her face warmed. "We're doing just fine."

"Is that all?" David suppressed a laugh at his sister's obvious discomfort.

"Come on, David. That's not the easiest thing to talk to you about."

"No? I can't imagine why not." He continued to laugh.

She swatted at him.

He raised his hands in the air. "I'm just teasing. I think Doc is a fine fellow. You just surprised everyone is all. But you wouldn't be Katherine the Great if you didn't."

Her eyes narrowed and he noted that her jaw clenched. "You promised."

Ever since they had learned about Catherine the Great in school, he had taunted her with that nickname. And she hated it. But he had promised not to use it again. What had prompted him to do so today?

"You're right, I'm sorry." His voice softened. "You seem to be doing just well. And I'm happy for you."

She became quiet. Maybe too quiet.

"What is it, Katie?"

Shaking her head, she looked away.

He put a hand on her arm. "I truly am sorry that I teased you. I didn't mean to upset you."

"It's not you." She focused on Susie, bouncing her.

"Well then, who is it? Is it Doc? Has he upset you? If he has, I'll..."

Katherine turned to him and laid a hand on his arm then. "No. I don't want you to do anything. It's not like that."

He eyed her. Was she being truthful? Doc seemed nice enough, but everyone knew what his father was like. If he ever raised a hand against Katie, David would ensure he never did it again.

"Honest, David, Wyatt has done nothing to hurt me. I'm just a little worn out."

David relaxed then. Newly married, two young kids, and a teacher . . . he wasn't surprised. "All right. Do I need to remind you to take care of yourself?"

She smiled. "Do I need to remind you?"

He frowned.

"I don't hear good things about the behavior of these miners on strike."

"It depends on who you talk to, I suppose." David focused his eyes forward, leaning his elbows on his knees.

"Is being a part of this strike that important to you? Is it better than swallowing your pride and . . . "

David stood. "I don't want to talk about it."

Katherine closed her mouth then.

"I need some air." He moved away from his sister and toward the door, not caring what Katie might think. Perhaps he was being rude, but he couldn't help it. She had pushed too far. And there were no answers for her. Or for himself.

Wyatt gazed out at the sun as it slowly lowered itself toward the horizon.

"It's good to have you here, Doc," David said, coming up behind him and clapping a hand on his shoulder.

Startled, he soon recovered. "Please, it's just Wyatt."

The men exchanged smiles.

Wyatt had stepped outside in desperate need of space. This whole family atmosphere . . . . it was just too much. They were so happy together. So caring. As nice as it was, he found it suffocating. Not so much the Matthews, but the memories. His parents. It haunted him.

The fights, the beatings . . . his lungs burned as he dragged a breath in. And he hoped David couldn't see how distracted he was.

David nodded. "I never did thank you for your help the other day. With the miner incident."

"Just doing my job," Wyatt said, thankful for something new to focus on. "How is the strike?" He was concerned about David, but his reasons for asking were also for his own benefit. His practice would no doubt continue to be affected by any future incidents.

David shifted his weight from one foot to the other. "It's got its good days and bad days."

Wyatt guessed he just didn't want to talk about it.

"Don't listen to him." It was Tom. He came up behind them. "He narrowly escaped being arrested for being present at that incident as he calls it. I think it's time David got out."

"Pa . . ." David started, turning on his father.

Wyatt tensed at the confrontation he saw coming.

Tom raised his hands in front of him. "Sorry, son. It's just that your Ma and I are awful worried about you."

Wyatt was surprised how Tom's gentle voice had diffused much of the tension.

"I gotta make my own way, Pa." David remained on edge, but his voice was not raised.

"I know you do, son." Tom laid a hand on his shoulder.

Wyatt almost couldn't believe what he had just witnessed. Is this what it was supposed to look like? A father and son? A solid lump formed in his throat as more memories of his own confrontations with his father flashed in his mind's eye.

A moment later, he realized they were standing in silence. So, he swallowed past the large lump and broke the stillness.

"How's the ranch?" He turned toward Tom.

"Good as ever. Cows are healthy and will bring a pretty price at auction time."

"That's good to hear." Wyatt looked out at the horizon, stuck for something else to say.

"How about you, Doc? How's the clinic?" Tom crossed his arms in front of his chest.

Wyatt was grateful for the interest. "Busy. This town needs another doctor. It's just grown so fast, I don't think they've been able to bring in enough of the right professions to fit a town this size. I think we're due our own judge, too, if you ask me."

"Have you brought it up to the town council?" David kicked at the dirt.

"Yes, but getting a judge requires more than a city's desire of it. And getting another doctor . . . well, that's a whole different matter. We have to search for one willing to come out to our town to practice."

"I'm sure it will all work out," Tom assured him.

Wyatt nodded. He wished he had the confidence and faith Mr. Matthews did.

The front door opened behind them and all three men turned in unison. It was Lauren.

"What are you three out here chattering on about?"

"Nothing of any importance," Tom said, smiling at his wife and exchanging a knowing look with both David and Wyatt.

"Well, then y'all won't mind joining us at the table for some food. 'Cause dinner is served." She made her way back into the house without waiting for the men to follow.

But they didn't need her to supervise, they moved into the house as requested. As they stepped into the dining room, taking seats next to their wives, Wyatt took a moment to soak it in. This was his family now. For better or for worse. And the past was in the past.

Katherine smoothed her hands over her long maroon skirt. It was one of her favorites, but she didn't often have cause to wear it. But today was a special day, Founder's Day. And the town hosted a big to-do every year with crafts, games, and excellent food. Even so, Katherine wished the waist wasn't cinched quite so tightly.

Turning this way and that, she admired the creaminess of the shirt fabric in the mirror, how it played against her skin tone and highlighted her chestnut hair, which she had left long for the day, pulling only the sides up. What a ridiculous color to wear on such a busy day! It was sure to be ruined. But she didn't care. Lifting her chin, she decided to be well pleased with the visage before her.

She checked the pins in her hair one last time, stepped out of the bedroom, and moved toward the sounds of Wyatt and the children. Before they were visible, she heard Wyatt telling Jack the history of Cripple Creek in the simplest terms possible. Susie gurgled and squealed along.

Now in the family room, she leaned against the wall, unobserved, to listen as Wyatt finished his tale. Jack did not seem so enthralled, but Wyatt sat near him on the floor as he played and told him nonetheless. Susie, having mastered sitting on her own, chewed on her hand not far away.

Katherine couldn't tear her eyes away from Wyatt. She followed the rise and fall of his voice and marveled, once again, at how gentle his interaction with the children could be. It caused her breath to catch. Why, she did not know. Was it because it reminded her of her own father? Or because of the stories she had heard about Wyatt's father?

Everyone knew the man by reputation. He was the town drunk. And, word had it, that bit by bit he destroyed his family in his drunken stupors. That was all she heard her parents say. As a child, she never understood what that meant. But as an adult, she could only imagine. The thought of what Wyatt must have endured . . . Katherine's heart twisted within her.

Susie noticed Katherine and squealed, causing Wyatt to turn toward her. His eyes widened as they set upon her. He rose to his feet, his movements slow.

"Katie, I . . . " He swallowed hard. "What I mean to say is . . . you are beautiful today."

She blinked at him. That had been an unexpected compliment. And she felt the corners of her mouth turn upward. "Thank you." Her face warmed at his words and at the intensity of his gaze upon her.

"I don't think I . . . rather, it's been a while since I've seen you with your hair down." He still seemed to be searching for words. "In the daytime, that is." Was it just her imagination, or was he blushing too?

"Thank you for getting the children ready." Katherine tore her eyes from his and looked to where Jack and Susie still sat not far from the fireplace.

"Of course." He did not take his eyes off her.

Her eyes met his briefly, then shifted to examine the floor. "Should we, um, get going then?"

"Yes." He jumped into action, seeming to remember they had plans today. "Of course." Wyatt gathered Jack into his arms.

The toddler protested being pulled away from his toys.

"It's okay, Jack-boy," Wyatt soothed. "We're going to go find more fun games. I promise. And we'll get to see Grandma and Grandpa!"

Jack's frustrated whimpers calmed, and he stopped fighting against Wyatt. Once again, Katherine marveled at how easy it was for Wyatt to redirect those tantrums. Would she ever win those battles as easily as he?

She picked up Susie and took the squirming bundle toward the door, followed by Wyatt and Jack. Maybe a little too closely. Katherine felt the heat emanating from Wyatt's body as he reached around her to open the door. It made her a bit light-headed.

Even so, she let him lead her to the cart and, in a matter of minutes, they were hitched to the horses and loaded up. The children secured in the back, Katherine sat next to Wyatt. She was close enough to reach back to Jack and Susie if need be and close enough to Wyatt to be uncomfortable. A few pleasantries were spoken between them on the ride to the churchyard, but she was too caught up in how alive her body seemed to be so near to his. And why that should be.

As they pulled into the yard where the other carts were parked, Katherine attempted to shift her attention from her thoughts of Wyatt to the celebrating townsfolk. Founder's Day had always been one of her favorite holidays growing up. Maybe because of the games and food and crafts. Maybe it was the celebration and sense of community together-ness that was never more keenly felt than today. The town had endured so much these last several months. But today there was no strike, there was no plague, there were no trials of life. There were just the festivities, the fun, and each other.

Katherine searched out her parents. She spotted them by the pie-judging table. Her mother had baked a pie to submit again this year. Lauren had held the first place ribbon the last five years in a row and there was no reason to think she wouldn't take it this year. Tom stood amongst the crowd gathered to watch the judging while her mother was at the table in front of her famous cherry pie.

So distracted, Katherine didn't realize Wyatt stood on her side of the cart, arms raised, waiting to help her down, until he cleared his throat. Turning her body toward him, she held out her arms to set on his shoulders. Then she dropped into his arms easily. Their bodies were so close, almost pressed against each other. He didn't release her right away, but held onto her waist. His eyes were on her lips. Was he going to kiss her again?

Her lips parted to speak, but no words came out.

He grunted and pulled away, moving toward the back of the cart.

She felt cold in that instant, as if all the heat in her body had been drained when he walked away. Her hands crossed her body and rubbed her upper arms. As she watched, Wyatt beckoned Jack to come so he could help him down. Then she moved over to stand next to Jack as Wyatt jumped into the cart to collect Susie.

Without a word, Katherine led them over to where her father stood by the pie table. They arrived in time to hear Mayor Jacobs announce that her mother's pie took the first prize ribbon yet again. Everyone clapped as behind her, the table was cleared of the prize winning pies and replaced with the pies for the pie-eating contest. The mayor announced the next game and one by one, men stepped forward to participate. Pa was among them. At length, all the spaces were filled but one.

"Do we have any other brave souls among us?" Mayor Jacobs asked from his spot behind a pie.

Several people around them began prodding Wyatt to step forward.

"C'mon, Doc, go on up there."

"I've seen you inhale food before, Doc. Give it a try."

At first Wyatt waved them off, uninterested. He glanced over at Katherine.

"Show them what you're made of," she said, winking at him.

He flashed her a smile that made her heart trip in her chest. Then he threw his hands up in surrender and stepped forward to claim the empty place.

Ma stood in front of the row of men and spoke. "Now the rules, gentlemen, are as follows: you must finish the whole pie and you must keep both hands on the table or behind your back." She demonstrated by putting her hands at the small of her back.

The men nodded in unison. Wyatt's eyes sought out Katherine's once more. They seemed to dance with amusement. She wanted to turn away, but found herself unable to.

"Ready, steady, go!" Ma shouted, waving her arm.

Katherine laughed as she watched Wyatt shove his face into the pie.

"Wyatt is quite the character," a voice near her right shoulder spoke.

She turned to see that Timothy had come up behind her. Her smile fell and she suddenly felt awkward.

He stepped closer, coming up beside her. Then he reached toward Susie with a finger that she grabbed and tried to move toward her mouth.

"How has it been with Jack and Susie?" he asked, turning his eyes from Susie to Katherine.

"It's been a learning experience." Katherine saw no reason to lie.

"I can imagine. You look as if you're handling it just fine."

"Most days," she smiled. And things felt easier between her and Timothy.

"You were quite brave," he said, his voice kind. "Taking them on, I mean. Blessed are those who take in orphans and show them love."

"Thank you." She gazed down at Jack by her side and Susie in her arms. They were so much a part of her. Already, they had begun to accept and trust her, and she had grown to love them.

She and Timothy stood in silence for a span of moments. Things that needed to be said hung between them.

"I'm sorry if I hurt you, Timothy," Katherine said, her voice quiet. "That was never something I wanted to do."

He looked down. "I know."

She put a hand on his arm to comfort him.

His eyes met hers. "You know, Katie," he said, his voice not much more than a whisper. "My answer to your proposal that day might have been different had I known the stakes."

Katherine looked away as she pulled her hand back from his arm.

She felt a strange emotion overcome her. Regret? Regret that he had refused her proposal? Or regret that he had said such a thing? It wasn't entirely appropriate.

She decided to try to lighten the mood. "Our story would have had a completely different ending. You might have been stuck with me."

"Yes, I would have," he responded. But though he smiled, his voice was serious. It did not put Katherine at ease.

She turned her attention back to the contest. Pa had been declared the winner, but as her eyes caught Wyatt's, she had a difficult time discerning what she saw there. His jaw set and his eyes stony, he was a mask of discontent. How long had he been watching her talk with Timothy? Whatever brewed in his thoughts, it wasn't pleasant.

David found a place in the picket line. His cohorts were in rare form, much more verbose and rowdy than usual. Their leader and fellow miners had indeed been tried and found not guilty. It validated for many of them that their actions, even the actions they had taken against the deputies that day, were justified. This concerned him.

There were also rumors. Stories about break-ins that were being blamed on the miners. Stores and warehouses ransacked for guns and ammunition. Did David believe it to be his cohorts? He would not doubt that some of these men would go to such extremes.

Sure enough, as the scabs made their way to the mines, the voices of the miners became a roar, taunting them, threatening them. How bold they had become. Once the strikebreakers were close enough, David spotted a stone being hurled from the mob of miners. It couldn't be! The stone did not find a suitable target, landing harmlessly on the ground near a couple of the men in the line. David sent up a prayer of thanksgiving. But it wasn't long before more miners took up rocks to throw at the scabs.

David wanted to yell for them to stop. But he feared they would turn on him, consider him no better than a scab, and exact some manner of violence on him. In that moment, David knew he had been wrong. *What have I allowed myself to become involved with?*

So caught up in his own thoughts, he never saw who threw the first punch, but the next thing he knew a fight had broken out between the miners and scabs. But he wasn't the only miner who hesitated. Those of the miners who were still grounded somewhat went to pull their friends and coworkers off the strikebreakers. It was a nightmare.

Katherine lay Susie down in her crib, humming the last strains of her favorite lullaby. Then she backed out of the room so that the tiny girl could rest in the quiet. She had some picking up to do. After the outing today, the family room was a mess. How could one toddler create such mayhem in one room? Susie wasn't old enough to participate with the toys yet. And she certainly hoped Wyatt wasn't tossing toys around.

She was about halfway through the family room, restoring order, when Wyatt emerged from Jack's room. Without a word, he came alongside Katherine and assisted in the cleanup.

Once that room had been picked up, Katherine moved over to the kitchen sink. The dishes were few, but they needed tending to. Wyatt followed.

"I can manage a few dishes on my own."

"I'm sure you can. Does it bother you for me to help?"

Did he have to be so difficult? "Not at all."

They stood side by side. She washed, he rinsed and dried. As the stack dwindled and Katherine reached for the next dish, she was startled by the feeling of cold water on her stomach.

Looking down, she saw that she had been sprinkled by her partner. Jerking her head to look at him, she pinned him with an accusing glare. Then she reached over to grab the dish. And was sprayed once again.

"I am not in the mood for such silly games." What was he thinking? It was too late for such childishness.

She reached for the dish once again and felt even more cold water upon her front. This time she dipped her hand in the soapy water and splashed him, not caring about spilling water upon the floors. Her efforts were met with success. He had been surprised and well drenched by her swipe. There, that should be the end of it.

He put his large hand in the soapy water and sprayed her. She closed her eyes against the water splashing into her face. Not good. Not good at all.

Eyes glued to his, she splashed him again, using both of her hands to cup the water and went back to scoop more. He grabbed for her hands to halt her. She fought against his grip, now laughing.

Her arms were a bit slippery as they were wet and soapy. She felt them sliding in his hands. In a moment, she would be free.

Wresting her wrists between them, he jerked her to himself. He, too, was grinning and suppressing laughter at their game.

The moment their bodies were pressed against each other, it was no longer a game. Their eyes locked and things became all too serious. His mouth was but a breath away from hers. And it pressed down upon her lips.

When he drew back, he did not apologize, he did not say he regretted the action. He laid his forehead on hers.

"I saw you with Timothy today." Did she hear him right? He kissed her and then spoke of Timothy?

She pulled back from him, but his hands held her body fast against his.

"Has he kissed you?"

Her brows furrowed. She attempted to pull away again. "If you're asking if I've been an unfaithful wife, the answer is 'no.'"

"I mean before."

"What business is that of yours?"

He made a growling sound. "I didn't like what I saw."

"Maybe I don't like that I'm married to the man who left my best friend to die."

His eyes became steel again. The hurt was naked, but they became hard.

How could she have said that? She meant it, but she hadn't meant to say it.

He released her then. So abruptly she almost tripped over her feet as she backed away from him.

"You're still stuck on that, are you?"

She caught herself on the counter. "How can I not be? It haunts me. It wounds me."

"And yet you refuse to remember the whole of it."

What was he talking about? The entirety of the event was seared into her memory. Not one detail was forgotten.

"You say I left Ellie Mae behind. You're wrong. Or you just choose not to remember that I went back in."

Katherine's composure dropped. Her face fell. The tight cords of her memory loosened, and a piece long darkened came to light.

"Yes, that's right. I took Ellie Mae's father back into that mine to bring her out. No one else could do it. So I volunteered."

She closed her eyes as the lost memory came together in her mind's eye. Betsy had refused and Katherine had been too sick with grief. But Wyatt, even with his injury, had stepped up. He hadn't wanted to leave Ellie Mae in there any more than she had. And he didn't. They got her out that same day.

Katherine opened her eyes and looked across the kitchen at Wyatt. His eyes were on the floor. Was he caught in the memory too? What must it have been like to go back in after having barely escaped that horrid, dark place? To help pull out Ellie Mae's lifeless body? With her grieving father?

"Wyatt, I'm sorry, I . . . "

He raised his eyes, but looked away.

"Wyatt, please. Let me just say how I . . . "

"Don't worry yourself. It's done." Then he walked out of the kitchen and back to his bedroom.

Katherine slid down to the floor. How could she have been so wrong?

Timothy finished the last bite of cornbread on his plate. He had been coming to the café more and more these last weeks. Perhaps for company. It became a dire need, it seemed, since . . . well, since Katherine's return from Denver, husband in tow. How he ever survived that shock was beyond him. Was he truly over it now?

Mrs. Abby came by and picked up his plate.

"How was it, Reverend?"

"Delicious as always." He blotted his mouth with his napkin.

Mrs. Abby put a hand on her hip and regarded him with her soft green eyes. "You know I don't like to meddle, Reverend."

How was he supposed to answer that? The truth was she did stick her nose where it didn't belong, often enough that she had a reputation for it. But instead of saying something that would upset her, he decided to remain quiet and wait for her to continue.

"Well, I have been watching you these last few weeks and I must say you are rather dour."

"Dour?"

"Yes. You aren't yourself. And you mope about, eating here alone. Ever since that schoolteacher and Doc eloped. What a scandal that was! Here she was, courting you and then up and runs off with the doc. Shameful."

Timothy looked down at his hands. He did not want to have this conversation. Not because he disagreed, but because of the emotions it stirred in him.

"But there are plenty of eligible ladies right here under your nose. Fine girls of good breeding. I'd be happy to introduce you to a few . . . "

That's when Timothy stopped her. Holding up a hand, he interjected, "I thank you, Mrs. Abby. Truly, I do. But I think I need to focus on my flock right now." He made sure his voice was firm enough that it did not invite further discussion.

Mrs. Abby stared at him for a full ten seconds. Then she shrugged her shoulders. "If you ever change your mind, you know where to find me." Then she sauntered off.

Even after she left, the sting of the wound she had hit on still hurt. Timothy put some money on the table and left the café. He had to get back to the one place he knew he could think things through—the church. Not only was that his place of vocation, it was where he felt the most free to be himself. To share his thoughts and feelings with the One he knew would listen. Except . . . he hadn't been able to pray about his thoughts and feelings surrounding Katherine. Not yet. Maybe because they weren't godly.

When she had shown up that day, storming into the church, and it was revealed she had married Wyatt, it was the first time he had felt such an intense ache in his chest. Worse than when he thought she might die in the typhoid plague. It was as if he was bleeding out on the inside and nothing could be done to staunch the wound. He became bitter and angry. How could he come to God with such intense anger toward someone?

She had betrayed him. He had opened his heart to her, and she had thrown it away. How he ever managed to preach those first couple of Sundays, he did not know.

But as he wallowed in his misery over his broken heart, he began to seek answers for his questions. Why had she done this? And he knew. She had done it for the sake of the children. After all, she had even come to him and asked him to marry her. Katherine had been desperate. That must be the only reason she turned to Wyatt. Not because she loved him.

She didn't. She couldn't.

So he allowed his thoughts to dwell on her again. And he began to have thoughts he shouldn't have about another man's wife. But, her marriage was a sham. A front.

And like any mistake, it could be remedied.

CHAPTER 12

Contention

A crisp, clear day settled upon Cripple Creek. Birds chirped, the flowers were in full bloom, spring was in the air. The world seemed alive and vibrant. This city, however, held its own secrets from the forward progress of nature. For within the boundaries of Colorado Springs, great tension was brewing. Men that cared not of the birds or flowers met to decide the fate of the miners and their strike.

David and his cohorts gathered, waiting with bated breath to hear the outcome of the negotiations. For Calderwood and representatives from the Western Federation of Miners, including the former leader of the Free Coinage Union, all sat at a table with the mine bosses. What would come of it?

The minutes ticked by into an hour, then two.

At long last, one man hushed their chattering. And in the quiet, hoofbeats could be heard. David stood, eager to lay eyes on their leaders as they came forth. Mere minutes passed before Calderwood and his representatives stood before them.

The miners were a roar of questions.

Calderwood raised his hands to quiet them.

"Men, I bring news that you may find unpalatable. They made an unacceptable offer to us."

A myriad of voices called out from around him.

"An offer? What kind of offer?"

"We want to hear the offer."

"Maybe we should have taken it."

"What a crock!"

"Gentlemen," Calderwood called out again, trying to silence the men. "We have refused the offer. I will tell you what I told them. We are not prepared to compromise with the livelihood of so many. You have put everything on the line for their clients. And you agreed to work at a certain rate of pay. For them to now demand you accept anything less is a breach of that verbal contract."

The miners did not respond. Except for some whispered comments here and there.

Not willing to compromise? They would fight for their full pay? Would that ever happen?

"They would not meet us there, and so negotiations ended."

Grumbles and shouts went up from around him. A few men stomped off from the meeting. And David understood. They had put a lot of hope and faith in these negotiations. He had, too. Why were the union leaders not willing to compromise? The miners were at this point. Striking had begun to wear thin and some of them were just as eager for a peace to be found. But they had put their trust in Calderwood and they were bound to his decisions.

David feared it would never end.

Katherine bolted awake. Where was she? As she glanced around her, she saw that she still sat at her desk in the classroom. But it was quite dim. The hour must be late. How could she have fallen asleep? She had been grading papers and laid her head down for just a minute. Rubbing the sleep from her eyes, she looked at the clock. It was past time to get Susie and Jack from her parents' house. Wyatt would probably beat them home, she realized to her dismay. Not only did she prefer to be home first to get the kids settled, it gave her a chance to start dinner. For whatever that was worth.

What was she thinking laying her head down even for a second? It must have been all of the interrupted sleep these last few nights with Susie. Wyatt had been faithful to take a feeding each night, but the children took so much of her energy night and day. And then she had to continue to give the school children everything she could. She sighed. No wonder she passed out on her desk.

Still, the fact remained that she needed to get to the livery, collect her horse and cart, and get to her parents' house. So, she gathered her things and made her way out into town. She became a little uneasy as she moved through the streets of the town. The saloons were quite rowdy, but she would only have to pass one. For that, she was most grateful.

As she walked by the saloon, she made sure to stay on the opposite side of the street, hoping to avoid notice. But two men stood outside the saloon. They glanced over at her.

She picked up her pace. But she sensed more than heard them cross the street and take up step behind her. Were they just walking the same direction she was? Or were they following her?

Katherine pushed her pace even faster.

They matched her steps.

Panic filled her. Where could she go? The livery was too far away. Her mind spun. Should she call for help? Who would hear her?

Then a thought struck her. Maybe she could make it to the clinic. Perhaps Wyatt was still there. But it was on the other side of the main stretch. She would have to turn down the alley up ahead. And the idea of going down the dark alley with these men in tow did not appeal to her. Although, if they were after her, it was her only chance.

Grabbing at her skirts, Katherine took off in a run. She heard the men behind her break into a run as well. Turning suddenly to the left toward the alley that would take her down her short cut to the clinic, the sound of the men drew closer. They were just behind her!

"Help!" she screamed. "Help me!"

Her cries were cut off as one of the men grabbed her. Then her back hit the wall of one of the buildings lining the alley. Hard. A firm hand clamped on her mouth.

Katherine's eyes sought the faces of her attackers, but much of their features were shadowed by the darkness of the hour and the alley.

"I'm going to move my hand. Don't scream," the man's gruff voice said.

The hand was removed and she cried out. He backhanded her. Heat exploded across her face and the ground rushed to meet her. She just caught herself with her hands. They stung from the impact.

Rough hands jerked her back to a standing position.

She cried out in pain.

The hand clamped on her mouth again. Only this time, with more force. She felt as if her teeth were cutting into the inside of her mouth.

"Do we understand each other now?" the first man asked, giving her head a jerk. The back of her head hit the hard wood of the building behind her.

She nodded, tasting blood in her mouth.

He slowly removed his hand.

She remained silent, her mind whirling, trying to come up with some sort of plan. How was she going to get out of this?

The man in front of her started moving his hands over her. "Where is your coin purse?"

"I . . . I don't carry one." She prayed that was all they were after.

"What?" He sounded angry.

She became afraid he would hit her again. "I'm the teacher. I don't carry one."

He cursed, taking his hands off her and moving a step back.

"Maybe it's not all for nothing," his friend said, stepping closer to her from his position off to the right. He trailed a finger down the side of Katherine's face, leaning in closer to her. His breath was hot on her face.

The first man turned toward his friend, but did not move or speak.

"Please," Katherine pled with the first man, hoping he would be reasonable. "Please don't do this."

"Oh, believe me, the begging has just begun," the second man said, pulling her tightly against himself.

Katherine squirmed in his arms.

A shot rang out, hitting the wall above their heads. The men put their hands up. Katherine almost fell, but caught herself, sagging against the wall for support. Her head jerked in the direction of where the shot had come from. A figure was silhouetted in the darkness, but stepped closer, coming into a strip of moonlight. It was Wyatt! She could have cried she was so relieved.

Wyatt held his gun trained on the two men. Jerking it to the left, he indicated that the man still a breath from her should move farther away and closer to his partner. He then held out his free arm for Katherine to come to him. Bruised, battered, and weak-kneed, she threw herself at him, falling on him more than anything else.

He began to back out of the alley, keeping the gun on the two men. Katherine tried her best to walk along with him, but found it hard to get her footing. Together, they moved out of the alley.

Once they were clear, Wyatt's voice was in her ear. "Run!" he said in a harsh whisper.

He pulled her along with him as he made his way to the clinic. Once they were safely inside, he locked and barred the door. Then Wyatt stood vigil with his weapon at the ready.

Katherine watched him, wide-eyed, trembling from her place next to the exam table. Were they safe yet?

David sat on the porch next to Mary. The children had been tucked in and all seemed at peace with the world. Only it wasn't. Not truly. For tomorrow would be another day of striking. It would go on and on with no clear end in sight.

Wrapping an arm around Mary, he cleared his mind and drew her closer. She leaned into him, resting a hand on his chest. He kissed the top of her head.

Here, at his home, there was no strike; there was no contention. But that wasn't quite true either. For he carried it inside him, wearing his troubles wherever he went. How could Mary not be affected by it? Or his children not sense it?

He sighed. "Mary, I think we need to talk."

Hoof beats and a horse whinnying cut him off. Someone approached the homestead. And fast. Should he get his gun? He hated being on alert and on the lookout for every intrusion to be unfriendly. Would he rather his conscience be clear or his family unharmed?

He stood and went for his gun.

When he emerged from the house, the rider was near. As he approached, David saw that it was his friend, Jonas.

As Jonas slowed, David came off the porch to greet him.

"Good evening, Jonas, what has you out and about so late? And in such a hurry?"

"My sister." Jonas breathed heavily, well exerted from his ride.

"Your sister? Is she well?" Why would he not seek out Wyatt?

"My sister works as a maid at a hotel in Colorado Springs." Jonas managed to get out.

David furrowed his brow, hopeful there would be more forthcoming.

"She overheard the mine bosses meeting with the sheriff."

"Our mine bosses? In Colorado Springs?"

Jonas nodded. "Yeah. Hagerman, Smith, and Moffat."

"Why would they meet in Colorado Springs?"

Jonas raised an eyebrow. "Why else?"

The hotel in Colorado Springs might have better accommodations, but it was a short trip over there. And the sheriff would need to trouble himself to sneak away. Why would they do so? Unless . . . unless they didn't want anyone to find out.

"What did she hear?" David's eyes were glued to Jonas.

"The mine bosses are intent on bringing in hundreds of nonunion workers and they told the sheriff they would fund a hundred deputies to protect their men."

"They're raising a small army." David felt the color draining from his face. What could they do against such a force?

Jonas nodded.

"We must tell Calderwood at once." He turned to Mary.

She nodded. "Go."

He pressed a kiss to the side of her face, handed his weapon to her, and raced off after his horse. Who knew what would come of it, but they would do what they could. Perhaps this would bring an end to the strike once and for all.

Several minutes later, Wyatt set his gun down and turned toward Katherine. "I guess those miscreants decided they were done for the evening."

He then found his way to Katherine, who leaned against the exam table in the middle of the room. "Are you all right?"

She nodded, sniffling.

"Can you manage to get on the exam table?"

Shifting, she worked her way up, but a whimper escaped her as she did so.

It gave him pause and filled him with concern. Were there internal injuries? He turned on a lantern so he could examine her. He brought the light near her face.

"Katie!" He grabbed a cloth to wipe away some of the blood that had trailed out of her mouth. One side of her face was swollen and would be bruised the next day. *What else had they done to her?* Anger boiled inside him as he continued his examination.

His eyes and hands moved swiftly over her body. Nothing seemed out of place. She grimaced as his fingers touched the back of her head and her arms. His hands shook as the ferocity of his ire filled him, and he imagined confronting the men once more. As his hands moved down her arms and he began to study her hands for cuts or abrasions, he realized that she trembled.

Setting the cloth down, he drew her into his arms. "It's all right. You're safe."

She slid off the table, clinging to him as the tears came.

The urge to hold her tighter was almost irresistible. But he forced himself to be gentle. As she cried, he stroked her hair, pressing kisses to the top of her head. "I'm here, Katie. I won't let you go." How he was able to be so tender with the intense anger inside him, he did not understand.

After some time, she pulled back, wiping the tears from her eyes. "How...how did you know?"

His arms ached to hold her just a little bit longer, but he relented, leaning against the exam table next to her. "When I went to the livery to pick up my horse, I saw that your horse and cart were still there. So, I went looking for you. I was walking down Main Street when I heard your screams."

She nodded, her tears now dried. "What are we going to do?"

Wyatt picked up his pistol. "Head home . . . carefully."

Katherine sniffled.

Wyatt feared she would start crying again, but it seemed to be the last bits of her gathering herself.

"I am ready." She turned to face him. Her green eyes wide, alert.

He offered her a smile. "Stay close."

She came up behind him as he placed a hand on the door to open it. They then made their way to the livery, all the while stealing glances behind themselves to ensure no one was trying to sneak up on them.

Wyatt first helped her into the wagon, and then climbed up to sit next to her.

Katherine looked at him strangely.

"We'll get my horse tomorrow," he said.

As they rode out of town, Wyatt felt relieved though his anger had not dissipated. He wished he had done more to those men who dared to threaten and lay hands on his Katherine. The muscles in his arms stiffened as he thought of what he would do if he could get his hands on them.

"I'm sorry I caused such trouble for you tonight." Katherine's voice was timid, small somehow.

Wyatt pulled himself from his murderous thoughts to focus on her. "No, Katie. It wasn't your fault."

"I know better than to be out on the streets so late unescorted. This is not the town we knew as children." She sniffed, but no tears came.

Wyatt frowned and looked ahead. She may have taken an unnecessary risk, but that did not mean she was to blame for what happened.

"I fell asleep grading papers."

Wyatt glanced over at her again, eyebrow quirked.

"It was senseless, I know." She didn't seem to be able to meet his eyes, her green orbs darting this way and that, before turning away from him altogether. "I've just been so tired of late."

He fixed his eyes on the road. She had been doing most of the night feedings. And Susie was in her room. Katherine probably stirred every time Susie made a sound. Then there was the amount of energy she had to put in to each day, both for their children and for the school children. It was just too much for one person. What could be done to remedy that?

There didn't seem to be much time to think on it as they were fast approaching the Matthews' homestead. Wyatt wanted to leave Katherine in the cart and gather the children himself, but that would only worry her parents. So, he helped her down. The grimace on her face as she released her weight into his hands did not escape him.

She glanced about. Was she fearful that even here, at her parents' homestead, she was unsafe? He reached for her hand and drew her closer. It had been meant to make her feel safer, but the closeness of their bodies flooded him with sensations of a different kind. Why should he be having such thoughts? And after what she'd been through?

They stood at the door and he raised a hand to knock. How would her parents react? Would they be angered as he was? Would her mother fall apart? He didn't know if he could handle two crying women.

Tom answered the door, light spilling out onto the porch as the inside illuminated the darkness beyond.

"We were starting to worry . . . " he began. But his eyes landed on Katherine. And though her face was downturned, it did nothing to disguise the early evidence of bruises. Tom's face fell.

"We're all right," Wyatt was quick to say. "Everyone is all right."

"What has happened?" Tom said, his voice soft, but firm and demanding all the same.

Lauren stepped up behind her husband, holding Susie in her arms.

Katherine raised her eyes to meet her mother's.

"Katie? What's happened to you?" her mother's features contorted. Brows furrowed, mouth opened. She raised a hand to her lips as if to contain further outcries.

She was going to fall apart. One glance over at Katherine and Wyatt saw his fears coming true. Pretty soon they would have two crying women on their hands. He needed to quell these out of control emotions soon.

Still holding Katherine's hand, he drew it across his body, so he could clasp it between both hands. "As you see, Mrs. Matthews, Katie is well. There is no cause for worry. We will explain everything."

Tom moved out of the doorway. Did he bid them enter? "We want to hear everything."

Wyatt and Katherine stepped into the house. He sensed more than felt that Katherine had started shaking again. Putting an arm around her, he attempted to soothe her fears. But it seemed to do nothing to assuage her.

Lauren stood back, eyes locked on Katherine's face. Susie started crying, but Lauren didn't respond even to that. Wyatt sat Katherine in one of the more comfortable chairs in the family room and moved over to Lauren, relieving her of the squalling bundle. He bounced Susie lightly. That worked to calm her.

Tom had drawn Lauren over to sit near Katherine, his hand on his wife's shoulder. Katherine sat, hands clasped tightly in her lap, drained of all color. Wyatt pulled a dining room chair over next to Katherine and sat beside her.

Then he met Tom and Lauren's eyes. How was he supposed to tell them about the events of the evening? It would serve him best to just be straightforward.

"Katherine was attacked this evening."

Lauren gasped, clutching her chest. Tom's expression displayed his concern, but his hands remained on his wife's shoulders.

"Two men followed her from the saloon."

"What did they . . . ? How did they . . . ? What did they want?" Lauren's voice trembled as she spoke.

"My coin purse." Katherine's voice was stronger than he would have expected.

Wyatt glanced over at her. That was certainly not what he saw. Had she lied to spare her mother's sensitivities and worries? Lauren did appear somewhat relieved.

"Are you . . . badly hurt?" Lauren's eyes became glassy.

"Nothing Dr. Sullivan can't take care of." Katherine looked over at him. He could not conjure a smile for her. Not tonight.

Lauren's shoulders relaxed. And though a tear escaped, no more followed.

"I think the best thing for Katherine is to get her back to her own bed." Wyatt spoke up.

Lauren and Tom nodded. Had he expected them to argue? To insist that they remain there?

Tom stepped forward as Wyatt helped Katherine to her feet. He embraced his daughter, saying something too softly for Wyatt to discern.

Next Lauren stepped in and hugged Katherine to herself. "I'm glad you are safe . . . " She continued speaking, but Tom stepped over to Wyatt, cutting off his ability to hear more of Lauren's interaction with Katherine.

"We're real thankful for you taking such good care of our Katie." He clapped Wyatt on the back.

Wyatt nodded at Tom, but looked over at Katherine and her mother as they held each other.

"I would do much more for her," he said absently. The words came out before he could stop them.

When he caught Tom's eyes again, he saw the kind appreciation there. It warmed him. His father never looked at him like that.

"It will not happen again." Whether or not Wyatt could truly promise that, he would do everything he could to ensure that this was the last time it did.

Katherine stepped over to where they stood just then, a small smile on her face. Soon enough, Lauren nudged Tom and urged him to get Jack from where they had laid him down in David's old room.

And so, moments later, Wyatt and Katherine were on their way to their own house, Jack and Susie in the back of the cart.

Once they arrived, Wyatt did everything he could to return them to their normal evening routine. With one exception: he insisted Katherine rest in one of the family room chairs even if she must help with Susie.

Jack had awakened on the ride home and insisted on a story, so Wyatt busied himself getting Jack into his bed and rushing through the bedtime story. But Jack was tired and precious little was required of Wyatt to send him off to dreamland.

As he came out into the hall, he spotted Katherine carrying a drowsy Susie into their shared room. But Wyatt stopped her.

"I think it's time to move the cradle to Susie's new room." He met

Katherine's eyes and held them. Susie's room had been completed for some time now, but Katherine had been resistant to moving her.

Even then, Katherine opened her mouth to protest.

"I know you don't want to, but I think she will sleep better. Perhaps even wake less. And I know you will sleep better. Please, trust me on this."

Katherine looked down at the sleeping child in her arms. Then she nodded reluctantly.

Stepping around her, Wyatt went into the bedroom Katherine and Susie shared to gather the crib. Then he walked it down the hallway into Susie's new room. He had expected Katherine to follow him. But when he stood up, he discovered she had not. So, he went back out to find her still rooted to the spot, swaying with Susie in her arms.

He watched the two of them for a handful of moments. The picture they made tugged at his heart. Wasn't this everything he wanted in a family? But something nagged at him and he knew, this wasn't quite what he wanted. No, he wanted, needed Katherine, his wife, to return his affection. And it was still a mystery to him where her heart lay. How could it not be? Wyatt didn't know where his heart was.

Katherine looked up and caught his eyes. They exchanged a meaningful gaze. One that warmed him. Then he stepped forward and slid an arm around her back to lead her toward Susie's bedroom, where they put Susie down together.

As they slipped out of the room, Wyatt noticed Katherine brush a tear away. She had been through much this evening. He put an arm around her shoulders in an attempt to comfort her.

"It'll be fine. Trust me."

She sniffed back more tears as he led her back toward her room. Pausing at the doorway, Katherine peered into the darkness beyond. It seemed her mind was turning. Was she thinking about the events of the evening? Of course she was. And now he had asked her to sleep alone, without even Susie's steady breathing to keep her company.

"Hey," Wyatt said, keeping his tone soft and reaching out with tentative fingers to touch her face. "Are you all right?"

She nodded, looking up at him. Their eyes locked. He didn't know how long they remained like that, but she leaned into him, pressing her lips to his. And he responded to her, moving his arms to pull her closer.

When she tilted her head, allowing him to deepen the kiss as her hands moved up the front of his shirt, it nearly drove him mad. His hands were on her back, pressing her body to his. Then his hands were in her hair, unpinning the tresses so they spilled down her back.

Wyatt pulled back slightly to look into her eyes. They were bright and eager, inviting. His mouth melted to hers again.

He wanted to slow down, but there was an urgency in him that wouldn't allow it. She filled his senses and he was overtaken. Leaning over her, he bent down and swept her off her feet and into his arms. One of her arms flung around his shoulder, her hand exploring the muscles there.

A few paces took them into her bedroom and he laid her on the cushion of the bed, breaking contact. Then he leaned over her, searching her face for any hint he should stop. His mind screamed for him to. Something wasn't right about this. But she wrapped her arms around his shoulders and pulled him back down to continue their kisses.

How could any hot-blooded man resist? He swept kisses across both cheeks and then leaned over to nuzzle the side of her neck. She made a small sound.

His hands, almost as if acting of their own accord, moved between them to begin unbuttoning her dress. Then he felt her hands on his shirt collar. Once there was a significant V opening, she slid a hand over his smooth flesh. He halted his work on her dress, surprised at her caresses.

Leaning down once again, he claimed her sweet lips. When he pulled back, he saw tears in her eyes. He wiped them away and kissed the trails where they had been before pressing another, deeper kiss to her lips. Their kisses soon became more fevered, hungrier, and hands began to work on divesting each other of clothing again.

In that moment, Wyatt was struck. This wasn't right. Did he have the power to stop himself? He had to. For Katherine. She deserved better. So, he placed his hands on either side of her head and pulled away, his breaths labored.

"I can't do this," he panted.

When he did chance a glance at Katherine, he saw that she stared up at him, wide-eyed, and he knew she was confused. And hurt. But he couldn't deal with that now. It was taking all he had to pull away.

He dragged himself off her and stepped to the other side of the room, turning his back to her as he leaned against the wall.

"Katie, I'm sorry . . . I'm sorry . . . " He kept repeating those words as he was kicking himself inside. How could he have been so selfish? After what she'd been through, then for him to take advantage of her. She was innocent and trusting, and he was a monster.

He heard Katherine sniffling behind him, and there was no doubt she was crying. Placing his back firmly against the wall, he glanced back in the dimness of the room to see her pulling at her dress, trying to cover herself. She rolled away so that her back was to him and her form shook with sobs. Did she think he didn't want her? It took all he had not to go to her, wrap her in his embrace, and comfort her. But he had to be strong. Wyatt knew where that would lead.

"Katie, I . . . " he started, but the sentence trailed off. What could he say?

"Just go," came her whispered, almost breathless response.

His head dropped, and he backed out of the doorway, closing the door behind himself. But he couldn't make himself go any further. So, he slid down the door to the floor. And tortured himself with the sounds of her sobbing.

It was a grim day. Nothing good could come from the happenings of this day. The miners, having heard about the meeting between the sheriff and the mine owners to raise an army of deputies, were arming themselves to create their own army. David looked at his own firearm.

I cannot be a part of this!

But yet he was.

A hush fell over the crowd of miners as Calderwood began speaking.

" . . . must go to raise funds for our cause! But I leave you in the capable hands of former United States Army officer Junius J. Johnson!"

Another man stepped forward. His features were hard, and his jaw set in place. It was clear he had seen battle and his share of war. But was he prepared to rally this collection of rapscallions into a group of troops? That became all the more clear as he started to speak.

"We find ourselves in a hard place. A place in which our livelihood is being attacked, in which our lives are being threatened. And how we react will determine what kind of men we are. We are only as strong as our weakest link. Woe is it to the man who is found to be that link. For he will have to answer to me!

"We shall go from here to Bull Hill where we shall build up fortifications in preparation for whatever may come from the enemy. If you are not with us, you are against us. And you'd best leave now, for there is no place for you among us. So, who is with me?"

A cry went out from all of the miners who also raised their weapons to show solidarity with Johnson. Not one of them wanted to be found to be a strikebreaker. Not even David.

CHAPTER 13

Danger

Lauren took a sip of coffee, glancing over the rim of her cup at Mary across the table. The younger woman watched her children playing in the family room beyond the dining area, but that's not where her mind was. No, she had been quite preoccupied these last few days. And it wasn't difficult to guess what had her so distracted. It had to be the goings on at the mines.

Thoughts of what may be happening bothered Lauren, too. She worried after her son's well being. While she didn't watch him walk away from her each day to join the picket lines, she knew he went. And she spent many hours just as concerned. Especially with all this talk of fighting and violence. What would it all come to?

Tearing herself from these thoughts, she shifted her focus back to her daughter-in-law.

"Mary, dear, you're awful quiet," Lauren said, setting down her cup and laying a hand on Mary's arm.

Turning her head to meet her mother-in-law's gaze, Mary remained silent. Only then did Lauren see the tear that had formed and was even then falling down her face.

"Oh, Mary, I know how you feel!" Lauren dug for a handkerchief. "But rest assured, that man is made of strong stuff. He comes from a long line of stubborn men. Much too stubborn to let something like this get him down." Finally laying a hand to a handkerchief, she surrendered it to Mary.

Mary nodded. "I know. It's just . . . I just . . . "

"There, there," Lauren patted her hand.

Mary blotted her eyes for a moment and took a deep breath. Then she seemed able to gather her composure. "Thank you," she smiled. "Unfortunate for you, it seems Katherine inherited that stubborn streak, too."

Mary was attempting to change the subject. Lauren allowed it. "Don't I know it!"

"And now Wyatt will be stuck figuring out how to navigate that stubborn streak."

Both women laughed.

"Wyatt is a good man," Lauren said. "I just . . . " She stopped herself, her eyes flitting over to Mary's and then away again. "I best not say such things."

"You wonder if he's good for Katherine?" Mary prodded.

Lauren bit her lip and nodded. This, too, had weighed heavy on her heart these last weeks.

"I think there's more going on there than they would like anyone to believe," Mary said.

"Be assured of that." Lauren had seen enough of the stolen glances between the two to know better. They may not even be aware themselves.

"But you wonder if it's made of the stuff that will last?"

Lauren nodded. "And keep them both happy as long as they both shall live."

Lauren returned to her coffee. Both of her beloved children faced many challenges. If only she could step in and fix everything as she did when they were schoolchildren. But no more. They were on their own. They had to find their own way.

Wyatt flipped through the pages of the latest medical publication, but he had read the same article at least three times. His mind just wasn't on his work lately. It hadn't been for a couple of days now. Things were still a bit awkward between him and Katherine. And he didn't like it one bit. Their near miss haunted him. That night, their kisses, and what had almost happened between them.

Had he made the right decision? Deep down, he knew he had. There was still so much that needed to be said between them. Things that were unclear, muddied by their past.

A tap on the window of the door drew his attention. The curtains blocked much of his view, but it was about time for Katherine and the children to come by for their dinner plans. A smile pulled at his features. Though things were a bit rough between them, he still relished every moment with her. Perhaps somehow he could help her understand what was going on in his heart.

He gathered his medical bag and moved toward the door. But as he opened it, he came face-to-face with Betsy Callaway.

"Betsy!" he said, taken aback. He glanced around her to see if he could spot Katherine or the wagon nearby. "How can I help you?"

She pushed past him and into the clinic.

"I have a little burn on my hand," she said, holding out her arm toward him.

She did seem to have her hand wrapped. He closed the door behind her, set down his things, and followed her to the exam table.

Betsy hopped up with ease, keeping her hand out for him to unwrap.

He did so carefully, not wanting to cause her burned flesh any discomfort. Once he had the cloth off, he saw what she was referring to —a slightly reddened patch of skin that might not even blister, the burn was so mild. But she was his patient and he would do his due diligence.

"How did you incur this injury?"

"Slaving over a hot stove," she leaned toward him, smiling.

"Of course," he returned her smile. "Are you in any pain?"

"Not at the moment," she said, her voice low.

"I have some salve I can give you to administer should you have any discomfort." He moved across the room to his cabinet of medicines and pulled out a small canister. Bringing it back to the table, he held it out for her.

"Would you mind, Doctor, showing me how to put it on?" Her face was tilted and he thought he saw her wink at him. Probably his imagination.

"It's quite simple." He opened the canister and dipped two of his fingers in the salve. "Just get a little on your fingers like this . . . " Then he held her hand in his while he rubbed the salve on the wound.

She leaned in even more as if to watch him rub on the salve more clearly. Their faces were mere inches apart. "I see, Doctor. Ah, that feels better."

Wyatt's face warmed a bit, and he began to feel uncomfortable with her closeness. He prepared to step away when she closed the distance between them and kissed him. So taken by surprise, he didn't know how to respond at first. But he soon pulled away, having gathered his wits about him. And he took a full step back from her.

"I am a married man," was all he could think to say.

"I know," she said, tilting her face down, gazing at him through her eyelashes. "But it's a sham marriage. Everyone knows that. You don't love her."

Wyatt's heart was racing. Was Betsy right? Her words felt wrong to him.

"Look, Betsy, if I have done or said anything that led you on, I apologize, but I cannot be involved in this."

Betsy shrugged. "You'll come around," she said as she got down off of the table. "But I won't wait forever." She moved to leave the clinic.

He picked up the small canister she had left behind. "You forgot your salve."

She looked back over her shoulder as she opened the door. "Don't need it," she said as she winked at him. Then she was gone.

Wyatt stood rooted to the spot. Had he truly just fallen for Betsy's scheme? How long had she been working him? And Katherine had seen it the whole time. Katherine!

She should have been here by now. Did she see? He hoped not. Stepping outside the clinic, he saw a cart carrying a dark-haired woman, a young boy who looked like Jack, and a basket. It had to be Katherine! But where was she going? They were supposed to meet here. He closed the clinic doors, hopped on his horse, and went after her.

Katherine gathered Jack and Susie, setting them securely in the cart for the trip from her parents' house to the clinic. Wyatt had suggested they eat in the boarding house café this evening and his timing couldn't have been better. It had been a long week for her, and a night with someone else cooking and cleaning the dishes sounded like heaven.

It wasn't long before they pulled up to the clinic. Katherine hopped down, telling Jack to stay put. She need not unload the children, after all. A simple knock on the clinic door to summon Wyatt while she kept a careful eye on Jack and Susie would be all that was necessary.

As she neared the clinic door, she caught sight of movement between the curtains. Her heart dropped. There, in the middle of the room, were Wyatt and Betsy . . . kissing. Katherine turned away.

It all made sense. The other night when he pulled away . . . How could he want her if he was in love with someone like Betsy? She was beautiful and graceful and . . . *everything I'm not.* Katherine's heart sank deeper into her stomach. What was she going to do? Stand out here with her and Wyatt's children until his and Betsy's romantic interlude was over? No, she couldn't bear to see Wyatt right now.

Though her vision blurred, she jumped back into the cart and encouraged the horse to go. Where to, she did not know. All that existed was this ache in her chest. And it was exploding.

Moments later, she heard hoofbeats trailing behind her cart. Rapid. Closing in. It had to be Wyatt, but she didn't stop. How could she face him?

"Katherine!" she heard him call out for her. "Katherine!"

He would catch up. It would behoove her to slow the cart. So she pulled on the reins and took the few seconds she had to wipe away her errant tears before Wyatt pulled up alongside the cart.

"Katherine, where are you going?" came his breathless question.

"The children are tired. I thought we might just go home." She kept her eyes facing forward, avoiding his.

"Home? Taking the scenic route?"

Only then did she realize she was going in the opposite direction of Wyatt's homestead. She looked down at her lap, but didn't say anything.

"We'll have to feed everyone at home. So, why don't we just head back into town and eat at the café as planned. They'll get fed faster, I think."

Katherine wanted to refuse. But she couldn't find any logical argument on which to base her reasoning. She knew he was right. So she nodded.

"I could tie Rusty here to the back of the wagon and drive if you'd like," he offered.

"No, I'm quite fine, thank you," she said before urging the cart's horse forward, leaving Wyatt in her dust.

What must he think of her actions? She was acting like a child. But the pain was real. And she felt raw and vulnerable. So, she had no choice but to harden herself. Only then did she stand a chance of making it through this dinner, this evening, this marriage.

Wyatt watched Katherine's back as she walked down the hall. What was going on in that mind of hers? She had been quiet during dinner. Too quiet. Standoffish almost. How had she become more so since the other evening? Things had been awkward, yes. But hostile?

She had not been that way for weeks. Since he had reminded her of the truth about Ellie Mae. Why did they break down walls just to build them up again? Was there any hope for the two of them? Was he willing to fight for it?

He continued to stand in the hallway just outside of Jack's room, waiting for her to finish putting Susie down. She did emerge moments later, but when her eyes met his, she let out a loud sigh and moved past him.

"I don't have time for this tonight."

Didn't have time? She moved toward her bedroom, but he stopped her at the doorway, catching her arm to halt her. "Then make time."

Pulling against him to free her arm, she shot him a mean look. "Let me go, Wyatt."

"Not until you talk to me." He stepped closer to her.

She backed up, hitting the doorframe with her hip. A grimace crossed over her features.

"Why do you fight me so?" He softened his voice and gazed into her eyes.

When she looked at him again, there was something different in her eyes. Sadness? Hurt? Why?

"Please, Katie. Tell me."

She turned away from him, pulling her arm free from his loosened grasp, but she did not escape into the dark recesses of her room.

He laid a hand on her shoulder, but she jerked away.

The words were on the tip of his tongue. He wanted to ask if he'd hurt her. But he knew he had. That night after she'd been attacked . . . What had he been thinking? By the time he'd had the good sense to stop himself, the damage had been done.

"I'm sorry, Katie. I didn't mean to hurt you. You must understand, I . . ."

"Then why play games with me?" she shot at him over her shoulder.

Katherine wasn't wrong. From where she stood, it must look as though he led her on only to put her off.

"That was never my intention. I . . . "

She spun on him then. "Never your intention? You married me. And then you played house with me. All the time you kept her on the side. Why? Why didn't you just marry her to begin with? I don't understand." Katherine leaned her head back, looking up at the ceiling.

What? Played house? Marry whom? He didn't understand. Unless... unless she meant Betsy. Unless she had seen Betsy's stolen kiss.

Katherine straightened her head, but turned to look toward her room. Did she want to get away from him?

"What did you see in the clinic?" He wanted her to say it. To confess it.

"What does it matter?" She crossed her arms in front of her chest and glared at him.

"How could you believe that? After all we've been through, you would think so lowly of me?"

She shook her head, sniffling, as she turned her gaze back toward the darkness.

"It was not what you think."

Her eyes were on his then. One eyebrow arched. She didn't believe him.

"Betsy came to the clinic. And then she kissed me."

Katherine did not look away. But her eyes did not soften.

"I stopped it, Katie. Honest."

She looked at the floor then, examining the toes of her shoes.

If she wasn't going to believe him, maybe it didn't matter. Maybe this was all for nothing. "If you don't care, maybe I don't either."

Her eyes met his again. But he turned away and moved toward the door. She started to say something, but it was cut off by the slamming of the door as he walked out into the night.

David marveled at how Junius J. Johnson worked the miners as if they were a military unit. As soon as they set up fortifications, Johnson had a commissary stocked and began drilling the miners in maneuvers. Clearly, the man was built for army life and treated the miners as if they were nothing more than a new unit under his command. And it worked.

Their first victory had been to take the mine on Battle Mountain. They did so without any resistance as there was no one to fight. Still, they knew the mine owners and their army were due any day.

Why hadn't he gotten out of this mess when he'd had the chance? In those early days of the strike. He could have slipped out, anonymously for the most part, and joined his father's ranch hands. Things would have been so much simpler. But here he was, away from his family, stuck in the miners' encampment on Bull Hill in some kind of made up war.

At that moment, Jonas rushed past him. "It's happening!"

"What's happening?" David had no choice but to follow the small crowd of miners. Anxiety filled him, but he waited until he could see around the agitated, shifting bodies in front of him as he came to the edge of their lookout. His heart stopped. There, at the base of Bull Hill, a large contingency of deputies, over a hundred, marched toward the miner's camp.

Johnson's voice called from somewhere behind them, barking out instructions. The men rushed to their lines.

"We have a plan. Stand your ground," Johnson commanded them.

David only knew part of the plan. It had to do with the miners at the captured Strong mine. They had been given explosives. What for, he did not know.

A loud *boom* sounded across the area. The miners hit the ground, covering their heads. David jerked his body in the direction of the sound in time to see the Strong mine's shaft house hurled into the air. He didn't have time to recover from his shock before the steam boiler blew. Had someone blasted it with dynamite? As David watched, wood, metal, and cable fell down upon the deputies, who, in turn, rushed toward the nearby rail station.

The miners went wild with celebration of their newfound victory. Johnson continued to give orders, attempting to stay the men, but it became more than he could contain. All Johnson and David could do was look on as a group of miners ran into the town. Exchanging a look with Johnson, David wished he had the courage to assist in rounding up the crazed miners, but he held back, fearful for his own safety.

He stood by as Cripple Creek became the playground of the miners. They broke into liquor warehouses and saloons. Eventually, shop-keepers were roused by the sounds of destruction and ran the miners out of their shops. The men then converged on the saloons.

As the miners carried on with their drinking, they roared with excitement. Some of the men wanted to keep going and blow up all the mines in the region. Johnson, now present and in command again, was able to stop that action. But the wake of their rampage would be unde-niable when people came into town the next day. This certainly wouldn't help their cause.

Pounding on the door echoed in the house. It dragged Wyatt from a sound sleep. His first thought was to grab for his firearm just over the door. Lifting the weapon from its perch and ensuring it was loaded, he felt reassured by the cold metal against his palms. He moved into the great room to find Katherine wide-eyed and clearly scared at the prospect of who could be at the door at this hour. She seemed so vulnerable. The sight of her tugged at his heart. But then he remembered their exchange the evening before.

"Go back to your room and shut the door," Wyatt said, fighting the urge to reach out for her. Why must his body betray him so?

She shook her head. "I'm staying with you."

He searched her sleep-drugged eyes for a moment. There was that fire, that determination that both frustrated and enticed him so. "All right, but stay behind me."

They moved toward the door.

"Who is it?" Wyatt called out.

"Jonas Anderson, sir. We need a doctor!"

Was it safe to open the door? Would there be a posse on the other side? "Are you alone, Jonas?"

"Yes, sir."

He had no choice but to trust the man. Wyatt opened the door, his gun at the ready.

As the door swung open and Jonas's eyes set upon the firearm, he raised his hands. "Honest, Doc, it's just me."

Wyatt glanced around Jonas and then lowered his gun. "What's happened?"

"Trouble. Come quick!" Jonas began to move back toward his horse.

Wyatt did not move. Something about this situation didn't sit well with him. "I'm not going anywhere until you tell me exactly what is going on."

"Some of the miners . . . they were drunk, Doc," he said as if it would excuse all bad behavior. "They stole a work train and went into Victor after some of the deputies we had on the run. And then a gun battle broke out. That's all I know. We were sent for the docs in the nearby towns."

Wyatt nodded. He stepped over to the table, set his shotgun down, and grabbed his medical bag before following the man out onto the porch. "Lead the way, Mr. Anderson."

Katherine caught Wyatt's arm as he passed by her.

He turned and caught her eyes. They were still wide and glassy.

When she spoke, her voice trembled. "Are you sure you should be going?"

Was she concerned about him? Despite everything that had happened? That touched him. So much that he wanted to promise he would stay. But he had a job to do. "There are probably wounded men. Maybe even some dying. They need me."

"But . . . " She hesitated. What was it she wasn't saying?

In a bold move, forgetting their earlier exchange, he cupped her face with his hand. "It will be all right."

The touch was briefer than he would have liked. And then he released her and went out into the night, following this miner into whatever remained of the confrontation. He would have given anything to remain with Katherine. To take her in his arms and kiss her the way he longed to and tell her he would never leave her again.

What had she wanted to say? Why had she held back? There were always questions with her. And he was determined to find the answers.

How late was the hour? Night had fallen some hours before and still some of the miners were ravaging the town. Johnson proved almost useless in reining them in. The saloons were packed with drunken miners who then came up with ideas such as the one that led to the shoot-out, leaving two dead and two wounded. But they were lucky. It could have been, should have been, much worse.

David had long since given up on any restful sleep. It had been too eventful, and with miners still out and about, it only promised to be more so. He wasn't surprised when he heard hoofbeats approaching their campsite. Who would come to this rabble in the middle of the night like this? Would it be friend or foe? Helper or instigator?

Lifting tired eyes to discern his fate, David attempted to make out the identity of the lone figure. As the rider neared, he saw that it was

John Calderwood. Taking in the situation quicker than David could have imagined, Calderwood was enraged by what he found.

"Help me round up the miners who are causing this violence," he ordered.

David and a few others obeyed, jumping on their horses and following Calderwood.

As Calderwood went around to the saloon owners, he asked, perhaps more demanded, they close. The miners who retained some sense of calm about themselves aided in rounding up the out-of-control ones. They were brought before Calderwood, who looked upon them with a disgusted eye.

"I can't believe it," he shouted at them. He appeared as if he wanted to say more, but seemed to realize it would be like talking to a tree stump.

Anyone with eyes could see that these men were too drunk to comprehend anything he would say.

"Ah, forget it. Let's take them over to the sheriff's office and lock 'em up," he hollered at his makeshift posse.

With a handful of rifles, they led the drunken miners to the sheriff's office. There was still no sign of the deputies.

"What are we going to do now?" David asked Calderwood as they stood in front of the city jail.

"I'm thinking. We need to put them somewhere. They are a danger to everyone, and we can't let them derail our negotiations with the mine owners."

Just then, they heard the door to the sheriff's office unlocking from the inside. They heard a voice call out, shaking, "What's your business?" The man inside seemed unsure about the situation, but perhaps sensed that this group wasn't on the same crazy rampage that had been sweeping the town.

"Officer, I rounded up the drunk miners. We were hoping to lock them up for the night and sort things out in the morning."

The door swung open wider, and a man carefully stepped out, holding a pistol and a lantern. He eyed Calderwood. Seeing the intoxicated men surrounded by weapons, his shoulders relaxed.

"I think we might be able to fit them in. Let me open the cells, and you start bringing them."

With that, all the rowdy miners were locked up. Calm was restored and sanity reigned again.

Another day was done. Katherine worked to clean the chalkboards and allowed her thoughts to wander. But she did not care for the places they went. As they so often did, they dwelled on Wyatt and her marriage. She had waited long into the morning hours for his return, until even sleep overtook her. So much so that she barely stirred when strong arms carried her from her place of vigil in the great room to her bed. They'd had so many ups and downs, she and Wyatt. Would it ever end?

True, it was not the typical marriage, but there had been times when it almost felt real. When it had seemed it could be real. Then there were moments like now, when nothing seemed real at all.

The schoolhouse door opened, drawing her attention away from her work. Turning toward the intrusion, she saw Timothy closing the door behind himself.

"Leave it open," she called. "It's a bit stuffy in here." She offered him a small smile. "I don't often have the pleasure," she said, wiping her hands off. It was true. Timothy did not make the regular visits to the classroom that he once did. Not since she and Wyatt . . .

She pulled her thoughts back to the present. And then she noticed Timothy still stood at the back of the room.

"What brings you this way?" She took a couple of steps toward him, indicating one of the empty student desks in the front row.

Timothy ran his hands over the brim of his hat, now in his hands. "I thought it was probably time for us to sit down and review your year. It's something the town council does with the teacher every year. And I thought I might help you get ready for it." He stepped toward her.

"That's a fine idea, Timothy. I appreciate your help." She moved to sit at her desk while he took the desk she had offered him. "Where shall we start?"

"Let's talk about the students and their progress."

They went down the roll, discussing each student, their successes and challenges throughout the year. Next they moved on to her goals for the year and how she had fared on meeting them.

As they went through everything, she noticed that Timothy became more and more quiet. Was there something on his mind? Should she ask him? But it was he who spoke about it first.

"Is everything all right, Katherine? You don't seem your usual chipper self today."

Katherine froze. How could she expect him to not notice? He was her friend.

"What's on your mind?"

She waved him off. "It's nothing. I don't want to bother you with it." In truth, she didn't know how appropriate it was to be discussing her marriage problems with her former beau.

"You know me better than that. We may have hit a rough patch, but I'm still your friend. And your reverend. You can trust me with anything. It will stay between us." His eyes searched hers, they were warm and kind. As always.

And he was right. He was a man of the cloth. A godly man. If she couldn't trust him, whom could she trust? She did so long for someone to talk to.

She sniffled. "It's my marriage. I'm not sure it's working out."

He nodded. "Tell me what's going on."

"We spend so much of our time at odds with each other. For the longest time, I didn't want anything more than a paper marriage, but then I started to think maybe, for the sake of the children, it would be better for us to try to be something more."

Her eyes sought Timothy's face for a reaction. She did not want to injure him with her words, but she feared her admission might do just that. His features held fast. He was reliable, trustworthy Timothy. So, she continued.

"But, I have come to accept Wyatt doesn't see me that way. He doesn't want me. And he never will because he has the attentions of a more beautiful woman." Her eyes stung and she felt tears welling.

Timothy reached out and placed a hand on her arm. "That cannot be possible, Katherine. You are the loveliest woman in Cripple Creek, if I might be so bold."

She smiled up at him, though the tears started to flow. "Thank you."

Why didn't she wait for Timothy? They were the match that should have been made. That would have lasted.

"You always will be, in my eyes." He reached forward with his other hand, grazing her face.

"I just don't know what to do," Katherine said, shoulders sagging. "But I know I can't live like this anymore."

Timothy opened his arms to her and she walked into his embrace. He soothed her with calm words of reassurance that everything would be okay, that things would work out, that she would find a way.

Whether or not she believed him, it felt good to be held by someone whose affection she did not question, someone who felt comfortable to her.

Wyatt watched all of this from the porch of the schoolhouse. His plan was to surprise her with a picnic. After the rocky night they'd had, he hoped to patch things up and move in the right direction. Perhaps even tell her his heart and his hopes for them at last. But he was shaken to the core by what he saw. And his anger burned toward the both of them as he watched her walk so easily into another man's arms.

A larger army of deputies was being raised by the mine owners. That was no secret. Large-scale recruitment like this could not be kept hidden. And it struck fear into the miners. David, along with his cohorts, were on the verge of abandoning all hope of success and disbanding when an edict came down from the office of the governor. The situation with this recruitment must have also unnerved Governor Waite.

Even now, they stood together as Calderwood prepared to read the governor's proclamation.

"The miners' encampment on Bull Hill is to be disbanded."

There was a mixture of reactions from the group. David could not stop his sigh of relief. So many wanted to stay and fight, but others, like David, were ready to return home to their families. They all, in some way or another, knew they could not stand up against a force of over a thousand deputies.

Calderwood cleared his throat. There must be more. "The force of 1,200 deputies being formed by Sheriff Bowers is hereby declared illegal and is to be disbanded."

A cheer went up from the entire group. Again, David's concern was greatly alleviated.

"The state militia shall be on alert for any move on Cripple Creek by any force."

A great sense of relief rippled through the collection of men.

How long had it been since he had held Mary? Seen Jessie's smile? Heard Peter's giggle? They would be worried about him. In the midst of all that had happened, did they even know he was alive?

But something seemed unclear in the midst of all this.

"What does this mean for us?" someone called out. Someone had just read his mind.

Calderwood didn't miss a beat. "It means we are to continue our strike. We will succeed and we will all be paid a good, just wage for our labor. But we must remember to not get foolish or violent and damage our chances of accomplishing that.

"For those of you with families, return to them and enjoy your time." His words were comforting to David. "But I expect to see every one of you Monday morning so we can resume our strike and negotiations."

With those last words, a big hurray came from the large group of men. Then the men parted and went about their separate ways, packing up their things and departing the camp.

David didn't know how to contain his excitement. He could almost feel Mary in his arms and see his children running to greet him. His eyes filled. Home. He was going home.

Timothy walked toward town with a spring in his step. He shouldn't be happy about a couple's marital misery, but he couldn't help himself. Katherine's disappointment with her marriage maybe, just maybe, could lead to an annulment.

Guilt crept into the edge of his conscience. This was most unbecoming of a pastor. If he were honest with himself, he should be praying for their marriage. And counseling them in the direction of unity. But he found he didn't care. All he could think about was the possibility that Katherine might be free to . . .

"Reverend! Reverend! I've got a bone to pick with you!"

Someone called to him from behind. He turned to see Wyatt Sullivan's fist flying toward his face.

Timothy landed solidly on his hindquarters. Colors exploded in front of his face and he worked to catch his bearings.

"Wha . . . What was that for?" He dabbed at his lip, trying to discern if he was bleeding.

"Stay away from my wife," Wyatt ground out, teeth clenched, posture still firm and statuesque as he glared down at the reverend.

Timothy's eyes narrowed. "Friend, you have more problems on your hands than you know. And if you think taking me down a notch is going to fix anything, you've got it all backwards."

Wyatt remained silent for several moments, his hands clenched into fists as if he wanted to hit Timothy again. "Just stay away from Katherine," he said as he spun on the balls of his feet and walked off.

Two men came from nearby to help Timothy to his feet, but he barely noticed. He looked after Wyatt's retreating form and couldn't help but smile.

Katherine laid Susie in her crib and stepped out of the room, careful to latch the door soundlessly behind herself. She moved across the hall to look in on Jack and assure herself that he still napped. In the hustle and bustle of the last couple of days, it seemed she'd not had a moment of silence to think. Even at night, she came to her bed exhausted and fell asleep before she could put two thoughts together. Between school and her duties here with the children and the home, there seemed to be no time for her.

But now all was silent. A Saturday at home alone with the children was just what she needed. There was nothing to distract her from her thoughts. Things between her and Wyatt had been so awkward that when he mentioned at breakfast that he needed to make some house calls, she was quick to agree. And this was her reward—a couple of hours all to herself.

Katherine sat in her chair by the fireplace. She stared at the hearth as if it would yield some answers to the questions that faced her. What was she going to do? What about the children?

One thing was certain, she could not stay in this marriage. Not when it was tearing her apart. Wyatt's face appeared in her mind's eye. The features she could trace without effort were before her, and her heart ached. Why had she opened her heart to him?

Katherine laid her head in her hands. How was she to get out of this? Could she care for Jack and Susie on her own? She couldn't leave them. They meant too much to her. There must be a way to make it work. And she was not totally alone, she reasoned. Her parents would help her any way they could. At the same time, she knew leaving Wyatt would mean leaving Cripple Creek. And she would have to face that.

In her heart, she knew she needed to turn to a source she had not sought in many months. Yes, this had been a season in which she had been the prodigal son. But now she was ready. And she wanted so much more than this on again/off again relationship with God. She needed a firm foundation. And the Bible said He was it. No more teetering on the edge. He deserved a commitment from her. So, she bowed her head and her heart before Him and prayed.

As she did so, the answers became more and more clear to her.

CHAPTER 14

In the End

David watched as Governor Davis H. Waite dismounted with all the grace he could muster. Then, with the broad smile of a politician, he went up to the closest miner and shook his hand. He moved on to the next, and then the next, and so on. There was a palatable easing of tension among the group with his warm greeting. The man certainly seemed to live up to his reputation as a "man of the people."

After Waite had made his way around much of the group, he worked his way back toward where Calderwood still stood, holding the reins of both horses. Waite inhaled to his full height, cleared his throat, and launched into his speech.

"Good men of Cripple Creek, I thank you for receiving me so graciously. I understand why you are here today. I know you have hopes . . . hopes that I will fulfill for you."

There was a stirring among the crowd, whispers among the men. Should he be trusted? David was unsure.

Waite continued, "There has been much ado these last weeks, and I know many of you are discouraged. Take heart. The end is near. Trust in your leaders. Trust that they are fighting for you. And if you will allow me, I will fight for you as well."

General utterances among the miners became more excited. The men seemed ready to believe him. Still, David reserved his judgment. He had been swayed too easily in the past.

"Remember, it was I who ordered the illegal force of deputies to be disbanded. This force which threatened your mission and even your well-being!"

The men nodded and the drone of their voices became louder.

"So, what do you say, men?" Calderwood interjected. "I know you are frustrated, and I know you are tired. I am, too. But we are nearing the end. It is in sight! Shall we take this last chance? Do we throw our hat in with Governor Waite?"

The crowd cheered.

Calderwood and Waite exchanged a smile. Another alliance had been formed. But would it be to their benefit or their detriment?

Katherine took a deep breath before she knocked on the familiar door that belonged to her parents' home. Footsteps sounded on the other side.

Lord, give me strength. She shot up a prayer. This would become a more common occurrence, this regular communication with God. It made her feel more connected. *Lead me not astray.*

The door opened and her mother stood before her, wiping her hands on her apron.

"Katie! Come in, come in." Ma moved aside and opened the door wider for her. "Your father said you needed us to watch the kids for the afternoon. What's going on?" The concern was evident on Ma's face. "Everything all right?"

Katherine nudged Jack forward. Once inside, she set Susie on the family room rug. As much as she believed she retained control of her nerves, one glance at her mother and her stomach rolled. She never could hide anything from her mother.

"No, Ma, everything's a wreck!" She attempted to calm herself by taking several deep breaths.

Ma's face was now etched with worry. She took Katherine's arm and led her to a chair. Placing a hand on her daughter's knee, her soft voice urged Katherine for more. "Tell me."

"It's Wyatt. It's no secret that things have been . . . up and down for us. I fear he doesn't care for me, and I can't pretend anymore. I can't keep trying to make a life with him. So I need to know once and for all if there's a chance." Katherine stared at her hands in her lap.

Ma remained quiet for several moments before she spoke. "What about the children?"

Katherine's head jerked up. "I'm doing this for the children. If it doesn't work between Wyatt and me, how is that good for them? To live in a home full of contention and lies."

"Lies?" Ma's eyes darkened, her voice serious.

Katherine waved her hand as if to dismiss Ma's question. "The whole of it is that if Wyatt doesn't love me or if he's in love with someone else, I can't keep living a lie."

Ma gave her a long look.

Katherine wished she could read her mother's thoughts. Or maybe not. There were many unanswered questions. It was a drastic step. And there remained the real possibility that Wyatt would not respond favorably.

Oh, God, what am I doing? Katherine bowed her head. *What can I do?*

A sense of peace washed over her and she knew she had to try. Her eyes met her mother's again. "I left a note for Wyatt. If he wants this marriage to work, he will meet me at the clinic after he gets home. That should be within the hour. And then I'll know."

Leaning forward, Ma took both of Katherine's hands in hers. "Your father and I want nothing but the best for you."

The tension in Katherine eased at her mother's reassurances.

"I just want to know one thing," Ma said. "Do you love him?"

Wyatt turned Rusty toward home. He had seen all of his homebound patients. They stretched across many miles. It would be a bit later when he returned home, but Katherine would understand. Not that they were on the best of terms right now.

As he made progress toward his homestead, he heard hoofbeats approaching. Turning, he saw a frantic Mr. Hatcher. Wyatt slowed his horse.

"Dr. Sullivan!" Mr. Hatcher called as he neared.

What could be the matter? Then Wyatt remembered that his wife's time for delivery was soon. Was it today?

Mr. Hatcher stopped his horse. He looked as if he could come out of his skin. "Nellie's gone into labor. She's in an awful lot of pain."

Wyatt suppressed a smile. First-time parents. "Pain is normal. But I'll come back with you just in case."

The man turned his horse and set off again. Wyatt urged Rusty to follow.

David found himself waiting, yet again, for negotiations that droned on for hours. But these negotiations took place in Denver. For just a week prior, these men, Calderwood, Waite, and the mine bosses attempted to convene in Colorado Springs only to be pushed out by a mob of locals who were out for blood. Apparently, it wasn't only the miners who were restless and tired of the violence that had disrupted their peaceful lives.

Today, the miners crowded outside the telegraph office, awaiting word from their leader. But David had long since tired of these proceedings. What if the mine bosses did concede and give them everything they asked for? What then? Would he go back to the mine and be happy there?

Not having been in those caverns for so many months now, he could not imagine going back. Would he return to the damp, lonely darkness? It was for his family. But there was another way. His mind had been shut off to it for so long, he recoiled against it.

Only this time, he considered it again. What would be so wrong about working for his father? Would inheriting a family business be so wrong? Why?

Just then the telegraph operator stepped out from his small office. "I have an announcement for the miners of Cripple Creek."

The miners stood and faced him. David did the same. He would face his fate head on.

"Negotiations over. Eight hour work day. Three dollars per day. John Calderwood."

There was an elated outcry and celebration such as David had never known. And he joined in. Their hard work had succeeded. They, the small-time miners of Cripple Creek, had outdone the mine bosses. It was unbelievable.

The strike was over.

He wasn't coming. Katherine's shoulders slumped. That was her answer. Wyatt wanted his freedom. And, as much as it pained her, she would give it to him. God would make a way for her and the children. But what would she do with a broken heart?

Katherine sat on the bed and faced the window that looked out over the town. So much had changed for her in this short time in Cripple Creek. But one thing was certain amidst the pain – she had hope. Hope that each day would bring something new, something better. Even if Wyatt was not by her side. And as much as her heart tore at that thought, as long as she breathed and trusted God, she had hope that she would make it through. Somehow.

Wyatt rode home at the end of an arduous day. For the last couple of Saturdays he had made up excuses to stay away—be it at the clinic, making house calls, or such as this afternoon, being called away unexpectedly by a long birthing. The awkwardness between him and Katherine was just too much. But being away from her proved almost more than he could stand.

Being near her caused his heart to constrict painfully, being away from her caused him to ache. Was there an answer? Of course there was

—the truth. But was he ready for the truth? And what exactly was the truth?

He feared trusting her with his heart. His father had all but obliterated his ability to trust anyone. And his desire to commit. What if he turned out to be another version of that man? His heart clenched at the thought of putting his hands on Katherine or on one of the children in anger. Their trusting, innocent eyes wide and frightened in his vision.

Oh, God.

Wyatt had not prayed since he was a boy. Since he decided God didn't hear him. Didn't care.

God, protect them.

And he would do whatever it took to protect them. He would die for them. Because he loved them. All of them.

But my father spoke of love. He always apologized and said he loved us.

Wyatt remembered Timothy quoting from the Bible once that love keeps no record of wrongs. And he knew. Something urged him to forgive his father. Slowing his horse to a halt, he stared up at the sky, already starting to shift color. The sun would set within the hour.

"I can't," he spoke out into the void of the sky. "Don't you see? I'm past that."

A gentle breeze flowed over him and it was as if his chest warmed and expanded. He felt loved. Completely. In that moment, anything seemed possible.

"I don't know how, God. But I am willing to learn. I choose forgiveness." Leaning over the pommel of the saddle, he felt tears prick his eyes.

But just as sadness washed over him, it was replaced with something sweeter. Something more pleasant. Hope.

And his heart exploded. Everything became clear to him, his feelings for Katherine, and his desire that their marriage be more than just a piece of paper. He was free now. Free to love and trust and give himself to this woman.

Eagerness filled him and he dug his heels in the horse's flanks, urging the animal into a gallop toward the homestead. No matter the awkwardness, he would make amends. He would make their family whole.

As Rusty flew through the meadow, Wyatt counted every second until he would arrive. Wyatt didn't bother to stable the horse when he came upon the house, but tied his reins to a post near the porch. Rushing toward the door, he burst into the cabin to find it devoid of any life.

He felt as if the breath was sucked out of him. Where were they? Had something happened? Moving from room to room, he searched for any sign of where they had gone. At last, coming back to the dining area, he saw a note on the table.

Wyatt,

I am sorry for so many things. But most of all for trapping us in this marriage. We were fooling ourselves to think it would be adequate for either of us. I think we find ourselves at an impasse, you and I. And I want more from this marriage than you may be willing to give. So, if you do care for me, you will find me at the place you first brought me flowers. The first time I thought there might be more to you. If not, I will understand that you need to be free to start your own life.

Sincerely,

Katherine

Free to start his own life? What was she talking about? She and the children were his life. How could she not see that? He had to find her!

When had she written this note? Probably many hours prior. He was much later returning than she could have anticipated due to Mrs. Hatcher's lengthy labor. Would she still be waiting for him? Where would it be? The first time he brought her flowers . . . He cringed to think he hadn't done so since they'd been married. The only time he brought her flowers was when she was sick with the typhoid. How would she know that?

Regardless, that had to be it. He turned and raced outside. Thankful he hadn't stabled the horse, he hopped on Rusty and rushed out toward the clinic.

God, help me find her. Don't let me be too late.

Wyatt came upon the clinic in due time. His heart thundered in his ears as he made short work of securing the horse to the post out front. Then he rushed inside and up the stairs. The hallway and rooms were quiet. And his heart fell. Stepping into the room she had occupied during the plague, he found it empty. But indeed the bedcovers had been disturbed. Perhaps she had sat there. A single white lily lay next on the end table. She had been here.

He had missed her, but he refused to admit defeat. It was not over. Not if he could find her and bring her home. If she took the kids with her, there were only two places she could have gone. Her parents' home or her brother's. The former was the more likely.

The trip to Tom and Lauren's home seemed to take hours, but he knew it was mere minutes before he stood at their door, knocking.

Lauren opened the door for him. He entered the house, his eyes scanning for Katherine.

"Pa!" Jack jumped down from his seat at the table and ran toward Wyatt.

"Jack-boy!" Wyatt lifted him in the air before tucking him into his right side. Then his focus turned on Lauren. "Where is she?" He attempted to catch his breath from his hurried ride.

"She's not here," came Lauren's sharp reply. Her arms crossed in front of her chest.

Wyatt's eyes searched hers. What did she know? He wagered everything. So she was not happy with him. In her eyes, he had stood up Katherine. But she was always one to have faith in their little family unit. "Lauren, it's not what you think."

"Oh?" Her reply was short, measured.

"I had a patient. A long labor. I'll explain later, but believe me, I only now found the note." He threw himself on her mercy.

Lauren watched Jack in Wyatt's arms and her gaze softened.

Wyatt hoped she saw that he truly wanted to make things right.

She reached out to touch Jack's hair and then she met Wyatt's gaze again. "She's by the stream out back."

Wyatt shifted to hand Jack over to his grandmother before moving to the door. He had to find her. And he prayed she would listen.

David brought his horse to a stop by the familiar barn and tied off the reins on a post. He took in the sight of the homestead that was almost as dear to him as his own. Then he began to search out his father. Shading his eyes with a hand, he scanned the field beyond the house.

A smile played across his face as he watched his father out with his horse, moving amongst the cattle. Tom Matthews truly loved what he did. And he was good at it, too. What a blessing. David dropped his hand and looked down at his shoes. Would he ever be so fortunate?

Life had thrown him quite the curve these last months. The strike, a new knowledge of God and prayer, a new appreciation for his family . . . lessons he would not soon forget.

The sounds of the cows drew nearer, and David raised his eyes again. Tom spotted him and waved. David returned his greeting and waited for his father to move the cattle to the south pasture. Once that was done, Tom rode over to where David stood at the fence line.

"Don't often get the pleasure of seeing you during the day." Tom pulled his hat off and rubbed his forehead with a kerchief.

David watched the cows, now spreading out in the field. "Don't often have the time for it."

"I heard talk that there are negotiations ongoing." Tom repositioned his hat and leaned forward over the pommel of his saddle.

"They came to an end." David examined a niche in the fence post, too nervous to meet his father's eyes.

"Oh?"

David met his father's gaze at last. "We got what we wanted. Our full pay at our eight-hour workday."

"That's great, son."

"And I've been offered a position as foreman at the mine."

"Glad to hear it." Tom smiled, but there was still that sadness in his eyes whenever they talked about the mines.

David put his hands in his pockets and closed his eyes for a moment. Sending up a silent prayer for strength, he braced himself for what he knew he had to say. "But I'm not going back to the mines."

"What?" Tom's confusion was evident.

Meeting his father's eyes once more, he continued, "No, that's not where I belong. Never has been." His heart raced in his chest. But he knew there was more to say.

Tom remained silent, waiting.

"See, I thought it was about me making my own way in the world apart from you. That was before . . . well, before life forced me to see a bigger picture. I now understand that it's more than that. It's about enjoying what you do. It's about family. It's about legacy."

Tom continued to watch David with a soft gaze.

That didn't make things any easier. David wished he would say something, anything.

"So, I was wondering, Pa, if you have any need for another ranch hand?"

Tom looked out toward the horizon and slowly shook his head. "No, 'fraid I don't."

David's heart sank. He had waited too long. Shoulders falling, he looked at the ground.

"But I do have a need for a partner. If you're willing."

Turning his eyes back toward his father's face, David could hardly imagine the love he found there. All he managed was a nod.

Tom slid down off his horse and opened the gate to step through and embrace his son.

David, completely overwhelmed, did not know how to thank God for such a blessing, so he simply let his heart return praise.

Katherine gazed at the late spring sky as the sun began to set. She loved this spot by the stream. It had always been one of her special places to come and think. After relieving her feet of all coverings, she dug them into the soft grass as she sat among the flowers. The water flowing by as it made its journey across the earth's surface tempted her. Should she dip her feet in? Would it wash away her hurt?

She could not make herself move. So she closed her eyes and let the breeze that rustled the grasses take her worries with it as it blew over her. Only, her ache remained. Would time be her only cure?

"I like your hair down." A voice intruded on her solitude.

Her heart stopped. Could it be? She turned her head. Wyatt stood in the dwindling sunlight. Was it her imagination or was it truly him?

She moved to stand. He was by her side in an instant, offering his hands to assist her. Her hands slid easily into his and he lifted her with little effort. They stood, hands connected, but separated by unspoken words.

Katherine could hold back no longer. "You didn't come."

He swallowed. "I know. I'm sorry. There was an emergency. But if I'd known, nothing could have kept me from you."

She looked down at his chest.

He hooked her chin with his finger and tilted her face toward his. "I'm sorry, Katie. For all the pain. For the walls between us. For everything. But right now and for always, I choose us."

She nodded, her lip trembling. Leaning forward, she buried her face in his chest. "Can you ever forgive me? For my anger and my selfish pride?"

"It is long forgiven." He stroked her back, pressing a kiss to her hair. Wyatt pulled back only far enough to look into her eyes. "How can you not know by now, Katie? You have captivated me . . . " His voice broke with emotion. "And I love you with all that I am."

Katherine made a whimpering sound, letting her eyes slide closed as fresh tears spilled down her face. Her hands slid up to his arms, and a smile pulled at her lips as a small laugh escaped.

"Good. Because I am lost." Her eyes opened to meet his. "I'm so in love with you."

His lips came down to meet hers. Gentle and sweet at first, but soon pressing and possessive. And she welcomed his affections. There, in that field, everything changed between them. The walls they had built came down. They were no longer Wyatt and Katherine; they became one heart.

Epilogue

Katherine's mother placed one more flower in her veil headdress.

Surely the thing would topple. "I don't think it will hold any more, Ma," Katherine said, smiling.

"I just want it to be perfect."

Of course she did. Didn't every mother?

Katherine ran her hands along the white fabric of her skirt. She longed for a mirror to check her reflection, but her mother insisted she needed to wait until everything was completed. Ma and Mary worked to prepare her for the ceremony that would start within minutes.

"Please, Ma. I think I'm quite ready. May I have the mirror now?"

Ma exchanged a look with Mary. They stepped back to look Katherine over. Then Ma reached over to the shelf, grabbed the silver-backed mirror, and handed it to her daughter.

Katherine sucked in a breath and drew the mirror toward her face. She was surprised at what she saw. The flowers created a lovely, colorful halo on her head, and her veil spilling down her back made the reality of this day come full force upon her.

She would be marrying Wyatt . . . again. But this time would be different. Had it been only two weeks since they had professed their love for each other? And they agreed not to come together until they had pledged themselves to each other. Only this time, it would be a pledge from their hearts.

"It's time, Katie," her mother took the mirror from her grasp and clutched her elbow, leading her toward the door.

They stepped out of the clinic and made their way toward the church where everyone awaited them. Including Wyatt. Katherine could not wait to lay eyes on him. After today, the waiting would be over and they would be man and wife in every sense of the words.

It wasn't long before they arrived at the church and it was her turn to walk down the aisle. And though friends and family surrounded her as she made that short stroll, her eyes were locked onto her groom. For she would never forget the look on his face as his eyes met hers. Love, adoration, and joy were easy to read among his features.

She and Pa stopped just short of Reverend Dawson. In the end, Timothy had not been able to stay in Cripple Creek. Katherine regretted that she played a role in his decision to leave, but it was, in all truth, for the best. For his ministry as much as for her marriage.

When her father gave her away, Wyatt's hands reached for hers. The familiar sensations flitted in her stomach at his touch. They moved through the ceremony they had been through before, but the words meant more to her this day.

And as she and Wyatt had their first real kiss as husband and wife, she knew that God had knit them together, heart to heart.

Keep reading for a preview of the next book in the Cripple Creek Series!

Thank you, dear reader, for reading along with me! If you enjoyed this story, I would sincerely appreciate if you would submit a review. It would mean so much to me!

To read more about these characters, follow along with the Cripple Creek Series. Find it at:
https://saraturnquist.com/cripple-creek-series/

<h1 style="text-align:center">Author's Note</h1>

This book has been an interesting one! For those that follow my books, you know that I like to take the love story and "marry" it to a historical event in most cases. This happens to be this rather historically unique and significant miner's strike.

My hope in the portrayal of the strike is to represent a few viewpoints of those touched by the strike and the many ways it can affect a person's life. Not necessarily to offer an "right answer," but more to pose questions and thoughts through my characters' experiences. Perhaps, even, there is no "right answer," but just experiences that people go through in the end.

But much of what is portrayed about the miner's strike is factual. Although the character of David and Jonas are of my own creation. The typhoid plague sweeping through Cripple Creek is another fabrication of my imagination, but is true to what happened in many places with limited knowledge of the necessity of good sanitation during this time period.

Katherine Sullivan had never been so pleased with herself. She stepped back and looked at the large tree, breathing in the scent of fresh-cut evergreen. Standing tall and proud in the center of Cripple Creek's main street, the tree was a testament to the merriment of the season.

Christmas was upon them with all its wonder and delight. It happened to be Katherine's favorite time of the year. Memories of brown, wrapped packages and peppermint candies flooded her mind. Her skin fairly tingled. Or could it be that she needed to pull her wrap more tightly around herself?

She did so, but it didn't take away the thrill that shot through her. Times spent around each tree placed in this very spot became tangible—with carols and hymns sung by the whole town as they surrounded the fir branches and ribbons with lit candles in hand.

And this year, she bore the responsibility of ensuring the town decorations were just so. How did she land herself in such a position? True, the mayor and his wife were off visiting their eldest for the next few weeks. But was she the best choice for the job?

"Mama!" A little flash of red ran straight for her legs.

Katherine turned as the small girl collided with her skirt. "Susie, be careful." She kept her tone soft, but firm.

The small girl looked up, a smile on her face. "For baby?"

Placing a hand on her rounded stomach, Katherine nodded. "Yes, love, for baby. We have to take care of baby."

Susie flashed her teeth. How could she scold that cute face? It was impossible.

Leaning over, she put a hand on the child's cheek. "I think we need something from the General Store, hmm?"

There was no pretense between them. While Katherine's purpose included checking on the red ribbon in stock, these visits always ended with a sugarcoated something in Susie's hands.

Susie's smile became wider. As did her eyes.

"Yes, please." Her blond curls bounced.

Katherine reached for her hand, and together they walked down the wide dirt-packed road toward the wooden planked sidewalk around the stores.

Breathing in the chilled air, Katherine's oversensitive nose alerted her that Mrs. Abby's café had stew roasting. Her stomach grumbled. Perhaps when Wyatt returned from his house calls, that could be lunch.

Maybe until then she would have to sneak some of that candy promised to Susie.

As they neared the boardwalk, a familiar vibration shook her knees. The thundering of hoof beats shot alarm through her. She jerked her head left and right. Where did it come from?

A cart rushed down Main Street, careening on its way. The driver pushed the horse to move more quickly. Did he not see her and Susie in the road?

The man flung indistinguishable words in her direction. Only she could not work them out.

Susie!

Katherine grabbed for the toddler. She pushed her legs to work faster than they ever had.

The out-of-control horse bore down upon them. Katherine leaped toward safety. She pushed her arms forward, shoving Susie as far out of the way as possible.

Hands gripped Katherine, swinging her farther from danger.

She blinked as the cart passed, pressing Susie's face to her chest.

Who had pulled her to safety? The arms still held her.

She peered up; the man's hands were only then letting go of her arms.

"You all right, ma'am?" The dark-skinned man tipped his hat up, giving her an excellent view of his amber eyes and concerned features.

"Yes, sir. I-I thank you. If you hadn't reached out and…" Tears pricked her eyes. These cursed mood swings!

"Don't you worry none about it. Just glad I could help." The man jerked the brim of his hat downward.

She turned back toward the cart. Where had it stopped? It sat just outside Wyatt's clinic. Why?

A deep voice spoke beside her again. "If you're sure you don't need anything, I best be finding my wife."

She looked at the man who had rescued her and her daughter as she wiped at her eyes. "Of course. Thank you again, Mister…"

"Jeffries, ma'am. Mr. Jeffries."

His deep voice soothed her frazzled nerves.

Katherine nodded. "Mr. Jeffries."

With another nod, he stepped off into the crowd, which parted around him.

She frowned.

In seconds, there was another tug on her arm. "Katie! That was terrifying!"

She knew the voice before she turned. Her brother's wife, Mary. Setting a hand to the one on her arm, she patted it. Though she wanted to throw herself into Mary's arms, she needed to contain her emotion now. That was best. For Susie and for these many onlookers.

"Yes, but all is well now, is it not?" Her words and hands may be shaky, but her features were set.

Mary's eyes widened. "But you can't imagine how afraid I…why I was certain you would be run over."

Katherine rubbed her sister-in-law's fingers as she attempted to look to the happenings at the clinic. "We can't think of what might have been. All we can do, is be thankful for what is."

Mary nodded. "I suppose…" Her voice trailed as her eyes followed where Katherine's gaze landed.

As they watched, the driver knocked on the clinic door.

Nothing.

"Where is Doc?" Mary seemed confused. Why wouldn't Wyatt answer?

Then Katherine remembered—Wyatt wasn't there. He was out on house calls. Katherine must tell this gentleman.

The thought of addressing the man who nearly trampled her made her stomach flip. But there might be an injury. An emergency. Could she find someone to attend to it until Wyatt returned? Perhaps someone should ride after Wyatt?

She pushed forward, handing Susie off to Mary's capable care, and moved toward the clinic.

"Excuse me, sir," she called as she approached, her voice hitching only slightly.

The man turned, his features displaying his urgency. "Where is the doctor, Mrs.…"

"Sullivan." She pressed a hand to her chest. "I'm the doctor's wife. He is out visiting his home-bound patients."

"What am I supposed to do with this here fella?" The cart's owner moved toward the back. "I found him out on the trail all busted up. He's in a bad way."

Dare she peer into the cart? She wasn't one of those doctor's wives that could stomach any manner of injury. But she swallowed hard and stepped up to the wagon's bed.

No!

It couldn't be!

Her hand flew to her mouth. She let out a muffled cry.

Flinging a hand to rest on the driver's arm kept her upright.

"What is it, Mrs. Sullivan?"

The world spun.

"S-send for the doctor in Victor."

"What?"

"Just do it!" she screamed.

The man ran off.

She prayed he would make haste.

Clinging now to the side of the wagon, she reached in, fingers grazing the unconscious face of her husband.

"Wyatt..." she cried. "Not now."

To read more, find *Christmas in Cripple Creek* here:

https://saraturnquist.com/christmas-in-cripple-creek/

Love in Cripple Creek (Book 4)

A woman burned by love. A man who has lost his way.

Betsy Callaway hasn't been the most upstanding person in Cripple Creek...and she has now passed the acceptable age for marriage. But something about her calls to Nikolai "Nick" Hammond's heart and draws him back home.

The antics that ensue between the pair and the obstacles they face--including their own stubbornness and becoming entangled in a bank robbery--threaten to keep them on separate paths, but their draw to each other pushes them together.

Will the prodigal find home welcoming?
Can Betsy hope for real redemption?

Acknowledgments

This part of the book is so important to me and so difficult to write at the same time. So many people have impacted my life and my journey along the way...and that's how I got where I am. I wouldn't be the person I am, the writer I am without the totality of their influence. For all of you, I say thanks. But there is no way I can thank each of you individually in this section. As much as I'd like to, it's not possible. I must confine my written thanks to those who had hands directly in the creation of this book.

I cannot thank my beta readers enough for their valuable feedback. Christina Horton, Hillary Harvey, and Stacy Schoenwetter—what more could I ask for? You are both honest and gentle. My writer's heart appreciates it!

Julie Sherwood, my editor, thanks for keeping me honest and kicking my butt on this manuscript. You pushed me to make it all it could be. And it is.

Amanda Matthews, your amazing cover makes the whole thing shine! Thanks for sharing your talent.

The photographer who makes me look good, VerBull Photography, I know I'm taking full advantage of your skills.

The Clarksville Christian Writers, my critique group, you make me smile and give me so much to look forward to each week. I so enjoy sharing the craft of writing with you all!

Hannah Conway, I have no clue where I would be on this journey if it weren't for your encouragement and mentoring. Probably still in my writing closet ;-)

My husband and number one fan, Greg Turnquist. You pushed me out into this writing world to begin with. And I could not be more thankful that you saw the potential and have believed in me every step of the way.

For my sister, you make me want to be better. For my dad, you make me feel so good to have achieved this dream of writing. For my mom, I will love you forever. And for my kids, you give me every reason to smile.

Last, but certainly not least, my readers, you give me a reason to keep writing.

Sara is a coffee lovin', word slinging, Historical Romance author whose super power is converting caffeine into novels. She loves those odd little tidbits of history that are stranger than fiction. That's what inspires her. Well, that and a good love story.

But of all the love stories she knows, hers is her favorite. She lives happily with her own Prince Charming and their gaggle of minions. Three to be exact. They sure know how to distract a writer! But, alas, the stories must be written, even if it must happen in the wee hours of the morning.

Sara is an avid reader and enjoys reading and writing clean Historical Romance when she's not traveling.

Please follow along with her journey through her newsletter at: http://
saraturnquist.com/list

Happy Reading!

facebook.com/AuthorSaraRTurnquist

instagram.com/sararturnquist

x.com/sararturnquist

youtube.com/@SaraRTurnquist

pinterest.com/sararturnquist

Also by
Sara R. Turnquist

CONVENIENT RISK SERIES

A Convenient Risk

An Inconvenient Christmas

A Less Convenient Path

A Convenient Escape

An Inconvenient Acquaintance

These Golden Years

A Less Convenient Arrangement

Ranch Hands Collection (ebook only)

LADY OF BOHEMIA SERIES

The Lady Bornekova

The Lady and the Hussites

The Lady and Her Champion

The Lady and Her Secret

RAILWAY ROMANCE SERIES

Laura, The Tycoon's Daughter

ACROSS THE YEARS SERIES

Among the Pages

Between the Lines

STANDALONE NOVELS

The General's Wife

Trail of Fears

Off to War

9 781956 410471